Necessary
Secrets

Necessary Secrets

Greg McGee

upstart press

A catalogue record for this book is available from
the National Library of New Zealand

ISBN 978-1-988516-63-9

An Upstart Press Book
Published in 2019 by Upstart Press Ltd
Level 4, 15 Huron Street, Takapuna
Auckland, New Zealand

The author gratefully acknowledges the assistance of a Creative New Zealand grant
in the writing of this novel.

ARTS COUNCIL OF NEW ZEALAND TOI AOTEAROA

Designed by www.cvdgraphics.nz
Printed by Everbest Printing Co. Ltd., China

For Mary

ABOUT THE AUTHOR

Greg McGee has written for theatre, film and television, in which he has won numerous awards. More recently he has concentrated on prose. Under the pseudonym of Alix Bosco he won the 2010 Ngaio Marsh Award for best crime fiction novel for *Cut & Run*, and was a finalist the following year with *Slaughter Falls*. He has since written his first novel under his own name, *Love & Money*, and the biographies of Richie McCaw and Brendon McCullum. He was the 2013 Katherine Mansfield Menton Fellow, where he wrote *The Antipodeans*, a best-seller in New Zealand which was long-listed for the 2016 Ockham New Zealand Book Awards. He lives in Auckland.

spring

I DON'T WANT to leave a mess. That would be unfair on Ellie, who'd no doubt be the one to discover me. Unless I leave a note on the bedroom door. *Don't come in, Ellie, phone for the ambulance.* But ambulances don't come for corpses. Best to keep it short. *I am dead.* Deceased? Why does Monty Python's parrot come to mind? *I am no more.* That's the essential problem: I am less, much less, than I used to be.

There's no guarantee this pistol will work. The armourer on that gig – what was his name? I have a feeling it began with B. Not Bob, Bill . . . on that shoot for . . . Was it biscuits? Mint creams? How could I have worked guns into a television commercial for mint creams? I wouldn't put it past me. Anyway, that armourer beginning with B on that shoot for, possibly, mint creams, gave me this snub-nosed Walther PPK. When I say 'gave', I mean I paid him several hundred for it. I told Bevan – Bevan! – I told Bevan I'd love to have it because it was James Bond's weapon of choice back in the days when Sean Connery *was* Bond. I haven't been able to watch any of those subsequent Bonds, those thoroughly wrong iterations. I persuaded that armourer whose name begins with B but is not Bob or Bill, against his better judgement, to leave one bullet in the magazine. B was nakedly greedy, and

11

open to monetary persuasion, as most people are. He could, I explained, take my cash, report it stolen to future-proof his, as I recall, considerable arse, *and* claim the insurance. His *additional* insurance, I told him, was that if I did anything silly with the pistol, he could deny selling or giving it to me and I would be prosecuted as a thief. I was good back then – when would that have been, the nineties perhaps? More likely the cowboy eighties, before Health and Safety started applying a tourniquet to our red-blooded mercenary endeavour. I was good at seeing the angle back then. Exploiting the crack the angle exposed. So here he is, my snub-nosed Walter, with his one bullet. My lead pill.

I did look at other options. Nembutal had its attractions: a glass of wine in accompaniment, being found asleep in one's bed. No mess. But I can't ask young Jeetan, my doctor, to compromise himself, with his brilliant career still in front of him. I would have to scurry around elsewhere. Exit might have helped in the procurement, but the police are on to them, with a woman recently arrested for doing exactly that.

The online option might have appealed. I do like online shopping. For shoes, mainly. I saw Paul Smith brogues with exposed stitching on sale for $299 at that corner menswear shop. I went outside, sat on the bench under the pin oak with my iPhone and found an online retailer who was selling them at $125. I bought two pairs as an up-yours to the rapacious margins of the locals. I will probably never get to wear them. I'm no longer on anyone's D list and don't leave the house much, except to do my rounds, clear the box, order a flat white, say hello to someone I know passing by, there's always someone – I used to know a lot of people, in a superficial way – sit in the sun, take home a sandwich. I always wear Nike Air Force 1s on my rounds, not as light as the modern trainers, but robustly structured. They provide the pneumatic cushion my knee cartilages no longer manage. I have a dozen AF 1s, fly-knit, suede and leather mainly, trainers, Ultra Forces, LV8s, Premiums, all colours of the rainbow, enough to rotate so that my bunioned feet, gouted toes, heel spurs and plantar fasciitis don't deform the inner soles. I order them online from ASOS and they arrive from Vietnam or China or wherever within ten days, plenty long enough for me to forget having ordered them, or even what I've ordered, and when the courier delivers them I am like a child at Christmas, full of anticipation and delight as I unwrap my treasure. When I do my rounds in my Air Force 1s, I get knowing thumbs-up from sneaker-nerds, like Ethan, the Tokelauan barista. 'Old school!'

Vain probably, brand-Nazi certainly – how could I be other? It's what I did. I've always been an enthusiastic consumer, able to effortlessly believe my own hype, buy whatever I was selling and much else besides. Shopping used to be such a mindless pleasure, but Ellie threw a wobbly when those Paul Smiths turned up on the credit card bill. 'How can I get it through to you, Dad? We have no money!' That sounded overly dramatic, even by my standards. I'm a fish who is used to swimming in a sea of money; I've never read a budget that didn't have a bit of fat secreted here and there if you knew where to look. But it seems to be a sincerely held belief, as all Ellie's beliefs are. No more mystery boxes from China or Vietnam or wherever.

An online order for a fatal dose of Nembutal wouldn't have much attraction, no matter what sort of wrapping it came in. But I was seriously contemplating it, until a couple of pensioners got arrested for importing it from China and Mexico. It wasn't the prospect of being arrested that put me off, it was being publicly named, and my intentions being known. When I go, it will be without a build-up. I'm determined there'll be no trailers before that feature, just a final video farewell after the fact, which I've already recorded and lodged deep in the pocket of my Rainbird jacket. It has no cumbersome fleece lining, just a thin-skinned waterproofing, protection enough for an Auckland spring, where squalls fly in from the west like children's tantrums, short and intense. I seldom venture out without it, so the little USB containing my last production should be eminently discoverable.

As is the way when necessity becomes the mother of intervention, I've become reconciled to Walter, my seventies artefact. It's begun to seem more appropriate to my own artefaction, to the life I have lived. My lead pill will be quick, dramatic and somehow noble in a way that shuffling off this mortal coil in a drugged stupor isn't. Brave rather than cowardly, I like to think. Active rather than passive. And, I have to confess, better in the telling. 'Old Den, eh. Never one to do anything by halves! Old school. What a dag.' A dead dag, of course – I'll not be around to hear any of it, but I can at least savour it in prospect.

When I was young, I lived in the future too much. The present really only imposed itself when Carol got sick. I was fifty when she died, in the first year of the new century. Much harder to calibrate is when I morphed from the present to the past and became a preterite. That was a slower process and harder to mark with a failing memory.

All this, naturally, isn't what it seems to be. It's not really what I try to present it as – a matter of rational choice. That's the lesser part of it. The larger part is a much more frightening driver: the logical end to inchoate terror.

It came again today. Whoever said it's not about forgetting

where your car keys are, it's about forgetting what the car keys are for . . . was right – metaphorically, at least. And cruel.

I hope no one who knows me, saw me. Sitting in the middle of the local strip with my hazard lights going. The cars banked up behind me, trying to swerve round me, until that most loathed uniform in urban Auckland walked across with his tyre chalk and asked if he could help me, sir. When I showed him that the starter button wouldn't go, there was zero ignition, obviously some dreadful electrical malfunction, he suggested I shift the auto from Drive to Park or Neutral and try again. When the engine started and I realised what I had done, I tried to smile at him as he said, 'No trouble, sir', but I could see the pity in his eyes, and my panic was subsumed by terror.

I've learnt nothing. That's as terrifying as the incident itself. That infernal iStop. I thought the engine had stalled and pressed the starter button, which did in fact stop it. So I pressed the starter button again and nothing happened, because it was still in drive. It looked like a complete electrical meltdown, I told Dr Jeetan. An easy mistake, surely? He said nothing, then asked me whether it had happened before? I conceded that it might have.

'How many times?'

'Twice,' I said. 'Or three times, maybe.' The truth is, I can't remember, but I don't want to tell him that. I need my licence, I love driving. When I can't sleep, I drive the perfectly canted sweepers from Murchison down the Buller Gorge to Reefton, or along the side-mirror squeezes of the Grande Corniche from Cap Martin to Nice, or the Big Sur from San Luis Obispo to Monterey, or along the cliffs of the Great Southern Ocean in Victoria, or my favourite road in all the world, from Fairlie across the Mackenzie Country to Omarama and over the Lindis to Wanaka, the stunning mix of land and lake, burnt sepia and snow-fed blue, with the Southern Alps overlooking it all. I was determined to drive that road again before I die, but I now know I won't get the chance. Dr Jeetan wants a brain scan. Precautionary, he says. But I know the black room that's waiting for me. I've been there before.

I stand in my eyrie contemplating my end. Revelling in the power. I admire the right-to-die brigade, the euthanasia advocates, but they've got it wrong. It's not so much a right as a power. Power is taken, you don't ask permission of your fellows to exercise it. I will not be denied.

My view of the world is powerful and privileged, I know. Carol and I took a punt on this wonderfully odd run-down transition villa, which had a long history as a boarding house and flats. At our big house-warming party, all kinds of people, film-makers, musos, actors, students, told us they had lived or partied here. There used to be lots of old ruins like it all around this suburb, peopled by penniless itinerants of various descriptions, before the monied eastern suburbs cottoned on to its proximity to city and to sea and reclaimed it. Carol was a voracious reader. Years later she found words that perfectly described our feelings when we first saw this loft, up in the shallow gables, crystallising *'those blissful Jungian dreams that everyone has, of finding in the house another room that you didn't know was there, high up under the roof, an extra storey, unused or neglected, but with more windows, sunshine pouring in, a glorious view, and more space than you've ever had before or imagine you deserved. You can't wait to sweep it out and furnish it and begin to inhabit it – to expand into it.'* We did expand into it, Carol and I, and we've been here ever since. Carol often said we'd only leave when carried out feet first. That happened far too soon for her, but will nevertheless be true for both of us.

***

THE barrel's cold against my temple. I put it in my mouth. It doesn't go in far. I warm it up like some old tart trying to suck life into a limp dick. What if I pulled the trigger now? What if the bullet ignited, or whatever bullets do, and it worked? Where would it go, exactly? What mess would it leave? I don't mind blood being found, and even a bit of brain tissue, but not popped eyes. I don't want to inflict that on Ellie, having some unattached eye on the carpet ogling her as she screams. Perhaps I could organise it so Ellie wasn't the one to find me. I should do that. It's the least I can do, give that some thought. I pocket Walter.

'Is that a pistol in your pocket or are you just pleased to see me?'

Uh oh, she's back. It's been a while. I tell her I *am* pleased to see her, of course I'm pleased to see her, but it is indeed a pistol. I pull Walter back out of my pocket. When she asks me what on earth I'm going to do with it, I tell her it's my lead pill.

'You always had a flair for the dramatic,' she says.

'One bullet. I'll die at my convenience.'

'And everyone else's, I imagine, if it's sooner rather than later.'

That's the thing about Carol. She can be conjured, but not controlled. I might will her into existence, but once here, she is as she always was. That's her beauty and my curse. I tell her I won't suffer like she did, I won't put everyone through that.

'I suffered,' she points out, 'you endured. Isn't suicide a form of cowardice?'

I reframe cowardice to courage, ecological responsibility, saving the health system from wasting resources, as I put Walter back in the bottom cupboard of the kauri roll-top, in the concertina box-file under W.

'Public spirited to the last!' she chortles. I don't remember her being quite this dyspeptic when she was alive. She didn't chortle back then. Not at me. That I can remember. She looks suspiciously at the drawer where Walter is now hiding. 'Will it work? Shouldn't you do a test run?' She seems to be inordinately entertained at the prospect of my violent demise. When I tell her I've only got the one bullet, she seems disappointed.

I suppose the Carol I conjured could have been a younger, more compliant Carol – the twenty-three-year-old postgrad journalism student I first met when she was working for one of the local giveaway rags, for instance. She interviewed me about Something Important, gender equality in the television commercial production industry or something. I didn't really know what she was talking about. I looked around me at our production office, at the production co-ordinator, the line producer, the production accountant, all at their desks, while over at the big table, the director went through the script with an actress and her on-screen daughter. Behind them, other actresses were being measured and fitted by the wardrobe mistress who, I now recall, I might have been fucking. I was the only man in the room. I said nothing, but young Carol followed my gaze and began to laugh. She didn't chortle in those days. It was, as they say, husky, sexy, unconstrained. As, I learnt, her opinions were. Are.

That twenty-three-year-old didn't share our history, of course. This Carol comes to me forty-two years old, about two years before she was diagnosed. She wears the strapless summer print I always loved, white with red and purple impressionistic rose petals, that shows off the brown sheen of her skin. It presses tight over her breasts and belly and bum before releasing at her groin and swirling just above her bare, tanned knees and feet. That overrated bloom of youth is gone, yes, and there are lovely little wrinkles of flesh just above her kneecaps, at her elbows, and where the bodice of the dress flattens the base of her breasts back towards her armpits. I loved her body and soul and remember everything about her, the things I cannot see: this is when she went unshaven, at her peak of sexual confidence, her areola looked huge, engorged, enlarged by the tugging lips of three children. I can scarcely bring myself to think about what became of those breasts, her body, in so short a time. But in this moment, she is perfect. She has laugh lines at the corners of her thinnish lips, and delicate striations running vertically from her top lip. I *think* I loved her body and soul. My disadvantage is that she, being so much younger, remembers everything with a clarity that sometimes dismays me, where I sometimes seem to be looking at the past through the sepia-tinted spectacles of age.

She is over at the balcony, looking down at the deck and pool below, where our children are gathering in the dusk for my seventieth birthday celebrations. 'Do you think they're waiting for you to die?'

'Not Ellie!'

'Not Ellie.'

'Not Stan,' I say.

'Who would know what Stan's thinking? Last and loveliest. Will?'

Oh. Will. 'Would he wish me dead?'

'They fuck you up, your mum and dad,' she says, perhaps in Will's defence.

'I remember how that goes,' I tell her. 'You think he's our fault?'

'I was being diplomatic,' she says. 'I think he's your fault.'

That stuns me. Before I can think of a defence, she says, 'Cancer got him too.'

19

'Who?'

'Larkin.'

Her presence troubles me. If she's my invention, how can she know stuff I don't? How can she have so many divergent views? Are these cues, I ask myself, to some other reality? Metaphysics and spirituality were never my strong suits, but I was, they say, reasonably intutive. Is that what's happening? Or is it just another symptom of my decline? That she can remember what I used to know.

She turns from the balcony and beams at me, then nods towards Walter in his drawer. 'You should do them a favour. We'd be together again, wouldn't that be sweet?'

From her tone, I'm not at all sure. 'Is that how it works? Death?'

But how would she know, being a figment of my imagination, apparently. She ignores me, staying out on the balcony, her tousled brown hair obscuring her profile, falling down almost to her breasts.

'Tell Ellie,' she says, 'that I love her garden. My garden. She's kept it just as it was. My Abraham Darby rose is in flower. I can still smell it.'

'She'll think I'm losing my faculties.'

'Are you?'

Admit nothing! Cover with a joke. 'I can't remember.' My tremolo gives me away.

She studies me seriously. 'What if you forget you've got a pistol?'

'I won't risk waiting for a last moment of insight.'

I retrieve a big joint, freshly rolled, from the top drawer of the roll-top kauri that's full of everything I need.

'That won't help,' she says. 'I'm surprised you still smoke.'

I thought I'd lit up before in front of her, but clearly not. 'Ellie disapproves.'

'Of course she does. She saw her smoking mother die of breast cancer.'

I tell her I don't care any more. I search for a light, and out of habit, or nervous twitch, ask her if she's got a match.

'If I had a match for you I'd start a circus.'

'Ha ha.'

'It's one of yours.'

'Groucho Marx's, actually.'

'Whatever. Like you, it hasn't aged well.'

'Have I not?' I turn and trap myself long-shot in the en-suite mirror. I see a portly shape with a full head of hair haloing my skull like an emeritus professor, I like to think. Carol isn't finished with me.

'When you were thirty,' she says, 'it was the new twenty. Forty was the new thirty. Time's finally caught up and passed you, Den. Your seventy is the new eighty.'

'Eighty?'

'At least you got a chance at it.'

I'm so completely at a loss that she takes pity on me, I think. She comes very close, so close I swear I can smell her perfume, Chanel, as always. Her hair falls past me, over me. My favourite position was her on top, with her hair enveloping me, her lips on mine, our tongues entwined, the world shut out. I can sense her hair, but not feel it. I try to kiss her lips but they're not corporeal. And yet. She breathes on my joint, I swear, and the end glows with sudden heat. When I draw on it, the smoke and chemicals hit the back of my throat. I hold it there and stare into her dirt-brown eyes.

'This joint is real,' I tell her, still trying to hold it in. 'You're not. How does that work?'

I can't hold it in any longer and exhale. She becomes a circling wreath of smoke and disappears.

***

MARIJUANA takes the edge off my anxiety about the forthcoming celebration. I used to love being the centre of attention, now I quail at the prospect – even, or particularly, of my family. I think I knew even before Carol died that she was the beating heart of us. When she was gone, we became thrashing limbs looking for connection and direction.

I look out at the inner harbour, a salt river full of traffic and interest, magnified if necessary by my Konuspot 80, waiting patiently on its tripod. Directly across the water at the Chelsea wharf, the plimsoll of the sugar freighter from Queensland lifts, bow first then stern, as the augur relentlessly sucks the raw crystals into the refinery. Earlier, when the sun was still glancing off the water, there were ferries, water taxis, evening after-work yacht races, upright paddlers, kayakers, and the occasional jet-boat giving the tourists a thrill with a 360 wake-whirl. A sense of life going on, at a comfortable remove. I may not be an active part of it any more, but I've liked knowing it's there.

One of the best things about my kingdom by the sea is that I have no neighbours. Well, of course I have people living adjacent, but none I have to engage with. There's a primary school to the south, the back boundary, and on weekdays I can measure my day by the arrival of children and parents clogging the end of my shingle driveway, and by the raucous joy of the children at morning interval. At precisely 10.45 the nuns' hospice further up the hill asserts itself with bells summoning the sisters for matins or whatever, and I break for a cup of espresso from the Rocket, a relic of the old Flame production office kitchen. The school kids wake me from my midday nap with their afternoon break, then just before three, the armada of parental black SUVs returns to whisk them away.

The other boundaries are obfuscated by mature trees and a dense wall of pseudopanax between. I can see nothing of the neighbours' backyards to the north as I look over them to the sea, and even to the west, where there are three storeys of concrete-block apartments, I see only the lights of the windows at night, glimpsed through the foliage like a montage of small television screens, and hear phantom chords from a Spanish guitar, or lines from a play being rehearsed into meaninglessness, or babies crying. Very occasionally I hear voices raised in anger, male and female, in a language I don't recognise. They stay at a ghostly remove, my neighbours: thankfully there's no prospect of awkward small talk, or of any social intercourse at all.

Marijuana also burns the bleach from old eyes. I can see Will having an evening dip, ploughing up and down the pool, bifurcating the blue. Ellie and I haven't braved the water yet – it's still carrying too much winter – but Will has always been warmed by an inner fire. He has an audience, a woman in a yellow floral dress and matching enormous brimmed sunhat, sitting primly on the end of a lounger. Can that be Claudia? If it is, where are the children, my two grandchildren, Kristin, the five-year-old, and . . . the toddler, the boy. I seem to remember something about them being separated, Will and Claudia. I could be wrong. I do remember asking her when they announced their engagement, 'Are you sure you know what you're doing?' She didn't appreciate it at the time, but she might now. Unless I'm projecting, thinking wishfully. But I don't want that for Kristin and whatshisname, I don't wish that on them.

'You've been at it again,' she says, sniffing the air as she enters behind me. 'You're a terrible old degenerate.'

Ellie's smiling. She fusses over me, buttoning up my button-downs. 'Why do they make the holes so small?'

'As the bishop said to the actress.'

'In his dreams. Now,' she says, 'a warning. Will is here with a new friend.'

'I saw. Of the female persuasion.'

'He *is* separated.'

'What about the kids?'

'You can ask him. Glasses?'

I look around hopelessly. The truth is I need my glasses to find my glasses. Ellie produces them. I put them on, peer about. 'My watch. I have a special app on my iPhone which will locate–'

'Dad, you're wearing it.'

I look at my treacherous wrist. Can I really have done that?

'Easily done,' she says. Did I unknowingly articulate that last thought? 'And Jackson's disappeared, no idea where. I don't want to get him into trouble, but I'll have to ring his case officer.'

I try to reassure her, ask her to give Jackson the benefit of the doubt. I wax eloquent in Jackson's defence, that he's a good kid, the best foster we've had, that there's something about him, a sense of humility and respect for his elders that I can't recall having at his age.

She asks me if I'm okay. I wonder why she thinks I'm not. Does she think I'm not? I can't ask.

Ellie's the fag-end of Generation X, a demographic I used to know a lot about. I studied it in a predatory way, like a lion sizing up a herd of antelope. Too late to be a slacker, Ellie nevertheless adopted most of the accoutrements: the sexless flannel shirts and camo trou, the anti-establishment attitude, the endless sameness of the garage band riffs and relentless jangling faux naif of Flying Nun, but never the cynicism or the cigarettes. She was a non-conformist anti-capitalist, and I was always proud of her, even when she was deeply embarrassed by having a father who made TV commercials to sell crap. She had a healthy disrespect for authority, but was never nihilistic. She wanted to live a long, healthy life. And, always, always, do good. She dresses differently these days – today, as most days, like a card-carrying Greenie, which she is – in khaki culottes and flat sandals, but is otherwise much the same as the teenager I remember from the nineties. Or think I remember.

'Remember our secret sign, okay?'

It's so secret I have no idea what she's talking about. Ellie is holding one finger up.

'Means we've heard this story before, change tack gracefully.'

I nod. 'Change tack gracefully.'

Ellie holds two fingers up. 'Means we've heard this story or joke more than once before. Bail immediately.'

I swallow my bile, try to nod. What new stories or jokes would I have at my age? Clearly what I need is a new audience. Ellie isn't finished.

'I'll stay in your eye-line, so just give me a quick glance when you start on one of your monologues.'

'Mum says to tell you,' I say, desperate to change the subject, 'that she loves the way you've kept her garden, she can smell the scent of the Abraham Darby.'

'You've been talking to her again?'

I may have leapt from the frying pan into the fire, but I plunge on in my asbestos suit. 'I can't just ignore her.'

'Does she talk back?'

'Of course she bloody talks back – your mother always had a lot to say.'

Ellie looks at me curiously. It's not a look I recognise. Is it new, or have I forgotten it?

'Dad,' she says, 'I can tell it's real for you, and if it gives you some comfort, fine. But it's not something you should share, okay?'

Because if I do, they'll all think I'm losing it. I get it. 'Message understood. I'll have a pee and be right down.'

Ellie goes. I wander towards the en-suite and catch myself in long-shot again. I still look okay, I think. From a distance. It's the close-ups that don't work any more.

The default expression on my face has always been a smile. I might have been worried, anxious, preoccupied or feeling neutral or nothing at all, but I looked happy. It's always been my biggest asset. Until recently, when my smile seems to be getting lost in other crinkles. I've noticed that my beatific visage may be sending out different signals in old age: the bafflement of dotage, the harmless bewilderment of the elderly duffer. Like most writers – which is what I essentially consider myself to be, despite spending most of my career directing and co-producing – I'm a natural catastrophist, but an upbeat one. My glass was never half empty, always full to brimming, but threatening at any moment to explode in my face. I grew up down south, in a spare, wondrous landscape stretched across an alpine fault. At primary school, we were taught about earthquakes and practised diving under our desks as, in our imaginations, the earth rocked. We knew, as New Zealanders, that nothing was permanent: that we lived on the flotsam and jetsam of molten magma.

***

I EDGE myself down the stairs and along the polished wooden floor of the hallway, from which Ellie has removed the carpets after I tripped on one of Carol's favourite Persians and fell, shearing a knee cartilage. Heart kauri from the 1920s those floorboards, golden syrup yellow, full of knots. Those knots date it as precisely as carbon. Before that, the sawmillers threw away wood like this, thought it was blemished. A hundred next year, this house, more than a quarter of a century older than me. In better nick too, its joints still straight and strong. The softness of those floorboards looked after me – if I'd fallen on concrete, I'd have needed a new knee. My knee may have lost some muscle memory, but the cartilage within it has full recall and it gives me a dig just for old times' sake. It knows I can't neutralise it with anti-inflamms like I used to. They play havoc with my ulcer, a result of all those years using Voltaren as a hangover cure.

I limp along the hallway to the big room, heading across to the french doors, which open out onto the deck. In late afternoon, the dying westerly sun refracts off the pool, sending light dancing across the plastered ceiling of my favourite downstairs room. The huge sofas in American maple covered in Belgian linen, bought by Carol in flusher times, are big enough to stretch out and sleep on. In winter, the early afternoon sun is so low it bathes the sofa nearest the doors in warmth, making it a great place for an afternoon nap. I still haven't read every book in the glass-fronted bookcase along the wall, and I would happily choose one right now and curl up with it on the sofa, rather than continue with my veneration. Celebration doesn't come easily to our culture: we're better at heavy irony and even heavier drinking. Being in the same space for too long seems to have a corrosive effect on my family's paper-thin scars over old wounds. But it's too late now, and I walk on, trying not to limp, telling myself not to precipitate any conflict. Let others cast the first stone.

As I step onto the deck, I see Ellie in the kitchen loading plates onto the sills of the Whitney windows that open out onto the deck. The table is already chokka – ham on the bone, cold chicken, potato salad, green salads, bottles of dressing and sauce. One end has a cluster of bottles like skittles, champagne and wine and beer, ringed with glasses and flutes. I told Ellie not to spend more than twenty dollars on any bottle of wine, because my palate's no longer worthy of it. She said we couldn't afford to pay any more anyway. There are a lot of bottles and glasses. It seems like overkill just for us. I wonder who's coming that I don't know about. I don't like surprises.

Will is out of the pool, in profile, adjusting the cock in his Speedos to best effect for the woman on the lounger. Who is not Claudia. I hear a grab of conversation as I approach: 'a bit of maintenance' from him and 'good bones, though' from her. This will surely be Will talking about himself – he's looking fit, carrying less weight than I remember. It's interesting looking at your middle-aged children, trying to read the clues as to which genes went where. Carol is right about Will, our eldest: he's more me than her, physically at least. My sturdiness, but not so heavy, taller and my thick once-black hair, with blue eyes that always take me by surprise. My fault? What can Carol have meant by that?

The woman who isn't Claudia sees me and gives a subtle heads-up to Will, whose expression when he turns is shadowed by something too fleeting for me to decipher. I'm still chasing it when he smiles, blue eyes shining. My blue-eyed boy.

'Rocket Man!' Still wet, he draws me into a considerate semi-man-hug.

It's important I don't rise to the Rocket Man bait, give him any opportunity to sing the ditty, 'Give yourself a lift/Take off with Rocket', tell the story of how I made my fortune with a TV commercial for a sugar drink that made our children obese, reduce me to claiming ignorance, making me look both pathetic and rapacious. I take a breath, look over his shoulder at the woman in the yellow dress and hat and limit myself to telling her that I'd prefer he call me Den in front of strangers.

'This is my friend, Georgina,' says Will, releasing me.

'Georgie,' she corrects him.

They can't have known each other long, then. I shake her hand. She has a thin, austere sexuality about her, about as far from Claudia's dark buxom earthiness as it would be possible to get. 'How's Claudia?'

'Seems all right.'

'I was expecting the children. You said you had them weekends.'

'Not every weekend. I've got to have a life.'

'Clearly.' I'm peeved. This is supposed to be a family occasion, with all the tiers. And in truth, I prefer my grandchildren, particularly Kristin, to my children. Perhaps because they can't answer back yet, particularly whatshisname, the boy . . . The other thing that marijuana does, after it eases the anxiety, is make me paranoid.

'I won't be staying long, Mr Sparks,' says Georgie.

'Den, please. I wasn't trying to be rude–'

'You should see him when he tries!' Will is still smiling, but under sufferance.

I confess to Georgie that I'm still adjusting to Will's change of marital circumstances.

'It's been months, Den.'

'Easy come, easy go, these days, I suppose.'

'I had your upstanding example before me.'

'I never left Carol–'

'No you rubbed her face in it and–'

'Will! Enough!' Ellie has arrived, thankfully, with flutes of champagne. We're too alike, Will and I: every exchange seems testy, exposing the fragile crust of our civility.

I hate champagne. Those infernal bubbles. I get drunker quicker and the hangover begins before I've even started pontificating and slurring. But it's my birthday, what can I say? 'Thank you, Ellie.'

Will also wants champagne. Georgie asks directions to the loo. Ellie ushers her towards the house, leaving Will and me standing awkwardly beside the pool. Over Will's shoulder, I watch Georgie walk towards the french doors, the surprising jiggle of her slim arse. I have the thought that if I was younger . . . but mercifully it passes quickly. I'm actually relieved that I'm no longer a captive of my reptilian sexual urges. I can't be the first old bastard to have had that thought: I must have read it somewhere. I sometimes wonder if there can possibly be an original thought that hasn't already been thunk, after thousands of years of sentient beings. The odds against an original thought still roaming free out there must be astronomical. Can I be the first person to think of that, for instance?

I consider myself a writer, yes, but there are writers and writers. No one would accuse me of having poetry in my soul. Copywriter says it all really – I wouldn't dream of claiming originality for anything I ever wrote. That wasn't what I did. At my best I tried to mainstream the zeitgeist, create some newish take on what already existed out there. Watch other people's behaviour, use other people's thoughts, remix old ingredients to look like some new alchemy. Incremental modification is what the best of us do. Did. Always with the same aim. Commodification.

Until the zeitgeist began failing me. I can remember the exact moment it struck me. My D-list celebrity got me a free ticket to a preview screening of the first *Lord of the Rings* film, just after the turn of the century. True, Carol had died not long before, so I wasn't at my most optimistic. I stayed for the duration because I hadn't paid for my ticket and didn't feel I could walk out. So I sat there for what seemed like several weeks, long past any appreciation of the stunning scenery, wishing for it to end – the surprisingly unsurprising confrontations with monsters, the hugely contrived set-piece battles with entirely predictable outcomes, the endless portentous exposition. It seemed like the end of drama and beginning of spectacle, and when eventually I was released into the foyer, I asked Branko and the group of minor celebs with me, 'Who on earth would pay money to watch *that*?'

'Millions,' said Branko, quite correctly. He'd just used the Flame Inc. umbrella to produce a documentary about his early Dalmatian forebears who had come here to dig for kauri gum up north and fallen in love with Māori women – a stunningly handsome genetic mix. He had this theory about television, which had seemed so cynical when he'd first espoused it: you tell the audience what you're about to show them, then you show them what you've just talked about, then you tell them what they've just seen. The documentary he made on exactly those principles was a ratings success, not on the global scale of *Lord of the Rings*, of course, but there seemed to be a synergy between what he and Peter Jackson did, recycling the same endlessly repetitive tropes. Not that I saw all the movies. I went to the second *LOTR* to try and prove to myself that my reaction to the first one had been a jaundiced off-moment between me and the zeitgeist. But it was worse, if anything, redeemed only by the introduction of a character called Gollum, who at least had *two* dimensions. When I found myself wishing fervently that he'd wipe those big-eared, hairy-footed self-satisfied little cretins from the face of Middle Earth, I realised that there was no hope for me and my time in advertising was about done.

I couldn't bring myself to go near the final movie of the trilogy, the one that won all the Oscars. I could have looked at that kind of success and asked myself, 'What have *I* done? Where has my taste and discretion taken *me*?', and tried to learn from the experience, get my finger back on the populist pulse. But, I was fifty-something, still hurting from the loss of Carol, and couldn't be fucked.

Which reminds me. I'm well shot of it, my testosterone. Insidious, insistent, it constantly undermined my intelligence and good intentions. I sometimes miss the mindless drive, the excitement of the chase, the filling weight of blood in my penis, but it always came at such a cost and was much diminished, strangely enough, after Carol died and I was free to do what, in all honesty, I had always done. Whoever said that guilt heightened the pleasure, might have been half right. Will's lips are moving. He must be talking to me.

'I don't mean to be antsy, Den,' he is saying. I can't remember when he last called me Dad. Maybe before he came to work at Flame, when he was sixteen or seventeen. Calling me Dad around the production office wouldn't have been cool. 'Leaving Claudia wasn't easy. Hasn't been easy.' He's facing the garden, more like bush, that begins at the eastern end of the deck, behind me, beyond a cute wooden fence and gate. He sees something that alarms him, and whispers to me, 'You carrying your phone, Den? Don't make it obvious but slip it to me.'

I unlock the iPhone with my fingerprint, and palm it to Will. 'Why the cloak and dagger?'

When I try to turn towards whatever he's looking at, he holds me by the shoulder. 'Don't move, keep me covered . . .'

'What're you doing?'

'Dialling 111.' He does so, then, with his phone to his ear, he steps to the side of me and holds his hand up towards the garden. 'Stop right there,' he shouts. 'I'm talking to the cops!'

I swing round to see who he's talking to and quickly grab the phone out of his hand.

'F'chrissakes!'

Jackson is standing at the garden gate. Will's clearly made some quick value judgements on the key elements he sees in front of him – an obviously part-Māori sixteen-year-old in T-shirt and reversed baseball cap, carrying a tomahawk. I suppose Jackson could look a bit out of context and vaguely threatening if he didn't also have an armful of dry branches. Jackson is as alarmed by Will as Will is by him and looks to me. 'What's up, Mr D?'

'Jackson, this is my eldest, William. Will, Jackson.'

'Someone Jackson, or Jackson Someone?'

'Jackson Collins,' says the boy.

'Works for West Indian cricketers,' I offer. My favourite double surname was Grayson Shillingford, but Vanburn Holder and the incomparable Garfield Sobers also had a grandeur about them.

'I was named after a league player,' he says.

'Of course you were,' says Will.

'Don't be a tit all your life, Will,' says Ellie, arriving. 'Jackson, we've been worried about you.'

'I haven't,' says Will.

'Where've you been?' Ellie asks.

As if in answer, another figure steps out from the grass pathway that winds its way through Carol's garden. She's dressed tough-arse in black, torn stockings, Doc Martens, like a cross between Goth and punk, with a big black coat hanging open, showing a white T-shirt with a graphic of Keith Richards displaying his own chest with '*Who the Fuck is Mick Jagger?*' scrawled across the front. Underneath all that, there doesn't look to be much of her. She's got Jackson's skinny face and build, wiry and wound like a cord. 'This's my older sister, Lila,' says Jackson. 'Say hello, Lila.'

Lila looks suspiciously at her brother. 'You sure?'

Jackson looks at Ellie. 'I'se gunna check it out with you if she could come over.'

'I wish you had,' says Ellie. 'One of the department's conditions is that you have no contact with your family.'

'Lila's sweet, miss,' says Jackson.

Lila looks anything but sweet, but Jackson's embarrassed and Ellie's clearly conflicted, so while her better nature struggles to assert itself, I jump in. 'Fine! More the merrier!'

'Of course,' confirms Ellie. 'Welcome, Lila.'

Jackson ushers his sister in front of him and says he'll get the pizza oven going with the kindling he's collected, and Lila can give him a hand. We watch them cross to the big outdoor fireplace. Watch Lila grab a fistful of finger food from the table as she passes. Watch her wolf it.

'Help yourself,' mutters Will. 'Make yourself at home. What the fuck is going on here?'

Ellie explains that she has offered to take troubled kids on respite placement, if the department can't find anywhere else for them.

'They? Them? How many–?'

'Jackson's our third short-term foster.'

'Thought this was a strictly family gathering.'

'Which begs the question of Georgie's presence,' I reply.

'Please, you two,' says Ellie. 'Jackson's family, for the moment. We're fostering him while his own family's in crisis.'

'What sort of crisis?'

'His father's been in jail for beating up his mother. Jackson's been in care on and off since he was eight, when his grandmother died.'

Will smells a rat. 'On and off? C'mon, what'd he do this time?'

Ellie shrugs as if she doesn't know or it doesn't matter, but Will is insistent. Ellie says that he set fire to his school, which *is* news to me.

'Arson?' says Will, turning to watch Jackson feeding the branches he's collected into the smouldering pizza oven.

'They caught it in time,' she says. 'There wasn't much damage.'

'Good news all round then,' says Will. 'Should he be anywhere near that oven?'

'He's sixteen,' pleads Ellie, 'right on the cusp. Any more trouble in the next six months and he'll be old enough to have a criminal conviction and go to prison, instead of a youth justice residence. Another lost boy. Not if I can help it.'

Ellie was a social worker before she came home to me, whenever that was – two years ago? Could be four. She said she'd had enough. Compassion fatigue, she said. Was that just for my benefit? Ellie's compassion seems inexhaustible. I support her, tell Will that Jackson is a good kid. 'Better behaved than you were.' That was a mistake.

'When were you around to notice?' asks Will.

Ellie leaps to my defence. 'Oh, give it a rest, Will, for God's sake. These are kids who have nothing!'

I wasn't going to cast the first stone, but now it's done. I pout, stamp my foot, tell him it's my party and I'll have who I want. It's a joke.

'Sure,' says Will, with not even a ghost of a smile. 'I'll go put some clothes on, so I can leave when I want.'

He takes his towel and walks off towards the house. Not happy.

Ellie excuses herself and heads across to Jackson and his sister, not happy. I stand there, sipping champagne I don't want at a birthday celebration I don't want. So far, so good. Normal family service resumed.

***

THE light has slunk off behind the alders and eucalypts lining the western boundary. When I look back towards the house, I notice for the first time plants growing out of the spouting. They must have appeared over the winter; no wonder there were waterfalls from the roof in the rainstorms. Then I catch a flash of yellow on the balcony of my room upstairs. Georgie having a nosey round the house.

Oh well, I used to do the same when I went out. Medicine cabinets were particularly interesting. That rich, suave couple serving drinks and canapés downstairs, he the perfect, relaxed mine host, she the happy hostess with the mostest? A medicine cabinet with large bottles of two different SSRIs, sertraline and citalopram, might betray them. Who'd have thought? If Georgie ventures into my en-suite, there'll be no surprises. You'd look at me and say amlodipine for blood pressure and statins for sure, but unless you saw my disfigured big toe in a sandal, you might not plump for allopurinol, nor perhaps paroxetine. I resisted the anti-depressants for a long time, until I had no further use for what I called writer's melancholia. I used to think it gave me an edge, an occasional discomfort with the world, an insight that I might not otherwise have had, similar to but different from the insights I got from cocaine and booze. Then being depressed just got boring and a waste of time, as time began to run out. I'd sold my share of Flame to Will, so the pressure was off, I didn't have to come up with any more concepts, sixty-second narratives with commercial cut-through. That was our schtick to begin with: a boutique agency with its own production arm, the one-stop bullshit shop, Branko called it. I came up with the copy, began directing, Branko produced. Dream it, pitch it, shoot it. As long as Georgie doesn't go into my roll-top and discover Walter. Where did I put that half-smoked joint?

I look across to Jackson, still feeding the fire, as Ellie talks to him and Lila. Jackson has a long visage, an old man's face atop his scrawny body. Lugubrious, until he grins, when the length of his face splits, and you see beautiful teeth, a credit, Ellie says, to his grandmother, who raised him in poverty and loving care before she died. But arson? Now there's a word with a bit of cut-through.

***

IN the gloaming, the pool looks luminous, as if the water is giving light back to slow the darkening of the sky. We'll have half an hour before the mozzies arrive and need the torches lit to help keep them at bay. I grab the oversized matches from beside the fire and head over to the nearest bracket. In passing, I hear Ellie suggesting to Lila that she must be hot, can she take her coat?

'I'm good,' says Lila.

Ellie offers her a glass of iced water.

'Can I have one of those?' asks Lila, indicating the wine glasses.

'Sure,' says Ellie, 'white or red?'

'Red makes my teeth turn purple.' Lila takes a white, unscrews the top and pours herself a full glass. She swallows most of it. Ellie is looking at Jackson.

'I'll give you a hand, Mr D,' says Jackson, looking to escape.

He takes the first bamboo torch from its bracket and holds it while I strike the match and light the paraffin wick. By the time Jackson is replacing the torch in its bracket, Ellie has joined us. There's an intense sotto voce between Ellie and Jackson as we work our way from torch to torch round the perimeter of the deck. I don't catch it all but I know Jackson's back story – or thought I knew it before Ellie dropped the arson word – so it's easy to piece together her concern about Lila turning up here.

Ellie is careful to fill me in on the kids who come for respite so I can make an 'informed decision', though we both know I have no say in these matters. If I did, I would tell Ellie that 'respite' is a myth perpetrated by do-gooders. These kids have to go back to their world, sooner rather than later. And when they do, they carry with them a knowledge they may not have had before, of a world they can never aspire to or access. How can that help them reconcile themselves to their lives? The art of advertising was to tantalise people with the *possible*, not flaunt the impossible. We at least tried to give people the key to realise a dream – buy this, *be* that. No good will come of rubbing these kids' noses in a smorgasbord of comforts they can never have. But to say that to Ellie would be cruel. People need to believe what they need to believe, and it's altruism that makes Ellie tick. I'd meddle with that to my own detriment, given that I'm her prime project. But at least I belong here.

Jackson is here 'in respite' from a brutal father, recently released from jail. Who was incarcerated for beating Jackson's mother with a lump of half-burnt wood from the grate, causing injuries that kept her in intensive care for several days. When she wouldn't or couldn't go to the cops, Jackson did. Stood in a witness box behind a screen, fourteen years old, and got his father three years inside. Now his old man's out, after eighteen months, on 'good behaviour'. Eighteen months during which a prison visit by his mother and Lila wasn't complete without a threat against Jackson, who never went. The son who 'narked' on him and put him away was going to be 'dealt to'. The father's warnings were carried back to Jackson by his sister. How the authorities could know he was threatening his son, yet still let him out, I've no idea.

That's Ellie's version of Jackson's story, anyway. Which I now wonder if she might have finessed to make it more compelling for me. I don't know. I can't say no to Ellie any more, whatever she tells me, but I'm not sure she knows that.

So here he lives, with us, in 'temporary respite', till what? What's going to change in Jackson's world? I don't ask, but I can see Ellie's concern that Lila now knows where her brother is. The father could beat that knowledge out of her, and then, according to Ellie, he *will* come for the boy.

As we work around to the torches along the back of the pool, Jackson's voice rises in defence of his sister. I can hear the high bleat of his pleading: 'He's burnt her with the pipe, miss.' I gradually piece it together: it's a meth pipe, and the father has been torturing Lila with it to find the address of her brother.

That leads to an interrogation by Ellie as to whether Lila's on P. Jackson denies it, says it's just his dad.

I look back across the pool towards his twitchy sister in the black coat, downing another glass of that god-awful gooseberry juice, Marlborough sauvignon blanc. What a crime against viniculture, when the same terroir, my own home soil, grows wonderful chardonnay and pinot noir. Lila projects a kind of fierce vulnerability: if she's challenged she'll either blow your lights out or burst into tears.

I don't hear everything Jackson says, but Ellie seems reassured.

I'm not. I think about intervening, but to say what? Chuck them both out, return them to their own world and to the certain and, surely, brutal revenge of their father? If what Ellie says is true, I don't want that on my head. I don't have any idea what Jackson's world looks like, but Ellie does. More than a decade as a front-line social worker with beaten mothers and vulnerable children in parts of this city I've never seen, before she came home to look after me. So I defer to her experience, of course I do. But what good can come of it? None. Yet good is what Ellie does.

Lila is standing with her bum to the fire, looking right at me, right through me. The look says she knows how the dynamics work here: *Watch it, you old cunt, I'm on to you.*

***

I FIND myself following Stan through Carol's garden, along the winding grass track, all that is left of the once expansive lawn. When we moved into this house in '78, she told me lawns were a waste of nature's time and energy and began planting until, within a decade, the grass was almost all gone.

It's too dark now to see Carol's garden in all its glory. It looks magical in full spring light and utterly transcendent in the hour before sunset. That was often a time of suppressed panic for me on set when I and the DOP would be trying to milk every moment of the soft amber light, while Branko would be more worried about the schedule and completing the day. Earlier this evening, I caught that light perfectly in my final production, shot on my mobile. I feel for the USB in the pocket of my Rainbird and remind myself to try to stay in the present, because there's not a lot more of it left for me.

I was looking away from Lila's stare, desperate for a change of focus, when I saw Stan, standing there at the garden gate, quietly beckoning me. God knows how long he'd been there, surveying the scene. Knowing Stan, quite some time – he's never been one for the grand entrance.

'Follow me,' he said.

I did, his long tramper's strides. He's got Carol's length of leg, with stringy muscle. The garden is only about fifty paces from end to end, but the meandering track must add half that number again. There are roses on either side, many in bloom. How Carol could distinguish the fragrance of the Abraham Darby from the others, I've no idea. I do know that, along the borders of the track, are phlox, bearded irises, violets, larkspurs, granny bonnets and lupins. And there are many more, all, at least to my eye, exactly as Carol had them, the flowers mixed with herbs – sage, rosemary, chamomile – and at the back near the fence the big melia tree, where Stan's umbilical cord is buried alongside those of Will and Ellie. Should I remind Stan of the historical significance of the tree whose newly leaf-laden branches we're now passing under? I have a feeling he wouldn't thank me, and say nothing. The main track leads to another wooden gate, which delivers you down some steps to the parking bay and double garage, but Stan turns onto a smaller track off to the left and we pass through a small grove of ponga and mamaku tree ferns guarding the north-east corner of the garden, where we stop in front of three citrus trees and a feijoa.

'White fly,' he says, lifting the leaves of the lemon, lime and grapefruit, revealing spots of what look like splatters of white paint on the undersides. 'And you can't eat the grapefruit anyway on that blood pressure drug, so why don't we rip them out?'

I have no answer, other than nothing must change. On that

Ellie and I are agreed. Everything here is Carol's. Those citrus were our first plantings: they're older than Stan.

He's not waiting for my reply, but indicating three bushy seedlings freshly planted in a gap between the lemon and feijoa trees. 'Happy birthday, Dad,' he says. 'I've just put them in for you. I've soaked the roots and given them crystals but they'll need watering in a few days.'

I'm staring at the plants, thinking that the leaf looks familiar, while Stan goes on to tell me that he's brought the plants up with him from Te Kurahau, that they're taken from a little trial patch he's growing. He sees that I'm not with him. 'Cannabis,' he explains. 'Weed. Though it's actually a cash crop with huge commercial potential. I know you enjoy it and come the end of summer you'll have your own supply, in bulk. You'll never have to buy the stuff again.'

I thank him, of course. Stan doesn't know that I can't recognise a marijuana plant in its natural state. I buy my reefers already packaged – they could be Cuban cigars. I no more know how to process a leaf into a reefer than how to catch a fish and cook it – if it doesn't come skinned, boned and filleted, it's no use to me. I've always been an iconoclast in this City of Sails, which by repute has more boats per capita than anywhere else in the world. There was a time in the early eighties when every man I knew who was coining it – and plenty were – bought a boat. Owning a boat, like the crash in '87, was a rite of passage to financial maturity. I've always hated boats. The idea of being trapped in a tiny capsule on a heaving sea with people I don't know – or even with those I do – fills me with dread. So I never fished. Carol and I were as one on that. 'Thank you, Stan.'

'You've already said that. You're starting to repeat yourself, Dad.'

'Thank you for pointing that out.'

'Just saying.'

I loathe that expression. By the time those words are uttered, we're no longer in the present. The words are said.

The sun is long gone, and if we were on set the DOP might be telling me the colour in the light has moved from maroon to blue to the darkest of greens. The solar lamps, also planted long ago along the edges of the track, begin tentatively offering their light. Many of them have given up the ghost, and the shadowy bush looms, but Stan's horticultural eyes are looking through the penumbra towards the glossy pseudopanax that screens the long northern boundary. 'See those blue flowers?'

'Yes!' They're the delicate powder blue of a David Hockney pool, woven through the verdant green. 'I've never noticed them before.'

'Morning glory. A vine. It'll strangle everything if you leave it. I'll try and rip it out before I go back down south.'

***

WHEN we get back to the deck, Ellie sees Stan for the first time. She rushes out from the kitchen into his arms. 'You've come! You've come!'

'How could I not?'

Ellie tightens her pincer hug. 'Christ, he's as taut as a rope!'

Their embrace is overtaken by a noise from the bowels of the house – Will, now wearing a short-sleeved shirt, shorts and boat shoes, from Nautica would be my guess. Whatever, the whole ensemble would have been bought from the same outlet at the same time with free parking for the first half-hour. Target shopping, he calls it. He's shouting into his mobile, swigging on a bottle of beer, oblivious, until he clocks Stan. 'Marlborough Man! How did you tear yourself away from bucolic bliss? Won't the cows be missing you?'

'We milk goats, actually.'

'As long as that's all you do with them, eh?'

'And it's Nelson, not Marlborough.'

When Stan takes Will's outstretched palm in his, Will draws him in for a manly hug. Stan's so tall that Will has to stand on tip-toe and reach up. 'Little bro!' says Will. It's awkward, ridiculous.

'Would anyone like a drink?' I ask. 'I would.'

Will drains his beer, burps. 'Good idea, I'm running on empty.'

Stan can't resist the opportunity. 'Still?'

Will manages a laugh. 'Just as well you're not living on your wit, little bro, there'd be no money in that.'

Ellie's already had enough. 'Grow up, both of you. It's Dad's day.'

I like to think I don't know how it got to this . . . But it was ever thus between them for as long as I can remember. Stan's more Carol than the other two: her length of limb, but not her certainty about her place in the world. He's always had a deference that got on Will's nerves. Stan was the unexpected afterthought, five years younger than Ellie. Carol hadn't wanted another baby and Stan, when he arrived, seemed to sense he was in this world on sufferance, that he should be on his best behaviour. He was sweet, compliant, beautiful, and almost from the start, his presence seemed galling to Will. On one of the few occasions I was home early enough, I was bathing seven-year-old Will when he asked me, 'Daddy, if someone sort of smashed that new baby right in the head and killed it, would that be a good thing?' I never told Carol.

Will always had a mean streak, particularly when it came to his siblings. He left school early, under a cloud, as they say. The principal of the local arty liberal high school called us into his temporary office in a cheap prefab on a stiflingly hot early summer's day to explain that Will had been caught having sex with a girl in the storage room of the gym, a younger girl who alleged he'd previously introduced her to marijuana. I daren't look, but I felt Carol's eyes burning me. It was made clear that if Will went now, of his own volition, he wouldn't have to be publicly censured and expelled and the girl would be spared the inevitable rumour-mongering and character assassination.

It was almost the end of the academic year anyway, and Will was never going to uni.

I had a talk with Branko at Flame. Nepotism rules, he said. Bring him in, we'll give him a start, see if he cuts it over the summer. It seemed like the perfect resolution and it was. It was only later that Carol told me that the girl Will had seduced at school was Ellie's best friend. Former.

Leaving school was the right move for Will. He proved adept at profiling his own generation, giving Flame an insight there, and then later, into the millennials who came behind him, of whom Stan was a classic example. For all his deference, Stan still had that millennial sense of entitlement and taste, which made them so hard to sell to. If they thought it was mainstream, they wouldn't touch it, but how do you make money from clique cool in a domestic market of four million, where the 'in crowd' isn't so much a crowd as a very small sect? Spending all day trying to corral millennial mercury must have driven Will mad. When he came home at night, student Stan bore the brunt of his brother's 'demographic research'. He used Stan as a whipping boy: pushed him, derided him, embarrassed him, called him a pussy. I should have stopped it, but even when I was there my attention was elsewhere.

Maybe Stan saw me as an enabler: he couldn't bolt fast enough as soon as he turned seventeen, to the other end of the country, to do a BA at Otago. I made sure he never needed a student loan, and he must have enjoyed it, majored in anthropology and stayed on in that academic holding pattern for another two years for a master's – about as useful as tits on a bull. He then took what he called a gap year, which became two, teaching English as a second language in China, before the prospect of Te Kurahau lured him back to the southern landscape of his paternal grandparents. They were both dead by the time he got back, so he was still about as far from his family as it was possible to be.

I look at the three of them still throwing barbs at each other in their middle age and feel depressed that such an old truth can keep reasserting itself: whatever we've become out in the world, we always come home to be what we were.

I want to call a halt, tell them to stop, to be civil, to try and accept the differences in each other, but instead I start obliquely on what I hope will be a cautionary tale about when I came home from university for the summer holidays after my first year away. Ellie is already holding one finger up. I can't remember what that signifies. 'We've heard this story before, Dad,' she mouths.

'Really?'

Ellie holds up ten fingers, bunches her fists and holds up another ten. Okay, I get it. But that wouldn't have stopped me. What stops me is . . . the story is gone. I ransack my brain but there's nothing there, neither the story nor the point I was going to make with it. In my desperation I remember another story, an old joke, a favourite that Branko and I often recycled. 'Have you heard the one about the Irish zookeeper and the orang-utan?'

Ellie gives me ten fingers again. 'Is that the one that ends with the zookeeper asking will they take a cheque?' she asks.

Well, that effectively kills that. I must have turned puce.

'Sorry, Dad.'

She means it to be consoling, but there's no consolation for what I'm suffering. I should take her into my confidence, but I can't, not now. I check again. My first summer home after starting uni, one of my favourite stories! Ellie could repeat it word for word probably, but from my brain it's gone. If I was eighteen that first summer holiday, it would have been 1967. I open my iPhone and Google '1967', thinking there must be a clue, maybe in Wikipedia, which I support with small donations, which Ellie doesn't object to. '1967 in New Zealand' lists things that happened: there was a gas explosion in the Strongman mine which killed nineteen miners, decimal currency was introduced – is that on the money?, Mr Lee Grant won the Loxene Golden Disc – I remember him, a lanky, lank-haired balladeer whose real name was Bogdan! That's promising! And Great Adios won the New Zealand Trotting Cup. All this is fascinating in its own write, as John Lennon must have said around about then, but is utterly useless in prompting any clues about my story.

Ellie is nudging me. 'Dad, please don't get lost in your phone.'

I want to tell her that it's not within my phone that I'm lost, I want to tell her what Dr Jeetan told me. I pull my eyes from the screen to my progeny. I've been absent for a swathe of conversation that seems to have extended and expanded the previous vitriol, so I've not missed much.

I'd hoped things would change with the passage of time. Marlboro Man? That wasn't a good opener from Will. He knows how much Stan would have been repelled by it: he was fourteen when he saw his pack-a-day mother die of breast cancer, and has never smoked, not even the marijuana he grows.

***

WHEN Georgie returns from the longest pee in Christendom, carrying her hat, she apologises for being so long, and for not previously wishing me a happy birthday. 'That's okay,' I tell her. 'We're not very good at celebrations.'

'At least this birthday is working out better than his fortieth,' says Will. He seems more nervous than usual about something, and turns his blue eyes on me. 'Don't you remember?'

I wish I could say yes, if only to forestall the bad news I sense is coming. But I don't remember anything at all. What year would that have been – 1989? Oh, shit. That decade with an eight in front of it. I fear the worst.

'Mum organised a surprise party for you at the office, kept me home from school so I could come. But you were out at a long lunch with the wardrobe mistress, discussing' – Will raises two fingers to telegraph irony – 'serious budget concerns.'

The mention of the wardrobe mistress raises a red flag, even though I tell him I really don't remember. I don't know how to stop him, even as Stan and Ellie join us.

'Convenient memory lapse, Den! When we got the word you were on the way back, Mum and me and Branko and Trish hid in your office en-suite with the champagne. We're all hiding there, waiting for the signal from Mum to burst out with the big "Surprise!", when we hear the unmistakeable sounds of serious rutting. When Mum bursts into your office, the surprise is on her – you've got the wardrobe mistress bent over your desk–'

Ellie, of course, is appalled. 'Dad!'

Georgie is clearly struggling to cope with what she's hearing. 'What?' she says. 'They were–'

'Discussing the Ugandan situation, yes. I was twelve years old.'

'I'm truly sorry, Will, and I'm sure I apologised to Carol many times.'

'Mum tried to break the bottle of champagne over your head.'

'Did she?'

'Missed and hit the edge of the desk.'

What can I say? I shrug at Georgie. 'You know what they say: If you can remember the eighties, you weren't there.'

'They were talking about the sixties, Den,' corrects Will.

'Well, the sixties didn't get here until halfway through the seventies, so we had a lot of time to make up.' I'm still, through the fog of embarrassment, asking myself why Will wants to abase me in front of this stranger, and my daughter and youngest son, when it all becomes very clear. I don't see it coming, even when Georgie dismisses further family reminiscences and tells Will she's waiting for her cue.

Ellie is clearly not in on the play. 'Your cue?'

I'm equally puzzled. 'You're not a thespian by any chance, Georgie?'

'I'm a prospective purchaser.'

It's Will's turn to look embarrassed in the stunned silence that follows, a rare expression for him. I'm the only one who doesn't get the subtext. 'Of what?'

Georgie explains that she and her husband know this neighbourhood, they live right on the water, one block down. I look at Will, still way behind the eight ball. 'Her husband?'

'We're not an item, Den,' says Will.

'We're looking to the future,' says Georgie. 'We'd prefer to have a glimpse of the harbour than be submerged in it. And have a beautiful garden.'

Ellie turns on Will, furious. 'How could you?'

Georgie waves her hat like a fan to cool her reddening face. 'Your brother was kind enough to let me informally appraise the place – under false pretences, I'll admit.' I'd not noticed, under the brim of her hat, how unnaturally high on her forehead her eyebrows were etched. Why would anyone do that to themselves?

'I was just trying to keep the real estate agents out of it,' says Will, finding his voice.

Now I get it, finally. Why Georgie was gone so long, what she was doing in there, sniffing every corner of the house, while we were out here, unknowing, celebrating my birthday. My eternal smile must desert me – Georgie senses my dismay. 'Your son told me I'd be doing your family a service.'

'We need to do something, Den,' says the procurer of this service. 'Or the place will fall around your ears and be worth nothing.'

'Your son said we could make an offer before the property actually goes on the open market.'

'Think about it, Den. No agent, no fees!'

I'm wondering what the connection is between Will and Georgie. They seemed from the first moment I met them such an unlikely couple, why didn't I twig? 'How did you two meet?'

Ellie is more direct. 'Where'd you find him?' she asks Georgie.

'Under a fucking rock,' says Will.

'I can believe that!' Ellie's now right in Georgie's flushed face. 'How did he know you were interested in buying this house?'

Will, clearly worried that she will disclose something, tells Georgie she doesn't need to answer. But Georgie is intent on retrieving some dignity. I'm not sure her next words do that. 'My husband's a proctologist.'

Will protests. 'That's a breach of confidence!'

Stan makes the connection. 'Will's a patient.'

His brother turns on him. 'You want to die from arse cancer? Do you?'

'So, he had his thing up your arse . . .' suggests Stan calmly, as if seeking clarification.

'Colonoscopy, yes. Burning off polyps. After Mum died–'

'And you started talking shit,' says Ellie, livid. 'How fucking appropriate!'

Georgie, alarmed at this scatological turn, rails at Will. 'You told me he was ready to sell!'

'Open to persuasion, I said. He is.'

Ellie is adamant. 'He's not!'

'He fucking should be!'

They seem to be talking about someone in another room, and I get the feeling that's where I should be. Georgie's clearly not the brightest of bulbs, but clicks that she's been sold a pup. 'I'm sorry,' she says. 'I was given to understand–'

But Georgie is ignored. Ellie and Stan have turned on Will. I can't bear the detail of what follows. Ellie is furious, Stan less so, more appalled that Will has consulted none of us. Through it all, Will is defensive, but unrepentant: someone had to make the call. 'Think about it f'chrissakes!' he repeats. 'No commission, no open homes, no advertising budget.'

'Not one more fucking word!' yells Ellie.

Georgie, I think, is not a bad person, just badly advised. When she sees the family up in arms, at one another's throats, she has the sense to take her leave, and disappears through the french doors, so distressed that she leaves her hat. I pick it up and hand it to Will. 'Have the courtesy to see your friend out.'

When Will goes, Ellie turns and makes for the kitchen, passing Jackson and his sister over by the fire. In her fury, she doesn't see or acknowledge them. They look stricken. They may not have understood the detail of what's happened, but the dynamic of a family pummelling each other must seem utterly familiar.

Through the Whitneys I can see Ellie trying to calm herself, lighting the seven candles on my cake with shaking fingers. It's coming, but I don't feel ready. What's the word? When that little whirling symbol appears on screen while my MacBook Pro tries to get its shit together? Bluffing . . . Buffering! I'm still trying to get a grip on all that's happened, my RAM, or is it ROM, overwhelmed. In shock. My oldest child wants me gone from my home.

***

THE deck lights have been turned off. There's some spill from the house, but most of the light is coming from the bamboo torches and the plaintive little candles on the cake Ellie has placed in front of me. As the strains of 'Happy birthday' finish, I try to summon up a mighty wind to blow the candles out. Unfortunately, as I poise myself over the candles, the build-up of pressure at one end begets release at the other. There's a loud fart, which appears to emanate from me, shortly before the catarrhal breath in my lungs rushes out, leaving me in a coughing fit.

'Shit, I'm not eating that,' says Lila before Jackson can tell her to shush.

Will bursts into song. 'Why was he born so beautiful, why was he born at all? He's no bloody good to anyone, he's no bloody good at all.'

'Thank you *so* much, Will,' says Ellie.

'It's traditional,' says Will.

'What about calls of "Speech! Speech!"?' I suggest. 'That's traditional.'

'We don't want to encourage you, Dad,' says Ellie.

I tell them *someone* should say something, I've made it to seventy after all. I'm tempted to tell them it's also my last birthday. There's an embarrassed silence, which gives Will an opening. He'd be prepared, he says, to say a few words, drop a few pearls of wisdom. That seems to help Ellie make up her mind. 'We've heard quite enough from you. I'll say something. Um. Just that we're grateful, Dad, for all you've done for us. We didn't have what others would call a normal upbringing but between you, you and Mum got us there.'

'The only question is where.'

'Shut up, Will. So, Dad. Thank you.' Ellie grabs a glass, and raises it. 'Here's to you, Dad.'

The toast is fulsome. This part of proceedings is going much better than I thought it would. But when Ellie sits beside me and hugs me, there's a yawning silence, until Jackson stands and begins what sounds like nervous mumbling, though I can hear enough of it to understand he's speaking Māori.

'He's thanking you,' whispers Ellie. 'E te rangatira – that's you.'

Like many of my generation, I came to te reo late, and with little application. I should have gone to classes with Carol and Ellie: it might have kept me in touch with the zeitgeist a tick or two longer. But I recognise odd words, and am flattered to be acknowledged by Jackson as the leader or chief. 'Kia ora, Jackson.'

He seems to lose his way, but comes back to it, as Ellie resumes her whispered commentary. 'I have travelled – I find myself in the Pākehā world,' says Ellie. 'I am grateful for your blessing.'

'Tēnā koe, Mr D,' he finishes.

I don't need Ellie to translate that. I'm dismayed by my earlier questioning of his being here. 'Tēna koe, Jackson.'

Ellie acknowledges him too, and I think that must be an end to it, but Jackson stays on his feet, seemingly unsure as to what might follow, until his sister rises beside him, and gives him the confidence he needs. He lowers himself into a crouch and launches into a haka, supported by Lila. 'Haere mai rā!'

Ellie can't keep up her translation and to be honest I don't want her to, as I let the passion and power of these two skinny kids wash over me. I recognise smatterings of the chant, the repetition of 'Awhi! Awhi!', urging us to embrace, but then I'm lost.

'Tautokotia – support, true support,' says Ellie at one point, clasping her hands together in acknowledgement, as Jackson rips into repetitions of 'mātua', the word for father, before their rousing finish: 'Tihei! Tihei! Tihei mauri ora!'

I'm drawn to my feet, more moved than I can say. 'Kia ora, Jackson, kia ora, Lila, I'm honoured, very honoured.' I feel that anything I can say after such intensity will be flat, but I know it's customary to sing. 'Carol loved this waiata,' I tell them. I try not to be deflected by Will's groan. 'It was her favourite. Bob Dylan wrote the hymns for our generation, y'know, and Carol and I, our first date was a Dylan concert, at Western Springs I think, or maybe that was Neil Young . . .'

Ellie is holding up two fingers. 'Just sing the song, Dad.'

So I do. 'May God bless and keep you always, May your wishes all come true . . .'

And am joined by Ellie and Stan, and eventually even Will,

standing together and singing those words of Dylan that Carol loved so much.

Unfortunately, it's not an easy song to sing, and as we quaver our way towards the end, I overhear Lila's stage whisper to her brother: 'Jeez, who's drowning the kittens?' Jackson tells her to shush, but she can't help herself, as we bellow our way into the last couplet, me trying to desperately make up in volume what we lack in harmony. 'How can they be *so* bad?'

'Kia ora, Mr D and all of youse,' says Jackson graciously once the cacophony has stopped. We all sit, except Lila, who resists her brother's attempts to pull her down.

Will groans again. 'Christ, we'll be here all night. Why don't I do a Morris dance and then maybe the Highland fling?'

'Thought that's what you were doing, bro,' says Lila, 'sounded like the bagpipes.'

'Cheeky bitch!'

'Cool it, Will, f'godsake,' implores Ellie.

Lila eyeballs Will, fierce, and whatever doubts she may be harbouring, go. 'For you,' she says to him. She steps back a pace from the table. The effect is accidental, but macabre, as the half-light strikes the angular planes of her thin face and her eyes get lost in dark pools. Her voice drops and takes on a rhythmic, insistent beat, like a bass drum, or, as the words begin striking me, the thump of my heart.

'One bullet in the chamber, one thought in my head, one press of the trigger, shoot and I'm dead.'

I'm panicked. I think I've been rumbled, that she must know about Walter. How can she be privy to my secret plan?

'One shot at happiness, one push at the dread, one shot at bliss, miss and I'm dead.'

One push at the dread. One moment of insight before the encompassing terror. She must know!

'I'm dead, I'm dead, I'm dead in the head, I'm dead, I'm dead, I'm lost in the dread.'

In the shocked silence, there's a muffled sob. Which I try to turn into a cough, to help cover my streaming eyes. I'm grateful for the lack of light.

Predictably, Will is the one to break the silence, laughing nervously. 'Jeezzus! What the fuck was that?'

Ellie tries to bridge with determined cheerfulness. 'Thank you, Lila. Who's going to help Dad cut the cake? Jackson?'

Jackson takes the knife from Ellie, who immediately crosses to Lila, still standing alone. I can sense Ellie wants to hug her, but Lila is still projecting a forcefield. Instead, Ellie tells her that she'll make up a bed: Lila can stay as long as she likes. The girl looks towards Jackson, who nods.

I feel relieved. I don't want her going back out into the world she's just described. My relief isn't completely altruistic, however. I have so many questions for her, but I daren't broach them. The questions aren't all about me. I am seventy years old and staring into an entirely natural abyss of degeneration and degradation. She's eighteen or maybe nineteen. 'I'm lost in the dread?' What on earth can she have seen to give her the same sense of impending doom?

***

THE cake is cut, the cake is eaten. I don't get to follow up with Lila. Will commandeers her, steers her away from us and into an intense conversation over by the pool, watched anxiously, I notice, by Jackson. At one point Jackson tries to casual his way into the conversation. 'Two's company, bro,' says Lila and Jackson moves back to cracking twigs and stoking the fire.

Will and Lila seemed so antipathetic, I wonder what they might have to talk about. I've never believed that hoary old cliché that opposites attract, yet Carol and I were so different. I suppose clichés become clichés because they're so often true – or is that another cliché?

Stan has also brought me a Chinese lantern, which he lights and hangs from the underside of the huge umbrella that spans the table. It gives off a rose-hued glow that softens everything around it, including Stan, who hugs his sister, tells her she's completely wonderful for offering Lila a bed. It's a lovely, rare moment, which I'm hoping bodes well for what remains of the evening.

I celebrate by helping myself to a second slice of birthday cake. Dr Jeetan has warned me that I'm showing some of the early symptoms of type 2 diabetes. Naturally, I checked them out on the internet, and discovered I've indeed got symptoms for that and half a dozen other incurable diseases. What the hell. Walter is waiting.

I'm so absorbed shoving Ellie's carrot cake into my gob that I don't see Will leave Lila and cross to me. 'You could have your cake and eat it, Den.'

'Ho fucking ho.' I tell him I'm in no mood to forgive him for shaming me in front of a stranger.

'That's a bit dramatic,' he says. 'Everyone loves a funny story.'

'It wasn't funny!'

'Not at the time,' he concedes.

'A stranger whom you'd invited to my birthday with the intention of selling my house out from under me!'

'Georgie's presence at least raised the subject of the house.'

'It's not something I want to discuss.'

Will looks like he's going to explode, but instead takes a deep breath. 'Den, the world doesn't stand still, circumstances change for all of us.'

'Yes, I'm old and weak, I get that, but–'

'I'm not talking about you, actually. My circumstances have changed, in ways I didn't intend and couldn't have imagined. I know you disapprove of my leaving Claudia, but you're not in the relationship, you can't make that call. I tried hard to make it work, for the kids, for me. But I couldn't. So I did the honourable thing, I think – walked away and left her and the kids in the family home, so they had as little disruption as possible, okay?'

What can I say? I do so agree that only those inside a relationship can say what's really going on in there. I have to admit that it's Will's call, of course it is. And that what he's done is right.

'But that's had consequences for me, Den. If I insist on my share of the matrimonial property right now, Claudia and the kids lose the house.'

I'm so familiar with this situation. In his early fifties Branko ditched Nadine for a younger woman, whose name I cannot recall, a publicist for an ad agency. The disruption to Branko's life, and those of Nadine and their daughter Yelena, was obvious, but the changes had unforeseen effects on the business. Branko's assets were suddenly halved. He held on to his shares in Flame by borrowing heavily against them so he could pay out their value as cash, and his sudden indebtedness put pressure on us in the early noughties, when the TV commercial business was becoming much more competitive. We'd been cruising along on our reputation with the big agencies, knowing we didn't necessarily have to submit the lowest quote to get the gig. But the environment was changing quickly, and Branko's marital woes damn near sank us.

Carol had died a couple of years earlier, at the turn of the century, and was at least spared having to take sides. I had every intention of maintaining my friendship with Nadine and Yelena, but that fell away quickly when the matrimonial property battles turned nasty. I tried to stay above it, but Branko was my business partner and closest friend, what else could I do? I think that Nadine, particularly, felt some deeper resentment towards me – I was part of the world that broke their marriage, a big cog in a lifestyle that had seduced her husband and corrupted him. And killed him, within a decade. By the time Branko died, he was, I discovered, my only true friend. When I retired it quickly became clear that all the others were in fact business colleagues, and when we no longer had any business to do, they were no longer collegial.

I'm no better. I remember promising Branko's new wife, widow, whose name I can no longer remember, that I'd stay in touch, but I haven't. She was so much younger, a trophy wife I suppose, and the only thing we had in common was her deceased husband. That sounds cruel. Is truth a defence?

I try to concentrate on what Will is telling me.

'I know the business isn't your concern any more,' he's saying, 'and I don't want to burden you with it, but there are big headwinds out there, Den, big disruption. It's hard yakker. I'm living hand to mouth in a rented shoebox and I wouldn't complain about that, but it's no place to bring the kids. I need to re-establish myself, and I've got no means of doing that.'

'Don't browbeat Dad.' Ellie arrives, with Stan not far behind. I assume they've spotted Will quartering me and have rushed to my defence.

Will's tone immediately changes. He and I are no longer confidants, it seems. 'Georgie's talking four mil,' he says to me, brusquely. 'So you'd walk away with two.'

'Two? You said four.'

'Mum's half would be distributed between the three of us, just as she wanted.'

'Mum wanted Dad to be able to live out his days in the family home,' points out Ellie.

Will carries on as if his sister hasn't spoken. 'This is an opportunity for a new life, Den–'

'I'm happy with my old life.'

'Isn't that a bit selfish? Not unexpected, but–'

'Back off, Will,' warns Stan.

'I've lived here for forty years,' I say, regretting the pathetic, plaintive note in my voice. 'I built this home.'

'You bought it,' says Will.

'We made it our home!'

Will is implacable. 'It's a house. It was here before you, it'll be here after you go, unless you let it fall down around your ears.'

'Mum's will made it clear that–'

'I know exactly what Mum's will did, sis. It left Den a life interest in her share of the house, until he dies, remarries or sells this house. In which event, Den, your life interest over Mum's half crystallises–'

'Crystallises?'

'Ends. And under her will, passes to the three of us, the remainder-men.'

'Jesus, Will,' says Stan, impressed. 'Who've you been getting advice from?'

I know exactly where Will gets his advice: Flame is still using the same legal and accounting firms that Branko and I set up. I feel betrayed in absentia by those vultures who profited so handsomely from our endeavours.

'So you're fine, Dad,' says Ellie valiantly. 'You can live here for the rest of your life.'

'Unless you choose not to,' says Stan. This is a surprise. I assumed my youngest would be fighting my corner as vociferously as Ellie.

Will, of course, delights in the chink that Stan has just opened in my defence. 'You could buy an apartment for a mil and have a mil in the bank to see you out.'

'To see me out?'

'Dignity money,' says Will.

'Cash *is* king,' says Stan.

Ellie is horrified. 'Jesus, Stan!'

'Just saying. I mean, Will is right about that.'

Just saying, just said. I feel beleaguered by Stan's change of tack, but maybe I shouldn't be surprised. He's talked about Te Kurahau needing a 'cash injection'. I imagine a long syringe with my home being squeezed out through the end.

I begin to ramble, I know I do. Talk about how hard I worked to make the money to buy this house, get into dodgy gender territory by minimising Carol's financial contribution, which is guaranteed to antagonise Ellie. But I needn't worry about her. Will launches into me anew, telling me I got the deposit for this house on the back of a ditty for a sugar drink that helped cause an epidemic of obesity and diabetes among school-age children. That might be cruel, as Ellie protests it is, but it's also true. It won't help me to say we didn't know about toxic sugar back then, because we did know about tobacco and we did know about booze, and that didn't slow us down. I could say in my defence that there were worse advertising crimes – the dancing Cossack TV ads that sank Labour in '75 and allowed Muldoon to ditch the superannuation scheme that would have made us, by now, the Norway of the South Seas. My children know none of this, but it might have been relevant. Would Will still hate our generation if we had left that sovereign fund intact and our little nation was farting through silk? Would Will actually give a fuck? Ellie does, but she's trying to defend me. Will cuts her off, tells her it's a straight choice between the past and the future.

'Except that it's not our choice, is it?' says Stan. 'It's Dad's.'

In some strange way Stan's putting it back on me. If I dig in and say no, I'm holding on to the past, all my privilege and power, which is way past its use-by date. That much is clear. I feel suddenly very tired.

I say something stupid, out of context, tell them Carol says she can smell the Abraham Darby. It says poor me. It says I've lost it. Even Will looks at me with a degree of pity.

Ellie, bless her, tries to seize the moment, tells Will and Stan that she's trying to do the right thing here. 'I can't affect what's happening beyond the garden gate, but I'm trying to do what I can within this tiny world I can control. Make enough money to cover expenses while doing some good.'

I presume she means the fostering of the likes of Jackson, though she doesn't get into specifics, which is just as well, because Jackson and Lila are now huddled together over by the fire, trying not to hear our frenzied sotto voce. Will is being provocative, telling Ellie that he appreciates her enterprise.

'It's not a fucking enterprise. I'm trying to save us money!'

'It is an enterprise and you're *costing* us money. You're looking at it the wrong way round, Ellie. The return on our capital asset you're getting from fostering waifs and strays is so low that *we* are in effect subsidising *you* and your good deeds. Is that fair?'

There, he's said the magic word. If Jackson and Lila didn't

hear that, they certainly hear what follows, because Ellie's reached tipping point and blazes at Will, calls him a selfish, scheming shit.

'Love you too, sis,' says Will equably.

'You're an opportunist, just using this situation to justify your greed.'

'How do you think the world works, Ellie?'

'It's not fucking working!' screams Ellie. 'It's not! Fucking! Working! Are you blind?'

I look away, towards Jackson and Lila. Will might be impervious to Ellie's pain and fury, but none of the rest of us are, as Will tells her she's living in her own little echo chamber, running round after me, making pocket money out of the house as a foster home for young wastrels.

Ellie belatedly tries to keep her voice down. 'They're guests here. How dare you try to embarrass them.'

'They need a reality check too.'

Ellie tells Will in a furious whisper that by any test of civilisation and humanity he's a barbarian. 'This is a home and it's not your fucking capital asset until either Dad dies or he sells it – and that'll be over my dead body!'

Stan goes to hug his sister, but she pulls away, turns her back on us and heads across to Jackson and Lila. I can see her as much as hear her asking them to help her clear the table. Both of them seem grateful to put some distance between themselves and the rest of us.

Stan stands awkwardly, looking after Ellie, grimacing. 'The remorseless logic of the neo-liberal creed,' he says, presumably to Will. 'Funny how some people just don't get it, eh?'

The irony is wasted on Will. 'Tell me about it,' he says.

Ellie comes back, red-eyed, sniffling. She bleakly surveys us and the detritus of the meal, our family celebration of my seventieth and last year on this earth. 'Mum once told me,' she says, 'that she fantasised about setting this place alight, burning it down.'

I'm stunned. 'Her own home?'

'Why on earth would she want to do that?' asks Will.

Ellie looks at him with a pure hatred. 'The symbol of her repression, she said, the ties that bind, the harness and the whip.'

It's a suitably miserable end note. I don't know where I am any more. My world has tipped. I was never more than a two-glass philosopher, even better on a full bottle, but I believed the hype, that I was part of perhaps the first existential generation, refusing to be defined by those who went before, by nurture, by class, by family or by circumstance. Yet here I am, captive to my progeny, mired in a desperate hierarchical struggle with my pride, like some old lion on the savannah losing control of his teeth, sinew and power. It's clear that I'll have to go.

***

IT'S late, way past ten, when I climb back into my eyrie. I'm usually asleep by 9.30, awake at 11.30, asleep by 12 if I'm lucky, awake by 2.30, and so on, until dawn, when I'm exhausted by my nocturnal micturitions and need a couple more hours. I do wonder about the merits of having the en-suite so close. Sometimes I don't actually feel like a pee but think that if I don't make the effort to get up and empty my bladder, it'll wake me in an hour anyway – in the event that I fall asleep, that is. I might lie awake for another hour or more, then feel I have to repeat the exercise in case I do, eventually, fall asleep. My deepest sleep is my afternoon nap, just for half an hour. When I come to, there are those wonderful few moments, when I'm no longer an old man with a black room waiting, no longer . . .

anything, really, just a pure, unfettered, age-neutral cloud of me-ness. Until reality kicks in. Tonight, reality has kicked me in the head. I feel groggy, not sleepy. Acrimony at least made it easier to say 'Goodnight' instead of 'Goodbye' to my children as I took my leave and made my way across the big room to the stairs.

By instinct I go to my kauri roll-top because I know it has everything I need. There's a moment of panic when I open the top right drawer, then I remember my cunning plan. Both the things I need are in the big concertina box-file on the bottom shelf, under W, for Walter obviously, but also, and this is the cunning part, for M upside down, which is where my head was at when the idea came to me. Walter and the marijuana are the keys to facing the future, the few minutes that are left of it, with equanimity. I shrug into my Rainbird, in case the weather is inclement where I'm going.

I know there's a black room waiting for me. The exact dimensions may have changed from the first time I was in it: it's so dark I can't tell. On my stag night, I was off my head, dead drunk in this club. My so-called mates left me comatose in a room out the back where the band warmed up. This, I found out later, had been completely soundproofed, no light, one blacked-out door. I woke up sick as a dog in a black void – completely black, not a shard of light, no sound. I thought I might be dead. I was terrified, I'd never felt such fear. Couldn't find the door, couldn't get out. It might have been only five or ten minutes, but that's a long time to be immersed in cold terror. But what awaits me promises to be so much worse.

I'd been planning to tell the family my secret tonight. But Georgie's presence and the 'discussion' about the sale of the house overtook any wish to reveal my news. In that context, sharing Dr Jeetan's diagnosis might have seemed opportunistic, it might have sounded pathetic, as if I was pulling the old tear-jerker out of my back pocket, a poor-me play. Or Will might have seen it as a weakness to exploit. Fuck them.

When Dr Jeetan suggested a precautionary brain scan, I asked him what it would be looking for. He tried to obfuscate, told me it was just part of a diligent diagnostic process.

I didn't buy that. 'Towards what end?' I asked.

He's a young man, Dr Jeetan, did I say that? Though 'young' is comparative these days: everyone is young. When I die tonight, I will have died 'young' in comparison with the soaring longevity of my generation. Anyway, Dr Jeetan's capacity to empathise was not prejudiced by his youth. Clearly he could imagine my fear at what he might find, and it was that perspicacity and resulting reluctance to tell me more that really got me worried, as he stared long and hard at me through his silver-rimmed glasses. Finally he took them off, as if he didn't want to have a clear view of me when the bad news hit. He said the scan would reveal, or not – preferably not – what he called multi-infarct dementia, which he explained as a series of mini-strokes, often called silent strokes, so small I don't even feel them. Each time it happens, it kills another piece of my brain – though that's my interpretation, not his exact words. As he talked, I began picturing these little dots of dead material in my head, gradually connecting, black spots of dead synapses, slowly spreading in 3D like a mad pointillist's vision. A slow death. Dr Jeetan didn't say that either, but what other conclusion can there be? There's seemingly nothing I can do, no virtuous circle I can belatedly join, to stop these unfelt lightning bolts in my head. They will continue, randomly, arbitrarily, creating dead matter where living tissue used to be. I asked him as calmly as I could how much I would know about where I was going. Would I know where I was and why I was there?

He pulled out his avuncular chuckle, the one no doubt designed to assuage fear, and gently chastised me for jumping to conclusions which had, at present, no empirical diagnostic basis without a 'confirmatory MRI'. I know language if nothing else: Dr Jeetan may not have noticed his movement from 'precautionary brain scan' to 'confirmatory MRI', but I did. And inside my imploding brain, I already know. When the past informs the present, you can feel confident of the future, take comfort in a sense of continuity. That seems to be my dilemma: my past is going, piecemeal but relentlessly – some of it already gone – until I am finally and completely lost in that black room without past or future. And this time, there will be no escape.

Other than Walter, of course. The advantage of instant death is that I'll become invisible, remembered as I was, rather than observable in my decline: muddled, befuddled, incontinent, a seventy-year-old toddler barely able to walk and talk, terrified of what he no longer understands . . . If I put the barrel to my temple, thus, aim backwards, surely the percussion of the bullet won't pop an eye.

'Party not go well then?'

Jesus! I turn on her, startled. 'Don't do that!'

'What, you might have pressed the trigger? I'd be doing you a favour, wouldn't I?'

How much does she know? Can she read my thoughts? She's dressed as before, as ever, that summer print, looking gorgeous. I wave Walter around, struggling for the words I need to say to her. 'There were things came up tonight, Carol. From the past. Embarrassing moments.'

'There were a few of them,' she concedes. 'Which ones are we talking about?'

'I don't want to be specific, but I want to make sure you know that I'm sorry.'

'A non-specific apology?'

'A generic apology, yes.'

'A generic acceptance then.' She smiles.

'Really?'

'Yes, if that makes it easier. So . . .' Her voice softens. 'This could be the moment, Den?'

I nod, nudge Walter against my temple. *This is it.*

'Might be very good timing,' she says. 'In terms of the travel arrangements. Everyone's here anyway for your birthday. Convenient.'

I look at her. She's still smiling. Her eyes are crinkling, which is supposed to be a sign of sincerity. I'm not so sure. 'Thanks.'

'You're welcome.'

For all her enthusiasm, it seems wrong to do it in front of her. She doesn't deserve such grisly horror after what she's been through. Would this be one other thing I'd have to apologise for? 'Are you sure you don't mind?'

'When did my minding ever matter?'

Aha! 'You haven't forgiven . . .'

'Forgiving doesn't mean forgetting, Den. How can I unremember?'

The thought comes to me that I won't have to unremember anything, if I stay alive. It'll all be done for me, like a hard disk being reformatted. Slowly. In small, arbitrary patches. How much does she know about that? I should give her an opportunity to reveal herself. I open my arms to her. 'Look at me. I'm fucking disgusting. The tyranny of age.'

She laughs. Chortles. Head thrown back, brown eyes sparkling.

'Not exactly an uplifting sight!'

That's certainly sincere! I'm a bit miffed, tell her it doesn't become her, this chortling at my degeneration, but I lie: it does. She looks happy, at peace with the world. That pisses me off more. I get a vision of Branko with his young wife, what he was grappling with. Carol and I now are even more disparate in ages than they were then: my seventy to her forty-two. I can certainly see why these big age-difference relationships don't work.

'You always behaved as if you were immortal,' she says, her smile leaving her. 'Guess what?'

Did I ever really think that? That I was never going to die? That I would live forever? I can't remember ever giving it much thought. It just sat there, my eventual demise, a deal that couldn't be renegotiated, finessed, derailed, gamed. There was no one to pay, to swindle, to persuade, who could stop it from happening, so what was the point of even thinking about it? But now it's here. And Carol is already there. 'One thing–'

'Shoot.'

'Ho fucking ho.' But it works, I lower the pistol. 'Since you're here, there's something I need to ask you. How does death work? Is there a God, for instance? Heaven?' I gulp. 'Hell?'

'If self-euthanasia is so courageous and right, why should you want reassurance before you do it?'

'What I'm asking is whether you're my proof that there's an afterlife?'

'If I'm a figment of your imagination, the only thing I'm proof of is that you've lost it completely.'

'Don't play these games with me!'

I must look as distressed as I feel, because she sits down in front of me, quite close, tells me she's not here to deflect me or divert

69

me from doing whatever I must do. Close enough to touch. I can smell her aroma, that Chanel number whatever, mixed up with something muskier, something I associate with the heat she always radiated for me. 'I have another question. A last question.'

'Will this hurt?'

'Only me,' I reassure her. 'All I did, those hurts, those things for which–'

'You've apologised generically.'

'Yes. Did you ever stop loving me? I mean, I can understand it if you did, but–?'

She looks at me for what seems far too long to gather any good news. 'I wanted to,' she says. 'Tried to.'

'But you couldn't – you loved me!' I don't mean to seize on it like a triumphant athlete, but I do.

'I did,' she says.

'You do!'

'Why is that important to you now, when it never seemed to be then?'

'I was young.'

'Not always. But foolish, yes.'

We're very close. I'm still holding Walter, but I reach out with my other hand, towards her breast. 'I still want you.'

She smiles. 'You can't have me. But you have the memory of me.' She indicates my crotch. 'Surely you can conjure something up?'

'It's been so long.'

'Shall I try to help?'

She leans back a little, opens her legs, draws the hem of her dress up. It's nothing really, but it's everything, *so* suggestive. I tell her it might work. I massage my unresponsive cock with my free hand, increasingly frenetically.

'Should you put your pistol down?' she asks, then smiles. 'Something hard to hold on to, I suppose.'

Not helpful. I wonder if the neural pathway between my brain and my penis is already zapped. Down. Out. Destroyed by one of those lightning bolts in my brain. I give up, but thank Carol for trying. I look at Walter, but he's drooping too, as if he knows his moment is gone. I cross to my roll-top and rummage under M before I remember, and retrieve the dead, half-smoked joint from W.

'So,' says Carol, 'instead of your lead pill–'

'Medicinal marijuana while I regroup.'

I mouth the joint and lean close to Carol. She shakes her head. 'Please – I love the way you do that!'

'It'll be the death of you.' She breathes on me, my face, that same magical breath. I swear I can feel the sweet waft of it. And my joint is alight. I draw deeply on it, close my eyes in almost instant ecstasy, the burn of the smoke on the back of my throat, the THC finding its way up what remains of those neural tracks to my brain. When I open my eyes, she is gone.

***

CAROL has left me in peace. I feel sure I can do what needs to be done. I walk out onto the balcony, joint in one hand, Walter in the other. One last look at the night sky, the moon lancing off the water. My eyes rove across the moonlit monochrome of sky and sea, and are drawn to movement in the foreground, down by the pool. There are two figures, hunched together, face to face, their profiles lit by a glowing ember between them. I can't see any detail. I turn and lean, trying to see more, and damn near trip over the tripod of my Konuspot.

I train it on the scene below, pocketing Walter in order to focus the lens. The frieze of two figures comes into sharp relief against the burning torches on the far side of the pool. I don't initially understand what I'm watching. Then I do. They're hunched over a pipe, a meth pipe. Lila is drawing deeply on it, before passing it back to Will, who takes his fill. Lila stands, does a little dance, turns away from Will and drops her big coat. She is naked underneath. So skinny I can see her ribs striating out from her spine as she walks down the steps into the pool. Her brown back is covered in small red welts. I remember Jackson's plaintive bleats to Ellie about someone, presumably the father, burning her. She's clearly feeling no pain now as she slides forward into the water. Will's watching, rising, beginning to remove his shorts.

Like most writers, I've a voyeuristic tendency, but I don't want to watch this. It explains so much about my elder son. I step back from the Konuspot, turn and cross the balcony to my inner sanctum. I remember another intense conversation, this one between Will and Lila, after Lila drummed her rap beat into my head: *One bullet in the chamber, one thought in my head, one press of the trigger, shoot and I'm dead.* I couldn't overhear what she and Will were saying but now I can guess what it was about. How do these people recognise each other? Is there a secret tattoo on their foreheads, visible only to other users?

I call out to Carol. *Where are you?*

I don't want to be alone.

summer

THE PUBLIC POOL sat on a burnt-grass promontory that pushed out into the harbour, ringed by pōhutukawa. The trees had long since shed their Christmas flowers, and the carpet of crimson cinders they'd left on the paths winding round the perimeter had been scuffed to the side of the hot tar. Officially, summer was almost shot – the end of February was a couple of days away – but the sun blazed on as relentlessly as ever, and would continue, Will guessed, right through March and most of April. The climate, he was sure, was as fucked as everything else.

The voice on his mobile had to compete with excited screams and splashes – the big kids doing bombs off the high board into the diving pool, the mash of water and bodies in the main pool. He glanced back to the more sedate action of the shallow pool, where Archie was still teetering about pursued by Kristin. There were mothers sitting in the shallows, playing with babies, watching their toddlers.

He'd been one of those babies. Carol had brought him here when she was pregnant with Ellie. He had no memory of that, but he did remember being in the toddlers' pool playing with Ellie when Carol was huge with what turned out to be Stan. He could remember Ellie screaming about something he'd done. Some things never change.

This pool complex had been the centre of his social life every summer until he was twelve or thirteen, when he and a couple of his mates had been caught by a security guard having a midnight swim after climbing over the fence. He'd nicked a bottle of blackberry nip from Den's liquor cabinet and he was so pissed the security guard damn near had to save him from drowning. His mates were too drunk themselves to see that he was in trouble after a mistimed tumble from the diving platform had flat-backed him onto the water so hard it took all the wind out of him. He'd been banned from the complex after that, never been back until today. Wonder they hadn't asked for ID before they'd let him and the kids in.

Moments ago, Will had been sitting there among the mothers until, restless and anxious, he'd pretended to be drawn away by his vibrating mobile, out onto the grass where blankets had been thrown down in the shade of a huge oak and whole families, mostly from the south or west, big, square brown bodies, were settled for the day. Families. Whole.

He pressed the mobile closer to his ear and tried to hear what Trish was saying, about a cameraman who wanted a daily rate they hadn't budgeted for. Who did these pricks think they were? There were guys out there putting iPhones on steadicam rigs bought off the net for two hundred bucks making *features* for sweet FA, putting them on YouTube, getting millions of eyeballs, selling them to Netflix for megabucks, and this prick was trying to extort them for a one-day shoot on a TVC they were obliged to quote for but probably wouldn't get? It struck him, not for the first time, that it was all a complete waste of time, the whole bloody thing. Used to be if you owned an Arri 16 mil you were made; now every cunt and his dog could make pretty pictures with an over-the-counter smart-phone. Turned out the song was wrong: video didn't kill the radio star, digital killed the video, *and* film, *and* all the pros who relied on it. It wasn't just the climate that was stuffed. 'Tell him fuck, Trish, there's gotta be someone else who needs a day.'

He doused that call and speed-dialled Lila's number. It didn't ring, went straight to her message. *Don't leave a message, text.*

Fuck her. But he texted her. *Takeaways tonight?* Who knew if she would turn up, but what else could he do? He pocketed the mobile and worked his way back towards the kids. Some of the yummy mummies were hot. One of them, in a pink bikini with her dirty blonde hair tied back into a pony-tail, was lifting Archie out of the water. He was crying, face red and crumpled, his pain distressing his sister. 'He slipped over and got a mouthful,' she was telling the woman.

'Where's your mummy?' the woman asked Kristin.

'Finishing a long lunch probably,' said Will, taking Archie from her. 'Come on, mate, the water won't hurt.'

'He fell over, Daddy. I tried to catch him.'

'He's fine, sweetie.' He patted his daughter on the head, wiped the snot from Archie's nose, back-handing it on the boy's rash-suit, and held out his hand to the woman, still hovering. 'Will.'

'They're too young to be left on their own, Will,' she replied, refusing his hand, and turning to her own little boy, a bit older than Archie.

'Thank you for helping out,' said Will, 'not to mention the advice. Cheque's in the mail.'

'You should try leaving your phone in the car,' she said, not unpleasantly. 'It works.'

He knew she was right. On the few occasions he'd come to the kids with no agenda, just gone, *Okay it's your time, we do whatever the hell you want*, he'd had more fun and got out of himself, chilled in a way that nothing else could do for him. Almost nothing else.

Archie started bawling for another ice block as they passed the cunningly positioned kiosk on the way to the exit. He bought them both one, then hustled out to the carpark. By the time the sugar hit their little receptors, they wouldn't be his problem.

The carpark was chokka with people movers, some already loading up, towels, flax mats, lava lavas, about to head back home, out west or south. The cool people wouldn't be seen dead in these minibuses, the cool people would rather pay a premium for an SUV, the mugs. He corralled Archie into the baby seat in the back of the waiting Kia Sportage.

He adjusted the seat, belted Archie in and was clicking the buckle when the little boy dropped his ice block on Will's forearm, then grabbed it back with sticky fingers. I'm over kids, he thought, wiping his arm and hands with the towel draped over Archie's shoulders. Had them too late, should have done all that ten years ago, fifteen. Kristin would be flatting by now, at uni or whatever. Archie would at least be a sentient human being, capable of conversation, not this loud, constantly demanding, caterwauling maker of messes. Too late now. Story of his life. *Too fucking late.* As he got into the driver's seat, he glanced instinctively out towards the house, and was grateful that the ruins were obscured by the big oaks and eucalypts covering the southern slope of the park.

The ice block was doing its evil work on Archie, distracting him from his wet togs and the damp, sticky towel around his shoulders: he couldn't be comfortable, but he'd be home soon enough. Kristin, little angel, had climbed in the back alongside Archie, to keep him amused once he'd finished. He belted up behind the wheel, pressed the starter button. The Sportage SUV had seemed like a good idea at the time, three years ago when he leased it through Flame, brand new. It looked stylish, designed, he'd heard, by some dude associated with Porsche, but closer acquaintance had revealed it to be a fucking bread-van with leather seats and pretentious accessories, powered by a 1.6-litre with the power-to-weight ratio of Kim Dotcom. Now the three years were up, he'd have to upgrade – at a premium – or pay out the residual bubble. He was *so* fucked, unless . . . If he did manage a financial miracle, there'd be no concessions to family this time: he'd get something sporty that went like a cut cat.

They were heading up to Jervois Road before Archie finished the ice block and started cracking up. *Please, shut the fuck up, you're hurting my head.* 'Hang in there, boy,' he said, 'we're nearly home.' He looked desperately for a distraction. 'Can you see the fire engine?' He made the sound of a siren. It was like turning off a tap. Archie began imitating his father.

'Where's the fire engine, Daddy?' asked Kristin.

'We must have missed it,' he lied. 'Maybe it went down a side street.' Archie's noise faucet instantly turned on again.

'He's upset he missed the fire engine, Daddy,' said Kristin, trying to keep the disappointment out of her own voice.

'Me too,' he lied. He made a right turn down Mackelvie, a short cut to Williamson, remembered running for his life down here, tearing out a fence paling to defend himself. When was that? He'd have been fourteen, fifteen, snuck out the bedroom window again, hooning around with his mates. The streets round here used to be fucking dangerous after 1 a.m. through to dawn. Big mean cunts who'd missed the last bus home after hitting all the bars and clubs in K Road, done all their dough, hungry or just looking for their bus fare back to Clendon or Kelston or wherever the fuck they came from. Roaming the streets of Ponsonby and Grey Lynn, waiting for dawn and the buses to start running again, looking for easy coin from white-boy stick-insects. The good old days. Might still be like that at dawn in the weekends. He wouldn't know – couldn't drag himself out of bed.

Left off Williamson and they dropped down into Ariki, pulling up outside a villa on the high side. Archie was wakening the dead as Will carried him up the steps. Claudia had the front door open before they arrived. 'Can you bring him in?'

He wanted to drop the kids and run, but he took the boy up the hallway to the kitchen in the lean-to addition at the back, which looked out onto a deck and water feature backgrounded by a burnt-brown lawn. Claudia readied the high-chair and he dropped the boy's feet through the stocks and sat him square. 'Has he had anything to eat?' Will shook his head.

'An ice block, Mummy,' said Kristin.

'That explains a bit.'

'Hey, we were at the pool . . .'

'Two ice blocks, actually,' said Kristin.

'It's okay,' she said, fussing over the boy. 'I'll feed him now. You could stay for dinner if you want.'

'Can't.'

'So busy, on a Sunday?'

'We're struggling to get a gig,' he said, seeing an opportunity. 'Everything's gone cold, which means we have to put ourselves out there, quote for every bullshit job. Have you thought over what we talked about?'

'Selling this?' She'd lost weight – the good old separation diet – and she looked gorgeous. 'Are we that far gone?' He said nothing, hoping his silence was eloquent. It seemed to be. Her eyes welled. 'My lawyer–'

'Your lawyer? You're lawyered up already?'

'I didn't know whether –'

'That's how dead in the water we are then,' he said.

'Can you cut some silver beet, darling?' she asked Kristin, handing her a little knife. Kristin went out onto the deck and he watched her wandering unhappily over to the raised veggie patch made by Claudia's father, Vince. Claudia was over at the sink, pulling out the chopping board, facing away from him. 'Barbara, my lawyer, says that it takes time to sort out matrimonial property, that usually the court allows about two years.'

'Two fucking *years*?'

'It's only been six months, Will. It's all still new. And–' She turned to face him. 'You used to say you'd be able to pay off the mortgage here with the proceeds of Den's house.'

'I might need that to keep the business afloat.'

'Oh,' she said, clearly dismayed. 'You know what I did this afternoon?'

'You don't have to tell me.'

'I went to visit Den.'

'Good on you.'

'He says you haven't been to see him.'

'He's forgetful.'

'You should go and see your own father.'

'I told you, he's–'

'He remembers some things. He told me you brought some woman to his party to make an offer on the house.'

'You can't rely on anything he says.'

'Is that why you walked out on me and the kids?' Claudia asked.

'Is what why?'

'That woman, whoever she was. You knew the big house was about to be sold and you didn't want your share of the proceeds to be part of the matrimonial property.'

'That's not Claudia-speak. Has Barbara been priming you?'

'That's not an answer, Will.'

'Are you serious?'

'Barbara might have raised it, but I wouldn't put it past you.'

'Such good faith and trust!'

'Good faith? You've just walked out on us for no reason you've ever given!'

'Things change.'

'Some things don't.' Her eyes finally locked into his. 'You're high.'

If only, he thought, as he slammed the front door behind him. *I'm crash landing, not flying.* As he picked his way back down the mossy steps he could hear Archie crying for him behind the closed front door. Daddy! There was some satisfaction in being wanted like that: the kid can't have had too bad a time with his old man.

He did a U and then a left onto Williamson, heading west towards Grey Lynn. Claudia's father had been a tough old bastard. You could see shades of the young man who helped drive the Moawhango tunnel under the Kaimanawas. If he'd still been alive, old Vince would be round like a shot door-stopping him, no matter where he hid. He'd forced them to do the Catholic wedding thing. Will had had to get confirmed, the whole nine yards of nonsensical ritual: *This is the body and the blood of Christ?* Yeah, right. How could anyone believe that shit.

Why *did* he leave? He didn't have a rational explanation. She hadn't done anything wrong: what was wrong was the picture he had of himself in his head. It didn't gel with a forty-something lock-stepped to a wife, two kids and a family wagon. He had tried. In his dreams he'd always been running, free, towards something, but now he'd begun ducking, weaving, dodging from some felt but unseen menace. It had become a waking nightmare, the need to flee. *Get out! Bail!* He missed her voluptuous warmth at night, the way she'd spoon his back, press her breasts and pelvis against him, a movement that quite often quickened and turned into something more urgent. What the fuck was he doing? *Keep running.*

***

HE climbed up the narrow wooden stairs to his flat through the cloying smell of frying fat. The downstairs tenant, a fish and chip shop, had a sign assuring customers that only rice-bran oil was used, and maybe it was true and maybe it made a difference to the customers' clogged arteries, but not to the smell of his stairwell: the hot breath from those boiling vats almost congealed on each step as it rose and cooled. He'd been put off fish and chips for life.

He washed down two tramadols with a beer and waited for his ragged edges to soften. When the beer was cut, he opened a bottle of jammy Aussie 'Reserve' shiraz, $8.99 at the nearest supermarket. How the fuck did those winemakers stay in business? He thought he might cook something up, but the fridge was sparse, so he settled for the liquid substitute and tried to find the calorific intake on the label of the bottle. He was on his second glass, the trammies were just beginning to take effect, when his mobile burped: *Here. Open up.* Fuck it, if he'd known she was coming he would have held off the trammies. He liked being edgy, scratchy, horny, when she came, not blissed out. Too late. He got up and descended through the pungent shroud to let her in.

Lila looked as she always looked: scrawny, lost in her big coat, which she wore even in the height of summer. The only thing that changed with the seasons and her mood was what she did or didn't wear under the coat. Her black hair was shaved short on one side; the other side fell across her face, thin and sharp but beautiful. He hadn't thought so at first, but she was, no doubt. Her beaky face looked more Italian than Claudia's – big black eyes and lashes over a hooked aquiline nose and full lips. He followed her back up the stairs in her boots, clomping loudly. She didn't give a fuck who heard her, she didn't give a fuck, she said, about anything any more. She told him once that she'd already given all her fucks, she had none left to give. And yet . . .

They did the deal, cash for the little ziplock, and as he stuck it in his pocket, she nuzzled into him. He didn't want to fuck, not really, didn't want to puncture the bliss. But she unzipped him, got him hard with her mouth, opened her big coat and pulled him in. She didn't take off her top this time, but he knew the scars on her back had healed, meaning the bastard had stopped hurting her, touch wood – maybe because of him, he liked to think, the money he paid her. He knew the old man was supplying. One of those nights when she didn't want to fuck, when she was anxious and dropped the P and ran, he'd looked out the front window through the leaping neon fish at a crappy grey hatch waiting down below, wiper blades going, engine running. His eyes were drawn to a man across the street, leaving the Indian dairy with a pack of fags, one of which he'd already lit. He was a scrawny bastard in a dirty denim jerkin showing sinewy arms with big ink, a white-trash whippet with a mullet. That was a surprise, he'd been expecting big and brown. The mother must be Māori.

Usually, Lila would have a taste of her product – 'a little fifty' she called it, like a courtier testing food for a king. He liked that. Most of all for the effect it had on her, even though it was a tab and didn't give the same instant rush as smoke. There was nothing about her that conformed to his template of sexy. She had big nipples but no tits, was so scrawny her hip bones dug into him. She looked boyish or almost pre-pubescent if it wasn't for the thatches of black hair under her arms and around her cunt. He loved that. Claudia had got the idea from somewhere that the feminine ideal was to shave everything. If it was true that women dressed for each other, maybe they shaved for each other too. There was never any foreplay with Lila, just stand and deliver – what he and his mates used to call knee tremblers, though he'd never had one before Lila. Front on or back to front against the cheap Formica table that threatened to collapse. Rutting not fucking. When she was coming, or sensed he was close, she'd call him, as if he was wasting her time: 'Come on, *come on for fucksake!*' Then last time, something he'd never heard her say before. He'd been horny and rough, banging her from behind over the back of the sofa, then, unusually, she'd turned round and lain down on the carpet. She told him she wanted to see his face when he came. That worked. But when he did, she locked her ankles behind his back as he thrust towards the custard stroke and her face was a painful grimace and what she grunted to him was 'Kill me! *Kill me!*' He'd been thrown, faked a come and pulled out. She didn't seem to notice, wiped herself with her knickers as usual and pulled her jeans back up. That memory, and the trammies, almost finished him now too, but he ground on and got there. She seemed to recognise his dogged lack of inspiration and said nothing. He offered her a trammie as she pulled up her pants. 'I'm sweet,' she said.

The first couple of times, he'd asked her if she wanted to use the shower, but she said no. A few times, she'd not wiped and run. A few times she'd wanted to stay a while, chilled with a trammie, and told him stories. One was about some kind of torture chamber in the CBD in a cellar under one of the towers, where girls were manacled and chained, beaten and force-fed drugs and cock. The way she told the story he never doubted it was true. He wanted to ask her how she knew, but he feared the answer. How could she know in such detail if she hadn't been there? And why else would she have been there, except as a victim? Once she'd told a story about her and that little shit of a brother, Jackson, being sent out of town to their mother's mother up north, how she hated the green and the wet. He'd tried to be casual when he asked her where the fuck her brother had disappeared to. She'd said she had no idea, that she hadn't seen him. He didn't believe that for a second, he was sure she was lying, but he didn't want to raise her suspicions – he had to keep her close. What Lila knew, her brother would know, sooner or later, if he didn't already. The boy was the menace.

She'd never asked about him in return. Maybe she'd picked up a few things at Den's seventieth though, because once he'd been complaining about something, and she'd said, 'Wife, two kids, nice home, new car – you're right, sounds like shit.' So he didn't go there again. She didn't want to share stories tonight. He pretended nothing had changed, but tried to change it anyway. 'I was thinking maybe we could go out?'

'Go out?' She looked gob-smacked. 'Like, *out*? Where?'

'Dunno. Tapas. Wine bar.'

She almost spat her disgust. '*Tapas?*'

'Whatever. A club, if you like.'

'No club I go to would let us in if I turned up with you.'

'Jesus. Somewhere else then.'

'Where else?'

He was a bit slow, the trammies, but he got there in the end.

'You don't want to be seen in public with me.'

'You know what you call this?' At least she tried to smile to soften it. 'It is what it is, and that's all it is.'

He might wish she wasn't so hard-arse but that was part of the attraction. She grabbed her bag and made for the door. 'Text me whenever,' she said, slammed the door behind her and clomped back down the stairs.

He'd always thought he knew what the transaction was between them, that it might be morally bankrupt but it was honest: the P, the money, her taste of the product, the first rush, the mutual sexual relief, that's how it went. And that maybe there were dynamics that went beyond the money: maybe having her own customer kept her father, literally, off her back. But after the 'Kill me' last time, he thought there might be another, more unsettling, element connecting them: self-hatred.

He took the ice out of the ziplock – what a dead fucking give-away those little bags were – and left the pills loose in his trouser pocket. He'd need them tomorrow. He finished his glass of red, poured another one, and used it to wash down another trammy. They were doing their stuff, those little bastards, mellowing him out. Even easier to get than meth, and cheaper, courtesy of ACC. Without an MRI, who knew whether a disc was herniated or not, whether the sciatic pain was real? They would do anything to avoid operating on the spine, it seemed. The tramadol left him floating above his own life, looking down on it like it was something far away and of not much moment. The contours of his anxieties, the crags that threatened to tear his wings, the deep valleys he might crash and drown in, were barely visible. It wasn't the complete unconsciousness of deep sleep, more a waking peace that gave him a break between rounds. He lay on the sofa, pushed up the sash window at the back, watched the sun go down over the purple Waitākeres and imagined he was someone else somewhere else.

***

MONDAY. The beginning of a week full of possibility. Possibly. He'd stitch up this director he was about to meet, possibly. On the back of that he'd get the electric vehicle TVC for Flame, possibly. On the back of that, he could possibly talk the bank into extending the OD to cash-flow them for another month until the production money for the EV gig began coming in. Or persuade newly lawyered-up Claudia that it was in her interest to put the house on the market . . . Was any of that *really* within the realms of possibility? A much stronger possibility before the week was out was the IRD slapping Flame with a section 271 for unpaid GST and terminal and the whole shebang turning to shit. Within six weeks Flame would be insolvent, he'd be bankrupt, with the public naming and shaming close behind. Possibly. Maybe it was the dregs of the trammies he'd taken last night, maybe it was the first spark from the 50 mil of crank he'd swallowed with his coffee before hopping in the car this morning, but the bankruptcy option no longer seemed as horrifying. The closer he got to putting his head in that noose, the more of a release it seemed to be. Swinging free. Finished, yes, but free. Off the wheel. Forty-something and fucked. That was still young, he could be anything, it wasn't too late. Possibly.

Will had woken to the mobile's insistent bleeps, still on the sofa where he'd drifted off on tramadol's soft shoulder. The morning sun was hitting the flanks of the Waitākeres, green and seductive, a beckoning quality to it. He'd pulled off yesterday's clothes, showered and found that he had no suit pants or shirts in the wardrobe. The suit pants didn't matter – you wouldn't turn up to a meeting with Anton in a suit if you wanted any shred of his bullshit cred. The clean shirt *was* a problem. He pulled on boots, dress jeans and a T-shirt, grabbed his computer bag and drove straight to the dry cleaner. Didn't have his ticket, but the young guy wanted the money and handed over the three white shirts Will rotated. He paid with the last of his cash, then stood in front of the ATM trying to calculate which card might still have some life in it. He'd need cash to pay for whatever the hell Anton wanted at this breakfast meet – probably fucking bircher and yoghurt, the fastidious fucker – because he couldn't risk pulling out the wrong card and having it die right there.

On the way back to Ponsonby he stopped by the park and tried to get his T-shirt off in the front seat of the car, then thought, Fuck it, fuck the leering fucking dog walkers. He got out, stripped the T off and buttoned himself into the newly minted white shirt, then climbed back into the car, checked himself in the mirror – thank God stubble was fashionable. He looked okay. You wouldn't know just from looking at him how comprehensively fucked he was. That was the key: don't let Anton smell the fear. He had to look like he was winning, not somersaulting into a high-speed train wreck.

Anton had refused to come to the Flame office for the meeting. That was a sign, that was a power dynamic right there: *I'm not coming to you, you come to me.* And Will couldn't begrudge Anton his moment. He'd paid his dues in the business, had been around long enough for his stocks to have risen and fallen like everyone else's. He'd begun in TV commercials as a cameraman, and still had a tendency when he was talking to make little box lens with his fingers in front of his eyes when he was describing scenes. He made the jump to director, made a name for being able to create and sustain atmospheric visual realities for one minute, which was all a TVC needed. But of course his deeper ambition was to make movies, and he took the traditional road to his first feature, making an interesting, witty, short film on the back of freebies from his mates in the industry, before, in Will's opinion, utterly losing his nerve in a dark little arthouse feature with no narrative spine that did no business, but had enough cinematic allusions and obfuscation to interest the critics. Will thought the feature had inadvertently done Anton a huge favour: shown him where his true talents lay. In any event, he never made another feature, and returned to TVCs and a lucrative career filming visual constructs that only had to convince and engage for less than a minute. In his text reply to Will, he had named some new place on the strip, which turned out to be a weird Scandi blond-wood combination of cafe, barber and clothes.

Predictably, when Will got there on time, Anton hadn't shown yet, so he grabbed a seat isolated enough to discourage any rubber-necking ear flappers. There were a few scattered patrons, all men, every last one of them staring into his MacBook, pretending to have pressing business. Will ordered a double-shot short black, pulled out his MacBook Air and joined the club. He had time to swallow the espresso before Anton showed, time also to appreciate how the space might work, how the relaxed cafe atmos might make waiting for the barber a good idea, and how that might engender a browse among the men's clothes. Diversification. People kept talking about it, but he'd never understood how it might work in his context. He'd done this schtick since he left school, he knew nothing else. Must be something else he could do. It might be worth a thought, he thought, once he'd dealt with this prick, now standing right in front of him, not a hair on his head, squinting at him through designer glasses, the rest of him neat as a pin in black jeans, black linen shirt, black boots. It was always winter in Anton's wardrobe. 'Anton!'

Anton didn't like Will's choice of table, offering the excuse that he needed to sit at an angle where his eye-line wasn't assaulted by the glare of the sun off the white chairs in the courtyard at the back. Delicate eyes, artistic. Whatever, thought Will, you're holding all the cards, and you know it. *Want me to hang upside down from the rafters and fart a sonata? I'll do it, just sign up, cunt, sign on the dotted line.*

That's not how it went, of course. There was no dotted line, never much certainty in the game Will played with Anton. Tap-dance, he urged himself, like no one knows you're a cripple. Anton made it clear he didn't do small talk, no use asking after the wife and kids. Will had no idea what Anton's domestic arrangements or proclivities were and that was fine. He didn't want any examination of his own situation and, besides, Anton could fuck goats for all he cared – he'd be more worried about the goats. So when Anton asked after 'old Den', he took Will by surprise. 'Great,' he lied. 'Loving retirement.'

'He gave me my first gig,' said Anton.

'The thing about Den was,' said Will, seeing an opportunity to turn it into a gratuitous compliment, 'he could always spot talent.' Anton grimaced and for a moment Will thought his ingratiating flattery had been seen for exactly that, before he realised that the grimace was a smile. He remembered Den telling him that sentiment was okay in a script if it was earned, but with actors and directors it could be dispensed like confetti. This was a better than expected beginning. So, down to business. He had to be careful how much he told Anton about the brief: enough to entice him, but not so much that Anton could take what he knew and shop himself somewhere else. 'The TVC is for an electric car,' he told Anton. 'Script already written, obviously.'

'Who by?' asked Anton.

'We'll get to that,' Will assured him, thinking, *none of your fucking business!*

'Which agency?'

'First things first,' insisted Will. He didn't want to tell Anton the agency was LSQN, because chances were Anton would be over there quick as a rat up a dead nun, touting himself and cutting out Flame. 'It'll involve shooting in a variety of scenic settings across both islands,' he said, going into his patter, 'if you take the brief literally. The idea, the controlling idea, is that this isn't a car experience, you aren't riding in a car, you're drifting along on a cloud. The car has a lot of autonomous driving features too.' *Next thing it'll be the fucking Flintstones.*

'Any CGI in the budget?'

Will didn't know, he hadn't done a detailed budget, that cost time and money he didn't have. 'The script *implies* a bit of computer graphics and green screen,' he told Anton. 'The complexity of the script, its varied settings and inherently high production values *imply* a proper production company with resources, facilities, and, of course, a talented director.'

'Thank you,' said Anton.

'It's not been posted on LSQN's website, so it's not going to be shot on spec by Some-cunt the guerrilla film-maker on his iPhone.'

'So the agency is LSQN,' said Anton. 'Is Nick the creative then?'

Fuck, thought Will, he'd given too much away, although in truth there was no way he could sell the thing without telling Anton who the agency was. He'd been at Western Springs high with Nick Preston, who he remembered as an arty streak of piss with explosive acne. Who'd have thought Nick would end up as the hot creative, *the man*, at an agency like LSQN? 'Yeah,' he said, 'Nick's across it.'

'Which car company?'

'Dunno yet. They want to keep the whole thing under wraps until they launch. It's a new model from a second-tier European company which has a good foothold in NZ but the big thing is they reckon the pictures they get here, they can use globally, which is why they'll spend real money.'

'But still get it cheaper than they could get anywhere else,' observed Anton.

Beggars can't be choosers, thought Will, but said nothing.

'I should talk to Nick,' said Anton.

'I'm talking to Nick,' said Will. 'I've got the brief right here.' Will pulled the plastic file cover from his bag. When Anton reached for the file, Will held it back. He saw a quick rush of bad blood through Anton's bland face. 'In return, I need at least an expression of interest from you.'

'I need to know what I'm expressing an interest in,' said Anton.

'The brief is comprehensive.'

'I need to fully understand where Nick's coming from. I want nuance.'

'If you're on for the job, I can get a sit-down with Nick. We can do lunch maybe.'

Anton couldn't keep the contempt out of his face. 'Lunch?

'Or whatever,' conceded Will. What the fuck happened to the idea of cementing relationships by going out to lunch and getting pissed? 'I'll organise something with Nick. Leave it to me.'

'Just me and him would be fine,' said Anton.

Oh yes, thought Will. I don't trust you, you little cunt. But what can I say? He knows we need him. He's the bankable element here, potentially. The only card I've got to play. He had to swallow it with good grace, try to keep some control. 'Okay,' he said. 'I'll make the call.'

'I've got his number.'

'It should come through me.'

'Let's not stand on protocol,' said Anton, standing. 'That wouldn't augur well for a creative relationship.'

Anton was smart, Will had to give him that. He'd turned the meeting, so that instead of Will holding out an apple, Anton had taken it, eaten it and was now throwing him the core.

'I'll give him a call, let you know,' said Anton, shaking his hand.

'So we've got an understanding?' asked Will. He knew as he asked the question that it was a step too far, giving Anton a glimmer of his need, his fear.

Anton understood it perfectly. He instantly dropped Will's hand and smiled at him with baleful, uncrinkled eyes that had no brows. 'That's exactly what I'm looking for,' he said. 'Understanding.'

Anton left without even the pretence of the old 'Where's my wallet?' Aussie haka, leaving Will, who had given everything in return for sweet FA, to pay the bill. On a purely monetary basis, it was good that Anton had eaten nothing, but on any other measurement, the fact that he hadn't wanted to break bread, or even fucking muesli, with Will, wasn't good. Anton was going to sell himself to Nick as the director he needed, and whether Flame got the producer gig, depended on . . . Who the fuck knew? It was now down to Nick at LSQN. Not for the first time, Will found himself wishing he'd been kinder to the gangling unco spaz at high school.

94

***

AS Will pulled the parking ticket from the windscreen wiper, screwed it up and threw it in the gutter, he tried to find the positives – though resorting to a biz-speak cliché like that was in itself a huge negative and even, he thought, a sign of desperation. WTF, he *was* desperate.

Anton had acknowledged Den, that was a positive. But did it *really* mean anything? Anton wouldn't have dared fuck Den over like that, so why do it to him? There was an obvious answer: because he could. That wasn't simply down to the fact, though it *was* a fact, that his father had earned a certain cachet in the industry that Will hadn't: times had changed. Entropy used to be the word people employed to describe a state of general and deep-seated fuckedness. Now the word was disruption. Maybe they were both right, Will thought. Entropy described the dynamic, disruption the result. An explosive disruption. That made sense: an explosion was just entropy at light speed, hurling everything outwards like a 360-degree projectile vomit. That's what's happened, he thought. Explosion. Fragmentation. Disruption. And it had begun happening way before Den had left the building.

Will cranked up the air con. The Bluetooth connected his mobile to the car-play and he saw a message from Yelena. *Urgent.* Fuck Yelena, she'd have to wait in line. He pulled out abruptly into the stream, cutting off some honking incompetent.

He'd arrived at Flame right out of high school in '95. Last fucking *century.* There seemed to be a shoot every couple of months back then, and Will had been the runner, the gofer, on whatever productions were happening. He'd loved it, driving round town, taking messages and people between the production office and the set, running errands for whoever needed something, picking up actors at whatever time the call-sheet dictated, delivering them to set, taking them home again. That had been particularly fascinating. Any overseas stars brought in would be staying at the Regent or the Langham, whereas he'd pick up the local 'stars' from some rented hovel at the dank end of Grey Lynn or Kingsland. He was always surprised at how needy they were – and not just the locals. A beautiful American B-lister on the wrong side of thirty had taken him back to her plush suite at the Regent after a trying day, cried about her lot, told him he had wonderful come-to-bed eyes and proved it by fucking him on her super king-size. He was sixteen, barely out of his high school short pants. How good was that!

He got to hang around on set, see how it all worked, the endless set-ups, the construction of a filmic narrative shot by painstaking shot. Exciting moving pictures created by a process that seemed paralytically slow and terminally boring. The magic of being where the action supposedly was quickly palled: everything happened at snail's pace, and you were out in all weathers, exposed to the elements, eternally waiting for the sun to go behind the clouds or emerge from them. It quickly struck Will that if you weren't *the man* on set, the name at the top of the call-sheet, the director, or maybe the DOP, or at least the sergeant-major first assistant director, you were at best a tradesman or, more likely, a labourer, a navvy, loading and unloading lights or cameras or tracks, setting them up, laying the cables to the generator truck, driving and parking the trucks, controlling traffic, getting coffee and food for spoilt fucking actors. He soon realised that the real action was happening back at the office and at the bars and restaurants around town. That was where the relationships were forged, where the networking with the ad agencies was done, where the deals were made that put all those people and equipment and celluloid into motion. And Branko and his father were the ones who made that happen.

Instead of putting him down in the ground-floor production office, Den had set up a temporary desk for Will in their open-plan mezzanine office, where he could see and hear his father and Branko doing their stuff, working their contacts on the phones and face-to-face – though a lot of that happened outside the office, at venues he wasn't initially invited to. That had changed on his seventeenth birthday, when Branko took him to a bar where naked women swam in a tank and there was cocaine on the bar tab. He knew Den hadn't wanted him there, but for Branko it was some kind of a test, that Will passed, right before he passed out. It was a lesson: if you had Mexican marching powder on tap, pass on the tequila.

Watching Den and Branko in operation was eye-opening. They worked the big ad agencies like a couple of sheep dogs: Branko the eye dog, the header, and Den the yappy huntaway. Will began to see the layers, and realise it was *all* about the layers, how they worked, the connections between them.

Within the big agencies, there was always a head of TV, usually older, often an ex-producer, who wielded huge power. The HTV took the brief and budgets from his suits to his team of creatives. He might have a few to choose from, but the creatives always worked in pairs, always, an art director and a writer. That team might bond for life, move from agency to agency as their stocks rose. The creatives were gold and Den was the miner. His smile was his pick-axe and his background as a writer his shovel. He knew these guys – they were all guys – he and Branko had rubbed up against most of them round the traps. And they'd done exactly the same kind of work before they set up Flame, Branko art directing and Den copywriting.

From their position inside one of the big agencies, they could see the eye-watering budgets the production companies were working with, and decided they could get a share of it if they jumped the fence and set up a hybrid agency-cum-production company. Besides, Den wanted to direct and the production company gave him the vehicle.

The hybrid concept didn't work – the industry was accustomed to a separation of powers – and the boutique agency part quickly withered while the production company took off and began minting it. By the time Will got there, Den had largely given up directing and was working in tandem with Branko, feeding the machine: wrangling the agencies, working the system of mutual grace and favours, the nexus of connections where the main players ate and drank, snorted and sometimes even fucked together. Back then, in endless long lunches or after-work drinks, they actually seemed to enjoy one another's company.

Will pulled into the lane to turn right from Ponsonby into Richmond. Four back, Will watched the first car miss the green. The bastard would be texting, unforgivable when you're the first in line. Will hit the horn in frustration, but too late: the first car got round, followed by two others, leaving Will stuck on the red. He took a deep breath, tried to calm himself, wondered how he'd ended up such a lone wolf at Flame.

While they divided their responsibilities, Branko and Den often overlapped, and were the perfect combination. Branko big and bluff with a face like a cliff, a face that showed complete assurance even when he was nervous or worried, even when, ten years later, he was diagnosed with type 2 Diabetes, and they started amputating bits and pieces of his extremities. Never seemed to have a worry in the world, and then he died. But Branko had been the best, the straight man to Den's smiling gadfly. Will had studied them closely, trying to pick up whatever he could. What were they really good at? Disarming people, Will decided. Making people feel comfortable. Making them happy to be sharing the space. And a big part of that was simply ridiculous, when you analysed it. They knew their shit, sure, spoke the ad industry patois, targeted the guys who counted, but the other big thing they did was tell jokes. *Really* well. They made people laugh, Branko and Den. The mystery was where they found them – jokes were open-open-source long before the internet. They seemed to drop from the ether. Way before email became popular, there seemed to be a network of people, men, who needed to hear the latest joke before getting down to business. For Branko and Den, once heard, a joke was never forgotten. Whatever the topic under discussion, it gave them a segue to the latest they'd heard, and when all else failed, they had some Default Classics – that's what they called them – which, even if the particular audience had heard them before, seemed, like *Fawlty Towers*, to improve on reprise. So Will heard some of these classics many times: *The Irish Zookeeper and the Orang-utan* and *Crocodile Dundee Walks into an Outback Pub with a Pet Crocodile on his Shoulder*, and *The Babysitting Gorilla* and *Roger, the Last Great White Hunter* and *The Girl Who Got a Job with a Scottish Laird*. It gradually dawned on Will that there was a science behind what Branko and Den would do. They knew an essential truth: that people, no matter how gifted and cool and talented and rich and entitled, liked to laugh. And there was always laughter when Branko and Den were holding court, and the HTVs and creatives, talented as they were, cool as they liked to imagine they were, couldn't resist a laugh. He remembered his father once telling him that when people opened their mouths to laugh, they were at their most vulnerable, and there was no telling what else you could slide in there.

Will couldn't remember the last time he'd laughed. Times had changed somewhere back there at the turn of the century. He hadn't picked up on it soon enough because there still seemed to be so much money around: there were still expense-account lunches that lasted all afternoon and kicked on into coke-fuelled parties, there were still $100,000 dollar days, big sets and art department budgets and travel.

Will had taken all the big meetings with Branko and Den, sat there and felt the tension as the HTV introduced them to rooms of maybe twenty people, up to six each from the client and the agency, assorted hangers-on. Then Branko and Den had the floor, to live or die, with these people hanging on every word. It was show and tell. Branko and Den might have storyboards, or just a script. If Den was directing, it was his show. If he wasn't, they'd have brought the director with them, but he might be articulate or he might be a visual maestro who had trouble stringing two words together. Branko went first, telling them why the money was so wisely spent with them, they'd see every dollar up on screen, then hand it over to Den, with or without the director. Den would sell the script, tell them what it really meant, describe the pictures, show them how it would work. He'd act out all the parts, the gunslinger, the child, the naif, the beautiful lover. He was so convincing that Will was often dismayed when he attended the first read-through of the same script with the actors. They sounded flat, wooden, they couldn't *read*: the words that had sung when Den did it in front of the HTV and the suits and the creatives, died a death round the big read-through table. 'You're so much better than them,' he once whispered to his father when they broke from the table for coffee after one of the disasters.

'I know the material,' Den told him. 'I wrote it. But in a week's time, I'll be at the same level, no matter how many times I rehearse it, but they'll have found all sorts of nuances and angles, and be a hundred times better. That's the difference.'

And Den was right, mostly: he was right if he and Branko had made the right decisions about the director and the cast and if the script was up to it. A mistake in one of those elements could tarnish gold in the other two. That was what the agencies saw in Flame back then: a safe pair of hands who could mould those elements into a magic alchemy.

But things began to change, tighten. Good ideas were leached through ten layers of market research till all the juice was gone. Clients began interfering in the creative process. Production budgets shrank. Will had seen Branko get it dreadfully wrong once and have to drop his budget estimation by half a million *on the spot*, in a nanosecond, right in front of an incredulous HTV. 'How the fuck will you do that?'

'I don't know,' Branko had said. 'What I do know is that we *will* do it. For you.' But the margins were getting stringy, even then.

He remembered Branko telling him after one pitching session that 'the only thing worse than not getting the job is getting the job'. At the time, Will had no idea what Branko was talking about, he put it down to the fact that he was ailing, already terminal. Now he knew. It was a tough business. You might be exhausted, you might be traumatised, you might be creatively bereft, but you couldn't stop, and then, having quoted skinny to get the gig, you had to find a way to deliver what you'd promised.

Will had a recurring nightmare where he was out in a wheat field, maybe at Stan's farm, though he'd never seen Te Kurahau and had no idea whether they even grew wheat. But Will was stumbling through the chest-high grain, trying to run, pursued by one of those massive combine harvesters that had a clown's exaggerated lips round a huge black hole where the wheat disappeared. As the thing closed on him, Will kept tearing off bundles of wheat and throwing it into the machine's giant maw, trying to slow it down, keep feeding it before it ate him. Will was real but the machine was an animation. The last time it was so graphic that Will had woken in a sweat.

At some point, Flame became a liability, rather than safe pair of hands. The big agencies wanted cool. They wanted the new boutique production companies, Robber's Dog, Sweet Shop, Curious, not old-school diehards like Branko and Den. The jokes had already lost their currency. When Branko died, Den lost the will to continue and Will saw an opportunity to reignite Flame. He'd done his best, took a punt on new directors, subsidised a few of them with film stock – those were the days! – and free post-production into music videos or short films to give them a calling card, but the directors who were any good fucked off to features, never felt they owed anyone and never came back.

Will had been hoping that Branko's daughter Yelena, by then an accounts suit at one of the agencies, would take over her father's share. She was smart and ambitious, and would have been the perfect partner. Too smart. She didn't want a bar of Flame, and Will had to persuade Claudia to mortgage the family home to pay her out. He'd had a stark choice: go it alone, or fold. He could see that, yes, he'd been sucked in by the glamorous peripherals, but the truth was he knew nothing else. Credit to Yelena, she saw what

Will couldn't, that the lucrative business model was at the end of its cycle, that the corporates were about to smother creativity, and that technology, available to anyone, would kill whatever was left. Had Den known what was coming? There was no point in asking him now. In any case, the die was cast. Will had borrowed to pay out Yelena for Branko's share, and Yelena had taken Will's money and put it down as a deposit on the building Flame occupied.

Back then it'd been a nondescript warehouse/office in an unfashionable cul-de-sac at the bottom of Richmond Road. Now there were lights controlling the entrance from Richmond Road, due to heavy traffic drawn by a posh boutique supermarket, three cafes, a shop selling faux Italian furniture and Euro toilet fittings and a huge hardware depot. He should have known: real estate was where it was at. He would have been better off sitting on his arse doing nothing, coining the tax-free capital gains on his house, rather than mortgaging it to run a business. Yelena was now his landlord and Flame was late with the rent, as with everything else.

There were two parking bays, clearly marked for staff only, in front of the double garage doors of the Flame Inc. warehouse, both taken, by the cars of his next two appointments, for whom he was already late. He kerbed the left front rim of the Sportage trying to park it against the footpath further along, and cursed the arrogant fucks who had taken his place. He hit the wheel with his fists, then grabbed his mobile, searched for the tow-truck number, imagined for one heavenly moment the faces of his lawyer and accountant when, after harassing him, they'd find their overpriced steel chariots in the can. Sorry, Rod, he'd say, and sorry whoever-the-fuck the current iteration of his accountant was, so sorry, the tow-trucks round here are quite predatory. Can't do a thing, you'll have to just pay the fine. He enjoyed the moment, then put the phone away. He needed to keep his cool, be confident and ingratiating, convince his advisers, who should know better, that he was solvent.

Will rubbed his eyes, tucked in his shirt and readied himself for the heat. There were no choices left: he'd jumped into this saddle, and now had to ride this broken nag until it staggered across the finishing line or died underneath him. He had to do what Den would have done: deal with the lawyer and accountant, then take Nick Preston to dinner, spend money on him, flatter him, play to his ego. Wine him, dine him, butter the bastard up, butter *himself* up if necessary, bend over the table and present his anus. Whatever it took. He had to do it quickly, before Anton got in Nick's ear. And before . . . At what point did the smell of fear metamorphose into the stink of failure?

***

THE interior of the warehouse was exactly as Branko and Den had configured it nearly forty years ago. A utilitarian production house, with the central well dominated by a huge table, around which a cast and director might fit for a read-through, or the heads of department, camera, lighting, wardrobe and art might gather, crossing the floor from their partitioned spaces around the perimeter. It was open plan, big connecting spaces built for fifty-odd people to collaborate closely in. As Will made for the mezzanine at the far end, his leather soles rapped the polished concrete floor and echoed back its emptiness.

Under the looming mezzanine, there was storage on one side, containing all kinds of production equipment, much of it now redundant: Branko had been an early adopter and an even quicker rejector. On the other side was a big editing suite, with all the bells and whistles, bought in better times when it had been state-of-the-art technology. Now Will could download software onto his MacBook that would do much the same things.

Will tried to remember when the suite had last been fully utilised. That $300,000 road safety TVC, Christ, when was that? Last year? Year before last? The edit had gone well. By day three there was real consensus between Will and the director and the HTV and creatives from the agency. In fact there was genuine delight – the HTV actually used the word 'genius' – and so much back-slapping and high-fiving that shoulders were in danger of dislocation. The client, the CEO of a fucking transport agency who'd personally okayed the script and the director's storyboard, was wheeled in for the final sign-off. He sat there and started clicking his tongue, then said at the end, 'This is nothing *like* what I was expecting.' The HTV from the agency immediately threw Flame under the bus, telling the CEO that he hadn't thought it was quite right either. And who was that HTV? Nick Preston, the ectomorphic fuck.

Another production came to mind, some years earlier, a shoot for a mobile provider. The HTV brought in three underlings, kids who'd done a marketing degree at Vic and had no knowledge of the world, no knowledge of film, no knowledge of edits. It was clearly the first time any of them had stepped foot inside an editing suite. This HTV played the fine-cut through three times, offered no opinion, then turned to the kids and said, 'What do you think?' They knew they were fucked. 'That was interesting, that was fascinating,' they said, and the clever-dick HTV asked 'Why?' Will had watched this absurdity play out, thinking this guy's company has paid 200K so that this dick can use a TVC to demonstrate his superiority over some pimply-faced graduates. Who was that turd? Nick fucking Preston. Will felt sick.

Guarding the stairs to the offices above, and commanding the central well, were the desks of the production manager, production co-ordinator and production secretary, but the only current occupant was the lone figure of Trish, the stalwart company secretary, who'd cross over to production co-ordinator when the cameras were rolling – a figurative expression these days. Trish had been with Flame longer than Will and she knew the drill: her piano calves, Boadicean chest and stentorian tones would keep the circling vultures from picking him to pieces, to the degree that this was within her power, given that two of the fuckers had already commandeered his parking space and the inner sanctum upstairs.

'How long have they been here?'

'Ten minutes. They've got coffee and water, they won't die.'

Trish was the widow of a grip, Pete, who'd worked with Branko and Den from the start, a strong, practical little bugger who laid tracks, set up dollies, made cranes and generally supported the camera and the lighting in whatever way was needed. Pete had been taken quickly by a melanoma, maybe from being outside so much. They never found the melanoma, only its metastasised tentacles in his groin and lymph nodes. Witty bugger, Pete, gallows humour. Will remembered visiting him with Den, and Pete grimacing or smiling, Will couldn't say which, telling Den to enjoy every breath while he still could: 'Rage, rage against the dying of the magic hour, boss.'

Pete had left Trish with two young boys who were now doing well, one in IT and the other an engineer who had been one of the abseilers on the cliffs above the Kaikōura road after the big quake, drilling holes to anchor the mesh nets that caught the falling rocks. Will had seen the photos – Trish was practically family, gold standard, part of what used to be the industry. Will remembered her wearing a T-shirt to a wrap party when Pete was still alive, with '*If these were brains I'd be a genius*' emblazoned across the front. But she was anyway. She took a lot of heat off Will at some personal cost. Will knew she hated lying to people on his behalf, obfuscating, saying he was out when he was in, protecting him when he was down or high or pissed, but she also knew Will and Flame were at rock bottom. Will had never told her specific details, but Trish sat there in that huge empty space day after day and she made Will's appointments, she knew who he was seeing, who was talking to him and who was not, and she knew the import of the two figures upstairs waiting for him. She'd hang in till the death, Will knew that, which was why he'd paid her last fortnight's wages out of his credit card. And he'd make sure she continued to get paid for as long as possible, and fuck the IRD.

***

WILL had spoken to Flame's accountant on the phone, but never met her in the flesh and had forgotten her name. He was grateful to be introduced by Rod, whose firm, Baigent & Son, had been Flame's solicitors since the year dot. The same accountancy firm had acted for Flame throughout too, but about every five years, it seemed, the practice would be sold and Branko and Den and then Will would get a letter from the outgoing principal thanking them for their custom, advising that he/she was moving on to 'pastures new' and introducing the new principal, a man/woman with CA after their name and an impressive pedigree and aspirations, whose 'focus would be on nurturing the best interests of Flame'. He tried to remember the original man behind the practice, a Dally mate of Branko's, but no image came. Then he tried to remember the name of the woman Rod had just introduced him to, who appeared to be well into a monologue to Will. Suzan Someone?

Other than her name, Will felt he knew everything about her just by looking. Keeping her cool, despite the air con being turned off, late thirties, shortish bobbed hair, blonde highlights, slim on top, a bit of width to the hips, but still fit, two children probably, married to another career numerant, a CA or maybe an engineer or quantity surveyor, someone practical and rational like her. The kids would be in care after school, but she and her hubby would take turns leaving early, picking them up, doing the supermarket runs and the cooking. They'd be mortgaged to the hilt to live the inner-city fringe dream and she'd go to Les Mills and have a yoga mat. She'd also have a mind like a steel trap and would have known before she came to this meeting that Flame was fucked and of limited future value to her practice: if Flame went into liquidation, some other accountant would be appointed receiver.

The only thing Will could *actually* remember was that she was ex-South African IRD. That memory might have been triggered by what she was saying, quite sternly, or maybe the harshness in her voice was just a remnant of Afrikaaner vowels. 'I'm happy to make a deal with the IRD, but I do not want to offer them something we cannot deliver on. That's *not* the way to go forward.'

She *would* say that, Will thought – if she's ex-IRD she doesn't want her clients shitting on her ex-colleagues. She had stopped talking and was clearly expecting a response. Will looked at Rod, but there appeared to be no salvation there, so he conjured up Den's smile, which he knew was there in his face in fleeting bursts, and began the kind of tap dance he'd learnt from his father

In Will's reversioning of this morning's meeting, 'top-gun' director Anton Gognik had been 'all over the brief', couldn't wait to get his hands on it, and all that remained was a 'pro forma meeting' with head of TV at LSQN, Nicholas Preston, an old school friend with whom Will and Anton had had previous successful collaborations. The gig was as good as signed off. Will had the figures, his producer's fee, Flame's production overhead. He ticked off the many and various ways Flame could draw money from the munificent budget for facilities and resources, like the bespoke production office they'd just walked through, the departmental spaces, the wardrobe storage, the editing suite. And so on. He was surprised by how much he was enjoying himself. This rosy picture he was painting was certainly working for him: the more he talked, the better he felt about his prospects. He'd heard the phrase 'talk therapy' – perhaps that's all it was, learning how to bullshit yourself.

When he stopped to draw breath, his shirt a dish-rag, Suzan simply said, 'What then?'

Will wanted to throttle her for puncturing the moment he had conjured, but instead managed, 'Fair point.' The future. One production, no matter how lucrative, wouldn't save them. So he detailed the bridgehead to more projects that this high-profile TVC for a class-leading, breakthrough high-tech EV would lead to. 'Regrettably,' Will said, 'this is an industry where perception matters as much as execution. Flame has always been among the elite production entities but this TVC will get a lot of exposure and will lift our stocks with the major agencies.'

Suzan was softening, he could tell, so Will got out the trowel and told Suzan about his marital woes. Traumatising, yes, they were, of course, but they also meant he could look forward to releasing equity in his matrimonial property. Then there was his parents' house, which was recently razed in a tragic fire, but which was fully insured, so there would be insurance proceeds on the immediate horizon, followed by the sale of the section.

'Which suburb?' asked Suzan.

'Herne Bay, actually,' said Will and watched with a mix of relief and contempt the effect of those two magic words. The country's richest suburb. *Game over.* He should have played that card earlier, saved himself some grist.

But he'd overread her: Suzan from Bloemfontein or wherever-the-hell was made of sterner stuff. Will's prospects were *so* much better than Suzan had been expecting that she couldn't hide her bean-counter suspicions, and looked to Rod Baigent for confirmation. Rod smiled, and said nothing, which prompted Will to lift an eyebrow to Rod. *WTF?*

'Sounds great to me,' said Rod, finally, 'and a good basis to negotiate a deal with the IRD, yes?'

Suzan agreed, if Will could just send her an email, confirming all the details in writing, so that she had something concrete to take back to the IRD.

'Oh,' said Rod, at last paying his way, 'I think we can take all those as read, Suzan. Tell IRD the story, and we'll look forward to you coming back to us with some idea of the quantum and T and Cs IRD would find acceptable.' He put a hand out to usher her towards the door to the stairs. 'The less the better over the longest term possible would be the ideal, obviously. I just need to discuss some of the more personal matrimonial details with my client, if you don't mind.'

'That's fine,' she said, as Rod opened the door, then turned for a last broadside. 'You might remind your client that it is an offence to trade knowing you're insolvent.' And she was gone.

Will could barely contain himself until the door closed and he heard her heels on the stairs. 'Why the fuck did you take so long to jump in?'

Rod carefully removed his jacket and rolled his cotton sleeves above strong, hairy wrists. Rod was the son of Clarry, the original lawyer for Flame, a mate of Branko's, and about Will's age, give or take, but affected a gravitas that made him seem, in Will's eyes at least, much older. One element of this was the formality of his speech. Over drinks, Will had heard him swear and curse with the best of them, but once he'd put on his lawyer's mien, he seemed offended by the fucks and cunts he threw around with abandon when he was off duty. Did jacket off mean off duty? Clearly not. Rod was grimacing, as if someone had kicked him in the nuts. 'There's no need for profanity, Will.'

'Fuck you, Rod, I pay you to cover my fucking back. You left me balls-out swinging in the breeze. Why didn't you endorse me on the matrimonial property proceeds and the fire insurance payout?'

'Because I find myself in a difficult position, due to—'

'*You're* in a difficult position?'

The other thing Rod disliked, when on duty or off, was being interrupted when speaking. He liked disgorging fully rounded sentences, with all the necessary qualifying clauses and phrases in place, he liked being heard *respectfully*, he liked launching into monologues, like some judge or schoolteacher or vicar who wouldn't brook interruption, as if every fucking word was a pearl. Will felt duty-bound to take every opportunity to break these perorations up.

'Unfortunately, Will, I'm privy to information which—'

'What fucking information?'

'Information which is material to the matters—'

'For fuck's sake, let's have it, Rod!'

111

Rod's incipient dewlaps were quivering. Will was sure he was about to remonstrate with him like a naughty schoolboy, tell him to put his hand up when he wanted to say something. Instead, Rod said, 'Will, you can be a complete and utter cunt.'

'That's better! What's the guts?'

'The insurance company's just come back. The fire investigator has made a preliminary report.'

'At last. When's the payout?'

When Will saw Rod hesitate and gather himself like a funeral director, he knew what was coming wasn't good. 'There's a problem,' said Rod. 'The fire investigator has determined that the probable cause was an accelerant, hot embers from the outside fire, carried into the kitchen, where the fire began.'

Will was aghast. 'It's taken this sensational fucking genius how many months to figure that out? That the fire was started by that little cunt Jackson, the arsonist, who was out there stoking the pizza oven?'

'The fire investigator has completed his interviews with everyone, including your father, who, as you know, was downstairs when the fire took hold.'

'There's fuck-all point in talking to Den.'

'He was downstairs at the relevant time.'

Will finally had a glimmering of disaster ahead. Rod's face had become longer, the dewlaps were extending in mournful sympathy, a sure sign that bad news was imminent. Suddenly Will didn't care any more how much time Rod took to get to whatever revelation he was about to drop.

'Since there's a genuine possibility that the fire was deliberately started by the insured and since there's a clause that specifically voids the policy if that's the case–'

'Den? Burnt his own fucking house down?' He didn't see that coming.

'Given your father's state of mind, or lack of, it's a possibility, that's what they're saying. And as long as it remains a genuine possibility, and until they have proof that the cause of the fire can be laid at someone else's feet, they won't pay out.'

Will sat down on the sofa, side-swiped, deflated. 'The cunts.'

Rod shrugged. 'That's why I didn't jump in, Will. And I'm also obliged to advise you that the matrimonial situation is unlikely to be resolved any time soon. Any proceeds from the matrimonial property are at least a couple of years away. With two very young dependent children, no judge will force a sale before then. I'm sorry, Will.'

'What can I do?'

'The delay in the fire insurance proceeds need not delay selling the section, now that the fire investigator has completed his inspection of the property . . . But of course, that's up to your father.'

'Up to Den? He's up to fuck all!'

As Rod began a bewildering off-the-cuff monologue about the dos and don'ts of powers of attorney, Will realised that the infinite possibilities of imminent disaster for him and for Flame represented just the opposite for the lawyer. Intractable shit-fights on all fronts promised ongoing dollops of moolah for Rod, given that eventual proceeds of sale would have to go through the Baigent & Son trust account, and would be quickly and quietly relieved of fees and disbursements before being passed on.

***

WHEN Rod Baigent finally took his leave, Will waved him down the stairs, then left the door half open so he could listen to the lawyer's leather soles reverberating up through the concrete canyon. He needed to know the fucker was irrevocably gone, that the lecture was finally over, that the talking was finished, that Rod wouldn't come back to nail a last codicil or qualifying clause to his bewildering off-the-cuff oral treatise on the vagaries of a power of attorney and the circumstances under which Den might sign one himself, or have a judge sign it for him.

Will felt an overwhelming dark lassitude and fingered the little lifters in his pocket. The sweat was running down the V of his spine into his jocks. He thought about going rogue and turning the air con on. Or he could take another half-gram, or . . . He looked across to the sofa. Or he could lay his head down on that cushion, put his feet up and, with a bit of luck, never fucking wake up.

***

WILL woke to a sound he hadn't heard in a long time. Laughter. Unbridled, raucous. He rolled off the sofa and over to the door, looked carefully down the stairs to Trish's desk. *Oh shit*. Branko's daughter, Yelena, his landlord – 'landlady' just didn't seem right for her – and Ellie, his sister, around Trish's desk, the three of them cackling together like a coven of witches. Yelena come to harass him about the rent, no doubt. But why Ellie? He seriously considered the fire escape, but Trish would have told them he was in, and they'd have seen the Sportage out front. He had to brazen it. 'Keep it down, f'chrissakes,' he called down. 'Some of us are trying to concentrate!'

'Yeah right, Rip Van Winkle, we could hear the snoring from down here!' That couldn't possibly be true, thought Will, but Yelena, with something of her father's powerful build and skin colour – a beautiful light brown satin, highlighted by her short blonded hair – also had her father's uncanny ability to invest everything she said with truth, or at least to divine what needed to be said and say it. She smiled up at him with her perfect teeth. 'Come on down, Will, the gang's all here.'

The gang? Will remembered with some embarrassment that they used to be exactly that, Yelena, Ellie and Will, at primary school and intermediate, often walking together back here after school, or being brought by Nadine, Yelena's mother, or occasionally by Carol. And Trish, childless in those early days, giving them the run of the place. Trish may have been low in the production pecking order, but the HODs knew she'd be here when they had moved on; she had the bosses' ears and these were the bosses' children. So the kids had unfettered access to the costume department for dress-ups, and Will could remember with some wonder his passivity as a mannequin on which Yelena, one year younger but always his equal, and his sister, two years younger, expressed their fantasies. Will had been more inclined towards the props department, where they could play with boltless guns and collapsible knives, and Yelena, particularly, had always been up for a bit of playful mayhem. When Trish's two boys came along, they were, like Stan, too young to be true friends of the older kids, but were always included. This warehouse had been their playpen for many years, and Trish had been their true north.

'A moment,' he told them. 'I have to make a call.'

'We all have to make calls, mate,' said Yelena. 'But fine, do it. You've got five.'

Will retreated to the office and into the en-suite. He leant forward over the basin to protect the front of his shirt, then splashed cold water on his face, which looked sunken when he towelled it dry. He'd look better with a few more kilos on him. And another couple of hundred thousand in his pocket. Failing that, he had half a tab there, the other half of what he'd taken at about six that morning. That used to be good for twelve to eighteen hours: maybe Lila's quality control was slipping. He'd need it to get the call done, then get through whatever was waiting for him downstairs. Time was slipping away. He swallowed the half-tab and sluiced some water directly from the tap into his mouth, then straightened up and grimaced again at the man in the mirror. He wished he had some smoke, wanted the big instant zap. Still, the conversation with Nick was likely to be long enough for the tab to kick in. He looked better already. *Now or never.*

Will crossed back to his mobile on the sofa, took a couple of deep breaths as he found Nick's number. Do the dance, he told himself, get those feet going. The steps for this one had to be all about Anton, the bankable element. He pressed the screen button, heard Nick's phone ring three times, then cut to voice-mail. *The cunt.* Three rings was just enough for Nick to have seen his name come up and react. Or maybe he was in a meeting and had forgotten to mute it. As Nick's bored, uncaring voice asked him to leave a message, Will tried to smuggle assurance and a smile into his voice. *Don't say too much. Keep it short, keep the need out of it.* 'Nick, Will Sparks. Had a great meet with Anton this morning. Look forward to talking.'

***

PUTTING on his smiley face after the Nick rebuff, he stood at the top of the stairs and said, 'Come on up.'

Yelena was having none of that. 'Nah, you come down,' she said.

'We've got a plan.'

His dismay must have shown. 'A coffee, all right?'

Trish was invited too, and could have come, but insisted on staying to 'hold the fort'. Will felt like telling her not to bother, the battle's been lost, the fort's been overrun, but she seemed adamant. Later, when Will became aware what Yelena and Ellie were up to, he understood that Trish must have been in on it. But when Yelena walked them to her car, not his, what could he say? When she opened the front passenger door and insisted he take that seat, when Ellie got into the back seat right behind her so she had a clear view of him, when he realised he was captive, what could he say? He was just grateful Yelena wasn't talking about the rent. Yet.

As they headed back up Richmond to the Ponsonby strip, he made some panicky small talk about Yelena's BMWi3, told them he was about to do a big TVC about an E vehicle. He couldn't reveal the brand, but the brief was big on cloud metaphor.

'Not a magic carpet ride?' asked Yelena.

Will wasn't sure whether she was taking the piss. What the fuck did she expect? It was advertising, for fuck's sake.

Ellie was saying nothing. Will noticed she'd cut her hair shorter. It lifted her face and she looked younger, happier, but not when she looked his way. He became aware that he was talking to fill a big hole when Yelena made it worse by falling silent too. They passed all the cafes on the strip, whispered down Franklin and Wellington, took a left to the on-ramp and into the motorway tunnel. There was nothing to look at, no engine noise, no conversation, just the whoosh of the air con keeping the stifling heat at bay. The safety belt started to feel like a straitjacket. 'Coffee wasn't the plan, then?' he asked. 'What *is* the plan, actually?'

In reply, Ellie said something in te reo, her first words, he realised, since he'd seen her at the bottom of the stairs. She sounded pissed off about something, but Will had little idea what it might be. Yelena had replied in kind. He picked up some words here and there, words he remembered from their kapa haka group at primary school and intermediate. That's all Will had left, along with a vague idea of some of the chants and dance movements they'd learnt, whereas Yelena and Ellie had, obviously, persevered. It was natural enough for Yelena, Will supposed. Her father had spoken Māori: his mother, her grandmother, was from some iwi up north. Will remembered Branko's mother visiting the Flame offices, bringing Kerikeri oranges and kiwifruit, which she called Chinese gooseberries, and saying things in Māori to Branko when, Will suspected, she didn't want others to understand. Which was exactly what Yelena and Ellie were doing now. Using code. Locking him out. *Fucking childish.* Words like whānau and mātua jumped out occasionally, but it was the repetition of his own name that gradually began to piss him off. 'You think I don't know who you're talking about?' he said, finally. 'It's just fucking rude.'

So they began talking in English. About him, as he suspected, but still in the third person as if he wasn't there.

'You remember how sweet Will used to be to us?' asked Ellie, draping her arms over Yelena's shoulders from behind.

So that's it, thought Will. They're an item. It made sense, he supposed. He could understand a woman's attraction to another woman. What he didn't get was why a woman would be attracted to a man, or, much worse, a man to another man.

'I *do* remember how sweet he used to be,' said Yelena. 'What I can't remember is when exactly he turned into such a self-obsessed arsehole.'

Here it comes, thought Will. The fucking rent.

'I was ten and you were eleven,' said Ellie. 'Will was twelve and went to Springs.'

'That's right! The next year, when I started there, he was a total prick to me. I was a newbie at this big high school, and all he did was shit on me.'

'I got it at home too. He stopped being our friend and became a . . . what?'

'A mean, treacherous little shit, who pretended not to know us.'

'My big bro. My friend.'

'Our bestie,' said Yelena, finally turning to Will. 'Do you remember?'

Will remembered being friends, but not how or why it changed. 'Dunno,' he said. 'We grew up. Things change.'

'Did you hear that?' asked Yelena.

'Things change,' mimicked Ellie.

'I think what happened was your balls dropped,' said Yelena. 'Your balls dropped and we went from being friends to being girls. Is that what happened, you reckon?'

Will was mute. Ellie started talking about him in the third person again, as if he wasn't there. 'Just another nasty little fuckwit boy.'

'Who grew up to be a self-obsessed arsehole.'

'A vainglorious neo-liberal shit.'

'A man for whom money speaks. Which, if you measure him by his own values, must make him a complete fucking failure.'

Here it comes, the fucking rent. 'Having fun?' asked Will. 'It must be *such* fun.'

'Does that sound like him?' asked Yelena.

'That's him, definitely,' confirmed Ellie.

They were at the top of the harbour bridge. Will looked out at the grey heat-flattened water and the distant blue hills and imagined the black beaches beyond, and the wide Tasman. He could just walk out through the break and start swimming west. He needed to get whatever journey they were on over and done with. 'Where the fuck are we going?'

'When did you last see Dad?' asked Ellie.

Will shrugged. 'Been a wee while . . .'

'Where was he when you last saw him?'

The truth was, at home, at his party, the night of the fire. But he wasn't going to tell Ellie that.

***

IT was happy hour at the Sunset Road Retirement Village, though Den looked far from happy. He'd spat his first gobful of wine back into his plastic stemmed glass. 'That's fucking chateau cardboard!'

'They do have some bottles of white wine there,' said Ellie, glancing back to the bar. Will followed her gaze and saw a dozen grey geezers and geezeresses in various states of physical degeneration making a show of being merry, standing in a tight wad because otherwise they wouldn't be able to hear each other wheeze and fart.

'You know what's in those bottles?' asked Den. 'Alcohol-free chardonnay. What's the point?'

'Try this,' said Yelena, offering Den a sip from her glass.

'What is it?'

'Sauvignon blanc, sans alcohol.'

'I might be losing my marbles,' said Den, 'but I haven't completely lost my palate.'

'Are you losing your marbles, Den?' asked Will.

Ellie sputtered on her wine. 'Jesus, Will!'

They were standing at a remove from the others in a large carpeted room, or hall, it might have been. The lighting was so low that the room might have extended for miles beyond the huge, deserted billiard table that loomed out of the darkness. Spaced regularly along the beige plastered walls were paintings of inoffensive rural scenes. The English ones looked a bit like Constable on a bad day, and the local ones were faux washed-out Grahame Sydney. Everything about the room screamed its desire to be least offensive to the largest number of people. It looked like a cross between a hotel conference room and the antechamber for a mausoleum. Which, Will supposed, it was.

Den didn't seem at all offended by Will's question about his marbles. 'It's strange,' he said. 'I don't know what's gone until it's already gone, and then it's too late, I can't remember what it is I've lost.' Then he gave them the Den smile, and that made it so much worse. It had become a rictus grimace and he looked terrified.

'You're doing really well, Dad,' said Ellie.

'Am I?' He shook his head as if to clear it. The shaggy mane seemed electrified.

'I'll ask them to give you a haircut,' said Ellie.

'They're not to touch me!'

'Okay,' said Ellie. 'Not if it's a problem.'

Den leant towards Will, conspiratorially. Will had forgotten how short he was, or perhaps his father had shrunk. He couldn't hear Den's whisper at first. 'This is a very strange hotel,' he said. 'Full of old buggers. Where are the kids?'

Will didn't know what to say.

'I'll tell you something else,' whispered Den. By this time Ellie and Yelena were leaning in too. 'Carol doesn't like this place.'

'She tell you that?' asked Will.

'She won't talk to me. That's how I know.'

'Right.' What the fuck do you say, thought Will. He looked at Ellie, whose eyes were brimming with tears.

'She hates it here,' said Den, oblivious. 'She won't come near it.'

Ellie had explained in the car – the rest of the journey from the bridge and up through the bays had passed civilly, relatively – that Den had entered an assisted living apartment on a ninety-day trial basis and sooner or later they had to make a decision about whether he stayed. When Will had asked what the options were, there weren't many, or any. Den had been assessed as not being able to safely live alone, so the autonomous villas and apartments were out. Some kind of care facility was necessary. Sunset had serviced apartments, where food and housekeeping was taken care of and trained staff were available twenty-four/seven. 'And,' said Ellie, 'Dad can shift from the serviced apartments to the actual rest home and then hospital care as part of the same complex. He doesn't have to leave and go somewhere else, as his condition progresses.'

Progresses? Will had thought it a strange way to describe the gradual disintegration of Den's mind, but kept his peace, as Ellie went on to explain that everything from dental care to pharmaceuticals to physio rehab was right on site, so Den wouldn't have to travel anywhere for anything.

'That's a plus?' Will had asked. 'He can't get out of there for anything?'

'He's lost his driver's licence,' explained Ellie patiently, 'so not having to travel is important.'

There was a pressing question, which Will did his best to delay while he feigned interest in Ellie's exegesis on the benefits of Sunset Road. But sure enough, when Will finally got it out and asked what all this cost, Ellie just stared at him. 'That's your first question?'

'Third, actually,' said Will. 'But a reasonable one, surely. I mean, presumably he doesn't get all that for nix. When the trial's over, and if it's the right place for him to be, how much does it cost?'

Ellie explained that the apartments were going for between 650 and 850, depending on their view and how much sun they got.

'Six fifty and eight fifty what?' asked Will, facetiously.

'Hundred thousand, doofus,' confirmed Yelena.

'He'll *own* the apartment. It'll be his, effectively,' said Ellie.

'Effectively?'

'They call it a right to occupy.'

'How does that work?' Will asked doubtfully. If it was ownership, why didn't they call it freehold like everyone else?

Ellie had turned to Yelena to take up the ownership story.

'Den gets to live in the apartment until he dies or moves on to, say, the rest home or the hospital, okay?' said Yelena. 'When he vacates the apartment, he, or his estate, get the purchase price of the apartment back, less twenty-five per cent.'

Will couldn't help himself. 'You are fucking kidding! He stays there, what, maybe five years, ten years, and not only gets *no* capital appreciation for all that time but actually *loses* twenty-five per cent of what he paid for it?'

'Yes.'

'So he buys for eight hundred thousand, say, he lives there for five years, say, which might be ten per cent appreciation per annum, *minimum*, which makes it worth, what . . .'

'One million two hundred and eighty.'

'And when he kicks the bucket or gets taken away to eternal care, these Sunset fuckers resell it to the next poor old geezer who turns up for more than one and a quarter million, thereby banking four hundred and eighty thousand fucking dollars' appreciation which should be Den's, *and* pocket another two hundred thousand of Den's original eight hundred?'

'That's the guts of it,' confirmed Yelena.

'Who do I fuck to get into this money-making carousel?' asked Will. 'Where do I sign up?'

'You might as well hear it all, so you can get all your frothing out of the way before we arrive,' said Ellie. 'Dad would also have to pay a weekly fee for his servicing and care.'

'How much?'

'Well, it starts at four hundred a week, but it's pegged to inflation so it might increase over time.'

'Jeezus!'

'That covers all the care and facilities, like food, housekeeping, laundry services, and all the engagement programmes and activities they provide, like gardening, arts and crafts, baking, aromatherapy, singalongs . . .'

Will jumped in with heavy sarcasm. 'Scrabble? Trying to remember all the words he no longer knows? What about trips down memory lane, to emphasise it's now a complete bloody dead-end? Sounds like value for money.'

Part of his anger had been precipitated by the quick calculations he'd been making as Yelena spelt out the financial conditions. He had a rough idea what the section might sell for, three mil say. Split those proceeds in half, give Den his share of one and a half, take his third of Carol's share, that's half a mill. That would keep the wolves at bay until the insurance proceeds came through, but he'd been counting on also getting the rest of it, his third of Den's one and a half, plus appreciation, in the short to medium term when his father carked it. He could feel the sun setting on any hope of getting his hands on that. 'Where's the fucking government in all this?' he asked, trying not to let his sense of disappointment show. 'What do we pay our fucking taxes for?'

'That's news,' said Ellie. 'I thought Flame's losses were just a way of evading taxes.' Yelena put a comforting hand on Ellie's forearm. She had taken a deep breath, disappointed, Will could see, in allowing herself to descend to her brother's level. That must have been agreed when they hatched this plan, the holier-than-thou fuckers. 'Sunset apply his pension towards the fee,' said Ellie, 'but that won't cover it, and the government rest-home subsidy doesn't kick in until his assets fall below about two hundred and fifty thousand.'

'This is intergenerational theft!' railed Will. 'Those bastards are stealing our money!'

'Dad's money.'

Will seethed in silence for the rest of the trip, as he came to terms with the idea of Sunset Road bleeding Den dry till there was no blood left for Will to siphon up. There was no justice, the world was fucked.

The sheer bleakness of happy hour, the bad wine, the stilted company, the bent, broken, deaf, blind old bodies clinging together, the nondescript paintings on the nondescript concrete cavern walls, dumped Will's spirits on the bilious floral carpeted floor. Fuck it, might as well spill it all, get it over with. 'Shouldn't we discuss the elephant in the room?'

'What, now?' asked Ellie, exasperated.

'Is it her?' asked Den. He was indicating a large woman close to the others at the bar. Her legs were withered but the rest of her threatened to overflow the green summer print she was wearing and submerge the wheelchair she was sitting in.

Is he playing me? thought Will. Den didn't look like he could take himself for a ride, let alone anyone else. His smile was, for the first time in his life, hesitant, as if his face couldn't quite remember which muscles to twitch. 'Den, the insurance company won't pay out on the fire because they think you started it.'

'Now's not the time,' began Ellie.

'When *is* the right time?' insisted Will. 'All Den needs to do is say on record that he doesn't remember taking a couple of shovelfuls of burning embers from the outside oven and dumping them on the kitchen floor.'

'I certainly don't remember doing that.'

'Great! I'll record that on my mobile.'

'I don't remember being downstairs at all. Last thing I remember was having a joint upstairs.'

'Wanna record that, Will?' asked Yelena.

Ellie gently corrected her father. 'But Dad, fortunately, you were downstairs when the smoke alarm went off.'

'Where was that little shit Jackson?' asked Will.

'He helped me rescue Dad from the sofa in the sitting room.'

'There you go!'

'Jackson raced past me in the downstairs hallway from the bedrooms to try to get upstairs to Dad. I had to call him back when I found Dad in the sitting room. We've been through this a thousand times, but if you have any alternative theories, Sherlock, we'd love to hear them.'

'Did I do something wrong?' asked Den.

'No, Dad,' said Ellie, then turned to Will. 'Back off!'

'I'm just trying to get some clarity—'

'Enough!' said Yelena.

That would have ended the conversation, except that after another sip of the chateau cardboard, which now seemed acceptable,

Den said that he remembered something else. 'I saw you and Lila,' he said, looking at him directly and, Will thought, not entirely innocently.

'You saw Will and Lila what?' asked Ellie, rediscovering some enthusiasm for the discussion.

'How is this relevant to—'

'Shut up, Will. Where were Will and Lila, Dad? Where did you see them?'

'I was out on the balcony having a toke.'

'But where were they?'

'Out by the pool.'

'Doing what?' Ellie asked.

'What the fuck business is it of yours?'

Yelena rounded on Will. 'You started this.'

Den seemed to realise he had somehow edged onto swampy ground, that whatever he said next was going to sink someone, perhaps himself. Will tried to catch his eye. In the old days, when Den was the pitching maestro and in full flow, but had forgotten some key element, Will or Branko would only have to catch his eye and he would pick it up, almost telepathically. Now Will stared into Den's opaque blue gaze and had no idea what was registering.

'You saw Will and Lila out by the pool,' reiterated Ellie. 'What were they doing, Dad?'

Den began nodding, as if he finally understood what he had seen. 'Lila went for a swim. In the pool. Will held a towel.'

That ended the conversation, until they'd said their goodbyes and left him there on the margins of happy hour, Den, suddenly old and unsure why they were going and not taking him with them. At a loss as to how to start walking away, Will asked if there was anything he needed.

'Where's Walter?' asked Den.

Will looked at Ellie for guidance. She shrugged. 'Who's Walter, Dad? Is he a friend we don't know? Does he live here?'

Den shook his electric mane again and changed the subject. 'Where's my roll-top? It has everything I need.'

'Your desk was lost in the fire, Dad,' Ellie explained. 'But tell me what you need and we'll get it for you if we can.'

Den shook his head. 'You can't.'

'We might be able to.'

'You can't,' said Den, emphatic.

***

ON the way back to the carpark, no one said anything. When they reached Yelena's car, Ellie, who was clearly still fuming, opened the passenger door, but barred Will's entrance. 'You were the one with the motivation,' she said.

'Eh?'

'The fire forced Dad out, released Mum's share under the will.'

'You are fucking kidding!'

She wasn't. 'There are still two people from Dad's party who were unaccounted for when the fire started,' she said, implacable. 'You and Lila.'

'I gave Lila a lift home,' said Will. 'It's all on record with the fire investigator.'

'She said she was staying the night.'

'She changed her mind.'

'Why would she change her mind? She was desperate for a place to stay. Where did she go?'

Will shrugged, suggested Ellie should ask Lila, knowing Ellie never would. He mentioned that it was Ellie who raised the topic of burning the house, when she talked about Carol's fantasy.

'You're *such* a cunt,' said Ellie, and turned and walked around to the rear door behind Yelena.

There's a lot to be said for clarity, thought Will, sliding into the front passenger seat. The killer seat, they used to call it, before air bags. Still, safer to know where you stand, or sit.

IT'S DARK OUTSIDE, but worse in here. I don't let them pull the blinds down or draw the curtains. I need to see the lights out there, the lights of the world, the one I remember. They keep me from slipping away into the black room. My memory of who I was is all I've got to help me claw onto the edge and hold fast. The trouble is, I seem to be able to remember my father's memories more than my own. His name was Lance, I remember that. He was in Colditz, I remember that. He'd been captured in early '43, I think it was, and for three years before that he'd been living in a tent, through Greece and Crete and North Africa. When we were kids we'd go over the hill to Nelson for the holidays. We had a campsite in the family part of the Tāhuna Beach motor camp, where we pitched our tent in the same spot every summer, and where our father made us sweep the grass floor every morning. Sweep the bloody grass! He was that kind of soldier, but not the kind who thought he had a duty to escape. So he wasn't one of those who escaped from Colditz. Charlie Upham, double VC, was there with him, and he never escaped either. Dad thought Charlie was a problematic bugger. He said you didn't want to be too close to Charlie on the battlefield because he had a death wish, and you didn't want to be his mate in Colditz either, because he was so contemptuous of the Germans that they hated him. Respected him, but hated him. Dad didn't hate the Germans, reckoned most of them were probably as reluctant to go to war as he was. Not Charlie. Dad got to know him better after the war, when he farmed near us, but he was always an odd bird, according to Dad.

I remember meeting him once when I was a boy, this crusty old bastard sitting on a horse during a communal DOC muster of some foothills near the Kaikōuras, up the Clarence River. He looked like a hawk, sitting on that horse, eyes glinting from under the shade of his hat, burning. But later I saw him walking about during smoko, and he was a small man, short, wiry. Dad said you didn't have to be a Charles Atlas to be a hero, you could be a Charles Upham. It was a joke, but I realised much later, he might have intended it as a salve or an inspiration: Dad knew I wasn't going to grow tall. If that's what he meant, it was probably the kindest thing he ever did or said. The thing my father knew in Colditz, he said, was that he didn't have to escape, he didn't have to risk being shot or electrified on the perimeter fence or falling from one of the high stone walls onto cobbles. He'd been picked up by the Afrika Korps after El Alamein, where they'd given Rommel a good root up the jaxie. That's how he described it. You don't hear that much any more. But he knew before he got to Colditz that we would win the war. Sooner or later, we would win, and he'd be free. It was more than hope, he said, it was certainty. But that was then. Here, there is no hope. There's no one coming to save me. When Ellie and my son and Branko's daughter walked away today, I knew I was lost. There's no way out. Unless I can find one myself. I'm sure I had a plan. Where is Walter? He was in my roll-top, under W. Or M. Why would I have filed Walter under M? It was part of a plan . . .

THE PERFECT SILENCE of Yelena's electric BMW was mirrored by a mute truculence inside the car, as Will was spirited back across the harbour bridge. Will looked out longingly at the city lights, circling the harbour like fluorescent beads. When they took the Cook Street off-ramp and swung off Pitt Street onto K Road, he saw his opportunity. 'Anywhere here would be brilliant, thanks Yelena.'

'We're having some kai.'

'I'm not actually hungry.'

'You need a feed. Doesn't he need a feed, Ellie?'

'That and a reality check.'

'Thought I was keeping it real.'

'Real? You're a fucking fantasist!' Ellie exclaimed.

'Would you two mind not trying to put me off my tucker?' said Yelena.

They sat in silence again for as long as it took to score a parallel park further along K Road, across from where the neon mermaid used to sparkle. Yelena pointed ahead to people and tables and light spilling out on the footpath, under a big sign, Kook A Chew. 'That's us,' she said.

Thank Christ, thought Will, I'll be able to get a drink.

Yelena walked them straight to a table just beyond the double doors that separated the serious diners inside from the party outside.

It was a table for two and Ellie didn't linger, waving to some people at a leaner further along the footpath. So this was part of the plan, thought Will. He was glad Ellie had taken her antagonism elsewhere. Yelena was going to get down and dirty with the rent, and he didn't need Ellie wading in too. One more tap dance for the day, he told himself, steeling himself and catching sight of Ellie, hugging a lanky, balding guy. Ellie offered her face up to him. They kissed. A lovers' kiss. Will looked at Yelena, who was looking too, smiling. 'Who's that guy?' he asked.

'The new man.'

Will couldn't help himself. 'What?'

'You mean who? She'll bring him over and introduce you if she wants to, I guess.'

A woman in her mid-thirties had arrived at the table and was kissing Yelena, the both cheeks thing. Yelena introduced her as Kath, one of the owners, then introduced Will to her as 'my dear old mate'. Will shook Kath's hand as she beamed a welcome at him. He felt suddenly emotional, tried to figure out why. He didn't much like the 'old', but the 'dear' in front of it damn near choked him up.

'Let me order you some drinks,' said Kath. 'The usual for you, darling?'

'And the same for Will,' said Yelena.

'On the way,' said Kath, disappearing into the restaurant.

'Something strong?' asked Will hopefully.

'Bitters and lemon.'

'Seriously?'

'For me booze was a gateway to drugs, which was a gateway to all sorts of betrayals and treacheries,' said Yelena. 'I lost someone I loved – she quite rightly decided that I was a flake and unworthy of her. That made it worse. I hated myself and the more I hated myself the more booze and drugs and sex I needed to make myself feel better. That's the way it goes, isn't it?' Yelena was smiling at him, and maybe there was something tender in that smile, but Will had to look away. Everyone around them was having a ball, even on a fucking Monday night, and he had to sit there with bitters and lemons and deal with this shit. 'They're placebos, aren't they, the booze and drugs?' continued Yelena. 'The pain doesn't go away, does it, Will.'

It wasn't a question, but Will felt he had to move the conversation away from this inquisition in the midst of the celebration going on all around them. He had to get it back on ground he knew, whatever the cost, so he could do the tap dance again. He never thought he'd be grateful to talk about the rent.

'I don't give a shit about the rent,' said Yelena. 'That's not what this is about.'

'This? What the fuck *is* this then?'

'The bullshit stops here, Will.'

'All I owe you is the rent. I'll have it covered, Yelena, this TVC I was telling you about for the new EV–'

'Who the fuck do you think you're talking to, Will? I'm Branko's daughter, f'chrissakes. Mum and I listened to that bullshit all our lives, till he upped and left us! You think I don't know how truly fucked you are? You can delude yourself, but don't fucking try to spin me. You know what we're trying to do here, me and Ellie?'

'No idea.'

'This is a fucking intervention, Will, for an old friend, who we can barely remember! People who love you trying to pull you out of a death-roll.'

'That's a bit dramatic.'

'Is it? You're high.'

'Jesus.'

'You're fucked up on meth and I don't believe a word you say tonight.' Yelena lowered her voice and leant across the table. 'But Will, I'm hoping some of this sticks, and when you wake up tomorrow, you'll ring me and ask me to sit down with you and find a way forward. Okay?'

Will could no longer hold her eyes. He looked down at the table, the gingham squares of the cloth, smudged and indistinct. Someone plonked a glass down in front of him. He drank it down and still couldn't look at Yelena. She reached across the table and took his hand. 'I'm fucked,' he said, gulping. 'Forty and fucked.'

'You're not alone. There've been legions of us through history. Started with Dante, but even when he was writing about losing his way in middle age, he struck a chord in readers, so the phenomenon was known way before him—'

Will's tongue seemed suddenly swollen but he finally got it out. 'Flame is fucked.'

'Yes,' said Yelena, 'it is.' She took his other hand in hers. 'So give up on that dream. Find another.'

'Just like that?'

'You inherited that dream from Dad and Den . . . You know the stats on entrepreneurs your age who fall over?'

Will shook his head.

'What I'm saying is, Flame's demise could be seen as a rite of passage to something else, not an end.'

'It's all I know.'

Yelena released his hands, took her drink and sipped, her eyes gauging him, measuring. 'You could apply some of those skills to something else,' she said. 'Another way of looking at producers is

134

as project managers. I'm doing eco retro-fits on my commercial properties as they come up for renewal: insulation, thermal windows, solar panels, storage batteries, sometimes even rainwater capture. It's time-consuming and distracting. I need someone to oversee that side of things.'

'Commercial real estate?'

'Why not? You can write budgets, you can read balance sheets, cost reports. You're dealing with businessmen, property managers, big numbers, you're not selling to Mum and Dad tyre-kickers and arguing over three dollars fifty. You could do a valuer's course. When you finish the fit-out, your next job could be to find a new tenant for the Flame premises.'

'Eh?' Finally, the fucking rent!

'I'll help you put together an advertising campaign and shadow you through the meetings. It won't be a production office any more, that's dead. We might be looking at warehousing, plumbing supply, or an architect's premises, or a boutique brewery. Or we could offer to fit it with glass doors and go for retail, a furniture outlet, say.'

'Why would you do that for me?'

'It's not all altruism, Will. When you sell the new lease, I'll deduct the Flame rent arrears from your commission. Win win.'

'Zero sum says that for every winner there has to be a loser. Who would that be?'

Yelena smiled. 'Do you have to practise to be such an arsehole, or does it just come naturally?'

'I'm a ray of light wherever I go.'

Yelena, still smiling, shook her head slowly, almost wonderingly. 'A deep, dark hole,' she said. Then she stood up. 'We're finished here, Will. I'm going to join your sister and some real people. Ring me tomorrow. But only if you're clean. I'm not working with a shithead.'

***

WILL wandered along K Road, past other bars full of deceptively happy people, starring in their own selfies, preening Facebook fakes who were as fucked as he was. Yelena was right: many fall, even in early middle age or before, and not all can pick themselves up. He could remember some tragics. Coming through arrivals a few months ago after a fruitless pitch to a government agency in Wellingdog, he'd passed the chauffeurs in suits standing in a row holding signs. His eye had been drawn to one of the faces, fleshy, shadowed with a late-afternoon beard, whom he'd known quite well as a hot young creative, early thirties at most. Will could no longer remember his name. The guy had blanked him anyway, a blessing for them both.

The bars petered out as K Road became Great North, and the caryards began. They used to stretch almost unbroken along the ridge to the Grey Lynn shops, but lately they'd been dug out and filled with massive concrete pads, supporting pillars that soared into apartments with steepling views of the city. And there was a giant Bunnings and cafes and a real estate office. It was some comfort to him that *everything* changed, nothing stayed the same, even commercial real estate.

Was Yelena serious about her offer? Yelena was serious about everything. He was flattered. There was a way ahead if he ignored the chasm in front of him and concentrated on landing safely on the other side. He remembered back in the day when Flame was coining it and he'd been advised by one of Suzan of South Africa's predecessors to buy a car he couldn't afford as a tax deduction. He'd taken the Aston Martin to Pukekohe for an advanced driving course, and he remembered the instructor telling him that if he got into a skid, he shouldn't look at the tree he was trying to avoid, but at the safe space he wanted to get to. 'You'll unconsciously steer towards where you're looking,' the guy had said, 'so look at the soft landing.' That's what he had to do. Look for a soft landing.

The problem, he realised when he climbed through the rancid air to his flat, was that his mind was in an extended skid and couldn't pull out. The late-afternoon half-tab at the office had put him out of sequence. He needed to come down, he needed to sleep. He needed to find some juice for Nick Preston tomorrow. He couldn't give in to the extinction of hope without a fight.

He sluiced down two trammies with his last can of Panhead, peeled off his soaked shirt and then his shoes, socks and trou, pulled up the old sash window and stared out at the lights sprinkled across the valley, all the way to the dark bulk of the Waitākeres, while he waited for the pills to give him some peace.

***

HE didn't sleep well. The meth and trammies fought for control well into the early hours, and by the time the trammies won, it was almost dawn. Maybe he'd slept: the only evidence he had were the nightmares. That combine harvester, the sheaves of wheat. Where the fuck did that come from? The only farm he'd ever heard about in detail was Stan's organic fucking wank, and there was no combine harvester there: they probably still used Clydesdales. He realised he'd left his car at the office, and it still had both his clean shirts in it. He showered and dressed the rest of him, then put on a T-shirt. It'd be wringing wet by the time he walked to Flame, which was mostly downhill, but he couldn't afford an Uber and he could have a Pommy wash at the en-suite basin and grab a new shirt before Nick Preston could diary a sit-down. Nick could call at any time. According to rumour, probably started by Nick, he was a Les Mills junkie and did three classes before breakfast, the spectral git. Will pulled on his trou and found the last little helper sitting loose in his pocket. He broke it in half and swallowed one. At the sink, swilling it down with a glass of water, he looked at the remaining half-tab, then tipped it down the drain with the rest of the water.

***

Will was late getting in to Flame, but his mobile hadn't rung; he had no reason to suspect he'd missed anything. But Trish had a slim courier parcel that had just been delivered, from LSQN, with a little card attached – *Compliments, Nick.*

Initially, Will couldn't imagine why Nick would send him a parcel or what could possibly be in it, but the contact, and the *thought* behind it had to be encouraging – it was far more difficult to send a parcel than make a call. He began thinking it could be a draft contract, or an amended script or spreadsheet . . . He asked Trish to open it.

She scissored along the dotted line, and drew out the contents. A newspaper, the *Herald*. Trish inspected the parcel to see if there was anything else, then shrugged and handed it to Will.

Will shook it to see if anything had been hidden inside it, then stared at it, uncomprehendingly, trying to divine its message. The front-page headline was pretty standard, another immigration scam, and Will couldn't for the life of him get the message. He was about to open the paper when he saw it, at the top beside the masthead banner. Will caught it like a blow. The date.

Trish read his face. 'What is it?'

'Yesterday's paper.'

When he finally looked back up to Trish, it was the first time he'd ever seen her tear up. 'Don't worry about me, Will. I've been very lucky to have what I've had for so long. You've got to do what you've got to do.'

***

THE mezzanine office was stifling. Will looked hopelessly towards the two windows along the western side. There used to be a view of empty wasteland, now the carpark for a boutique supermarket. That view had been gone for ten years. For ten years he'd been remembering that view, while looking at the firewall of the warehouse that had gone up next door. Those windows used to open and let in the late-afternoon breeze from the sea. Now it was air con or nothing. *It was nothing.* He was on a wheel, and was losing slivers of himself with every revolution. This is it, he thought. The end of the line. Flame is doused. Or, as Yelena would have it, a new beginning. What choice did he have left?

He heard his phone burp, and realised for the first time that it didn't ring any more.

U fancy take-ways to nite at yr place? I cld bring some smoked? x

autumn

ELLIE TURNED ON the gas fire, though the temperature hardly justified it. The evenings were definitely cooler, the mozzies gone, the cicadas' mad thrashing becoming more ragged with each passing night, but the days were still hot, summer not giving up easily. She'd had enough of that, of Auckland's cloudless grill and overcast oven. She wanted autumnal, she wanted *Season of mists and mellow fruitfulness*. What was Keats' second line, she wondered? She Googled it, skipped over the next few lines and landed on *And fill all fruit with ripeness to the core.*

> *To swell the gourd, and plump the hazel shells*
> *With a sweet kernel; to set budding more,*
> *And still more, later flowers for the bees,*
> *Until they think warm days will never cease,*
> *For Summer has o'er-brimm'd their clammy cells.*

She mulled them over, those beautiful words. Clammy cells o'er-brimmed. *I wish.* So eloquent and rhythmical. Fill all fruit with ripeness to the core. Perfect, she decided.

The kids were finally asleep, Kristin like a lamb after one story, a Margaret Mahy that she had read for Ellie, softly, falling asleep

143

before she'd finished. Ellie had wanted to bring her own childhood favourite, Frances Hodgson Burnett's *The Secret Garden*, and leave it with Kristin, but it had been lost in the fire along with the rest of their books, most of them Carol's.

Claudia had put Archie down before Ellie and Yelena got there, so that he wouldn't be alerted to his mother's impending absence. It was the first time Claudia had been out in the evening since Will left, and Ellie fervently hoped that Archie wouldn't wake. She'd projected a confidence in front of Claudia that she didn't feel now that she was alone in the house with two sleeping children. She daren't watch TV or listen to music, lest the sound wake Archie. Was it wrong of her to see in a child so young, intimations of his father, to see an embryonic Will in Archie's wilfulness and tantrums? To be so anxious about a baby waking and becoming enraged to find his mother gone? On the other hand, Archie's responses to his father's departure might be healthier than Kristin's, who had become the perfectly compliant child since the separation, seemingly aware of her mother's anguish and not wanting to add to it in any way. Was Kristin compensating? Was she feeling guilty for somehow causing her father to abandon her mother? Ellie reminded herself that she was no child psychologist: that seeing so many battered and beaten children didn't make her one.

What sort of parent would *she* make? Would she be strict, a maternal martinet? Laissez-faire would likely best describe her mothering: she'd be so grateful, she'd be a pushover. At every moment of every day she'd be conscious of the miracle of their being. How could she be anything else? Her children would have whatever they wanted, do whatever they wanted. It would be enough that they were there, that they existed.

144

She had a couple of hours, probably, before Claudia and Yelena got back from Claudia's Saturday-night date, unless it went very badly, which it easily could.

Kath at Kook A Chew was an inveterate matchmaker. Her personality, which made very quick connections with a diverse range of people, and her engaging curiosity meant she soon, but not inquisitively, came to know her regular customers in quite intimate detail – who was new in town, who might recently have lost a partner. And then she saw the potential connections. Kath's instincts were at least as good, and infinitely less brutal, than the various online dating apps Ellie had tried. *Left swipe, who's next?*

It was Kath who had suggested that Ellie have a drink with Richard, and her instincts had been almost right: Richard had been close to . . . What? Ellie's ideal? She doubted she had an ideal man any more. Whatever configuration she might once have fantasised about had long since subsided under a pall of . . . Not cynicism exactly. Reality. Based on recent experience, her type might be described as pale, intellectually whimsical wastrels. There'd been Howard the Greenpeace wonk, christened by Yelena the social policy bonk, because that was his word for sex. Ellie hadn't thought she could ever get too much intelligent discourse on ecological concerns, but Howard found her plimsoll line and damn near sank her under his endless enthusiasms for party political policy abstractions. When, at a vegan restaurant, Yelena had called him a boring wanker to his face, he had just blinked away and carried on as if she hadn't interrupted. Later, Yelena had asked Ellie, 'just out of interest', where she found 'these earnest lame-arses'.

She had a point. Before Howard, there'd been Victor, who was a junior lecturer in film theory. He was completing his PhD and

145

asked her to read his thesis. Ten pages in her eyes were bleeding and she never wanted to watch a movie again. Much more interestingly, she'd caught him watching porn on his laptop. He'd maintained that monitoring pornography trends was part and parcel of his research, that if she'd bothered to read further, she'd have seen the section of his thesis entitled 'The Democratisation of Pornography'. When she asked him how that actually related to variations of White Slut Bred by BBC, he'd struggled manfully, but couldn't really explain how devouring inter-racial mmf and mmmmmf liaisons contributed to his thesis. Ellie developed her own thesis: that sex with Victor was interminable because he masturbated so much his cock was more accustomed to his hand than a vagina. She'd left him to it.

It hadn't always been that way. The love of her life in her mid-twenties had been a passionate jazz saxophonist who worshipped Jah and weed (but was also, she realised, a wastrel). It did seem that the older she got, the more insipid the men she met. She wouldn't use the term leftovers without, in fairness, applying it to herself, but sometimes wondered where all the heartbreakers had gone. She'd had her heart broken so many times in her late teens and twenties, ravaging experiences at the time, but now, perhaps warmed by nostalgia, they seemed infinitely preferable to the lingering depression engendered by the current men. She seemed to always be the one doing the rejecting, and if one more married friend said, 'There's someone for everyone', she'd scream. That's why Yelena's adage, 'There's plenty for everyone!', was so refreshing. But Yelena had limited sympathy for Ellie's tales of woe about men. From her point of view, the more dorks out there, the more women for her.

So Ellie had been cautiously optimistic when Richard, on first acquaintance, hadn't conformed to what she had come to see as her doomed template. He was five years older than her, which once would have seemed quite a lot, but now seemed nothing. His manner was older than that, though. It wasn't a physical thing. Although he was balding and his height diminished by a slight stoop, he was slim and athletic. Strong hands and forearms particularly, which, when she remarked upon them, he attributed to being a 'carpenter of sorts'. His little joke: he was an orthopaedic surgeon, who did knees and hips – yes, 'hammer and saw stuff'– but his speciality was the spine. There he operated in some kind of cross-over zone with neurosurgeons, arthroscopic surgery guided by miniature cameras, discectomies and stuff – hugely delicate and precise. He'd tried to explain the demarcation – or lack of – between what he and neurosurgeons did, but Ellie ended up none the wiser. Richard's nearly twenty-year marriage had only recently ended. Ellie convinced herself that this was a good thing, even a progression of sorts, from leftovers to recycled, though maybe she was just moving into a different age bracket.

If she'd been honest, she might have called it from the start, but Richard spoke well, had a lovely deep voice, a self-deprecating humour, soft, undamaged skin and, importantly, in those hands, a tender, knowing touch. That had been enough for Ellie to start projecting. Yes, he had an ex-wife and three children, but might he not want more of the same? They'd never had that kind of conversation in the places they went together, ethnic cafes, boutique movie theatres, the art gallery – where he showed a comprehensive knowledge of modernist Polynesian painters like John Pule. At a play once, an interminable 'update' of an Ibsen that was, if anything, more boring than the original, Ellie had accidentally met the ex-wife, a regular theatregoer, a subscriber.

Maureen, all coiled, coiffured and bejewelled, which should have sounded warning bells, had been icily courteous and it had been instantly clear, though Richard had never discussed it, who had left whom. To Ellie, that spoke volumes – that he had left his wife, but was honourable towards her and had never tried to justify what he had done by speaking badly about her, or cynically about his marriage. It was far too early to discuss commitment or children, which left Ellie free to fill the void with her own speculations, based on the clues she was only too pleased to pick up. That he loved his children, whom she'd never met, but who were old enough, at twelve, fifteen and seventeen, to be almost self-reliant, which *might* make him ready for more. And that when they made love, he wore condoms, religiously. It wasn't something she'd asked for, in fact she disliked condoms and preferred skin on skin, but she'd been encouraged to believe that he was still potent, fertile and at least open to the possibility.

It had been a huge moment, last week at his duplex apartment on the top floor of a beautifully converted 1930 Art Deco department store, when she'd told him that he needn't wear a condom if he didn't want to, that she could take care of herself. Richard had smiled a bit sheepishly and admitted that he'd been wearing them as a precaution against STDs, not pregnancy, that in fact he'd 'had the snip'. At first she didn't know whether to be reassured that he would take such care about STDs or insulted that he could possibly think she'd be a risk. But the feeling that overwhelmed both of those was dismay.

She hadn't seen him since. He'd rung – she hadn't taken the call – and then left a message saying he'd be up at KAC tonight. She couldn't face him. Now she remembered his kindness and attentiveness as more that of a doctor with a patient, than lover to lover. Had he simply been applying his bedside manner to her?

She'd known, as he'd paused while rolling that satin sheath up his shaft, that it was over, that she'd been living a lie of her own making. It wasn't fair on him, he'd done nothing, but there'd been a seismic slip between her romantic projections and reality. She'd leapt off his bed, crossed to her clothes, muttering some *really* unoriginal excuse about headaches, cramps, whatever. Her last view of him as she closed the door had been of this curiously forked creature standing, arms wide in bewilderment, like a hirsute version of da Vinci's Vitruvian Man, but with a plastic sac hanging forlornly from the end of his wilting penis. As the lift descended, she had almost rung him, but then put the phone back in her bag. It was the end of a certain kind of hope and the beginning of a different one.

Three years ago, when she'd given up work and returned to the house to look after her father, she'd decided to buy 'insurance'. It was her thirty-fifth birthday and she'd had suspicions about her fertility. It was anecdotal evidence of the worst kind, sure, but she was the only woman she knew who had *never* had recourse to the morning-after pill or a termination. Given that she'd had the usual mishaps and passionate heat-of-the-moment accidents, it was strange that she'd never once had so much as a late period. Tests at the clinic had, to some degree, confirmed her fears. She was producing fewer eggs than normal, and at her age that could only get worse, perhaps quickly. Carol wasn't around to ask about early menopause, and Den couldn't remember, so Ellie made the decision, dug into her savings for eleven grand, took the prescribed drugs and went in for same-day egg extraction. The clinic had warned her that success was far from certain: she might have few or even no eggs to be harvested. Her relief that eight were recovered was huge. She'd been able to put her preoccupation with motherhood on the back burner and hope that she'd find a mate who would make the banked eggs redundant. Richard had been the end of that dream, but it had been coming for some time. The day after she'd walked out on Richard, she'd rung the clinic and told them she wanted to proceed with a sperm donor. There was usually a waiting list of nearly a year, but her frozen eggs meant she'd effectively been in the system for three years, so she was given priority.

Early the previous afternoon she'd driven out to the fertility clinic at Ascot Hospital, taken the lift to the third floor and been shown to a room facing east, a small room barely accommodating a round table and four chairs. Teresa, with a bob framing a kind face, had put three sperm donor non-identifying information sheets on the table in front of her and told her that, ideally, she should choose now, because donors were in short supply and this trio were also being made available to the network of clinics throughout the country. As Ellie, left on her own, tried to concentrate on the information in front of her, she felt a rising panic, like trying to book a motel on the internet with the 'selling fast!' sign flashing. *Only three left!* After taking a deep belly breath, she'd decided to read the sheets comparatively, and spread the opening pages across the table, side by side.

All three men had been screened and were low risk for cystic fibrosis, spinal muscular atrophy and Fragile X, whatever the hell that was. In terms of physical characteristics, none were excessively tall or short or overweight. Two were dark with brown eyes and one was blond and blue-eyed, but all had answered yes to '*Tan easily?*'. Was that a trick question? They were all heterosexual, New Zealand-born and had some tertiary education, one a master's in anthropology. None had allergies, chronic conditions or mental health issues. None smoked or used recreational drugs, natch.

When Ellie had enquired whether the clinic screened the information given by donors, the answer had been no, which might explain why they seemed so exemplary. She couldn't help seeing in her mind's eye a beauty pageant where all the unnaturally attractive contestants wanted world peace, to meet people and to travel. Overwhelmed by the choices in front of her, unable to read and understand the details properly, she'd asked Teresa if it would be okay to take the information sheets home and consider them over the weekend. If the clinics were all closed until Monday, the risk of missing out on one of the donors was pretty small, wasn't it? Teresa, who had no doubt seen it all, had been sympathetic and encouraging and looked forward to seeing Ellie on Monday morning. When Ellie had told her she'd be working, her first day back at her old job, Teresa had reassured her that it would be fine to ring with her choice.

Now, settled on Claudia's sofa in front of the fake log fire, she went through the information again. The ages. One was mid-twenties. Ellie thought back to herself ten years ago and wondered whether that was too young to make such a momentous decision. Another was forty. Ellie had read somewhere that sperm was affected by age in a similar, but less drastic way, as ova. The third donor was thirty-five. Just a little bit younger, thought Ellie, but not enough to notice, then chided herself for her Cinderella complex and for what? Anthropomorphising sperm, as if it was a person she'd have to relate to? But that's what it was, she thought, *this* sperm from *this* man, through *his* baby she would carry.

That third one, Donor Code SD 00007982, also had the freshest sperm, donated this year. The young guy was last year, and the older guy, the anthropologist, was two years ago and he had a wife and two children, which Ellie also found unsettling. Teresa had explained that any child resulting from a sperm donor had a right to request the identifying information kept by Births, Deaths and Marriages. The donor had no rights, so any future contact would be in her hands, or her child's hands, when he or she was eighteen. Ellie felt some discomfort she couldn't rationalise about her child becoming part of an existing, potentially enfolding, family. Existing families had existing problems – she knew that better than anyone: Ellie wanted to create her own family, not add to an entity whose dynamics she didn't know.

She couldn't help looking at her own family. Didn't she and Will and Stan prove that genetics were entirely arbitrary, even from the same parents and brought up in the same environment? Didn't that make this whole agonising choice thing redundant? She resolved to put aside her anxiety and concentrate on doing what she could: self-determination might be a complete fallacy, but was also a necessary self-deception. She had to be as diligent as possible in choosing her baby's father. What happened after that would be what happened after that.

There was another factor, which sent her back to SD 00007982. Under ethnic origins he'd identified himself as Māori, and under iwi as Tūwharetoa, which, she thought, came from the central North Island, round Lake Taupō. The tribal connection wasn't important, but there was something fundamentally attractive to her in having a child who could be what she and the rest of her family could never be: tangata whenua.

Ellie put the other sheets aside and began reading SD 00007982 in detail. He was hardly loquacious. Under *Social History*, he was asked: *How would you describe what kind of person you are (Introvert, extrovert, a thinker, a doer, anxious* (who would admit to that?), *easy-going, imaginative, practical, risk-taking, cautious etc.)?* He'd written nothing in the box, just circled *easy-going, imaginative* and *etc.* Etc, for god-sakes? He'd describe himself as *et cetera*? Might this mean that he had a sense of humour, was self-deprecating, or just lazy?

When she looked down the sheets at the other random questions, his answers were similarly cursory and, possibly humorous. *Do you like animals?* He'd written: *Who would admit to not liking animals? Even Hitler liked horses.* Did he? Ellie thought. That showed a considerable knowledge of history, if it was true. *How do you get on with people?* The answer: *So far, so good. I've been lucky with family, and friends. I have a no dick-heads policy, but, funnily enough, I haven't met any yet!*

Never met a dick-head, thought Ellie. Does that mean he's extremely tolerant or that he has no social filters? She liked that he thought he'd been lucky with family and friends. She liked his irreverence, she liked that he didn't seem desperate to sell himself. Or was that an indication that he simply didn't care?

SD 00007982 was a chef by occupation, a sous-chef he specified, which meant he wasn't trying to talk himself up. *What do you like doing in your spare time? I don't get any! Watching Netflix and chilling!* Wasn't that a euphemism for sex? There was something childish about the extravagant exclamation marks, but also playful – a sign he was joking, that he didn't take himself too seriously, perhaps.

Do you have any special talents (Musical, artistic, sporting, creative)? He'd written: *Yes!* Then qualified it with: *If playing the ukulele counts. And singing. Plus playing touch footy to rep level. Oh yes, and a fine arts degree, blah blah.* Blah blah? When she searched back to the section on education and occupation, he hadn't mentioned any degree, just the cooking diploma. She was intrigued: a picture was forming of an athletic, laid-back, musical, artistic Tūwharetoa chef with a sense of humour. She could almost hear his voice through his answers. *Are you left or right handed? Right handed, but ambi-footerous – I can kick with both feet!*

With a rising sense that she was on the verge to committing to a destiny, Ellie went to the last page. *Why did you want to be a donor? What thoughts and feelings led you to becoming a donor?* He'd written: *I've been lucky. Why not share?*

Ellie found herself staring at the fake glowing embers, the controlled flame, the ease and comfort of it. *I've been lucky. Why not share?* She couldn't imagine a better answer.

She heard the key-lock on the front door being punched and slid the sheets back into her bag, as Claudia and Yelena came in. Claudia was radiant, which made it safe to ask. 'How was he then?'

Claudia thought about it for a second. 'He was . . . sweet.'

'Sweet? Will?' Her date had been Will, who had told Yelena he wanted to come home.

'More like his old self.'

That didn't sound much of an improvement to Ellie. 'Is that good?'

'Not high, and not drinking.'

'She wanted to bring him home,' said Yelena.

'I did,' admitted Claudia with what looked suspiciously like a dreamy smile, 'but bossy britches Yelena said, "Not tonight, Josephine."'

'Make him work for it, I say!'

'I just don't want to discourage him.'

'And you don't want to make yourself a doormat, either.' Yelena softened, took Claudia by the hand. 'Claudia, darling, one step at a time. You and the kids are the best things in his life and he knows it. He's been straight for the past six weeks or so, as far as I can tell. But the thing is, once you've been to the dark side, you know the address and it's easy to find your way back there.'

**

YELENA told Claudia that she and Ellie had to dash: 'There's someone in the car.' Inevitably, the someone was a young woman. Yelena's playmates were often bi and sometimes even previously exclusively hetero; her enthusiasms were infectious, and her taste was catholic. Her one constant was younger: mid-twenties was her sweet spot. This one's name was Luissa, exotically Pasifika but with the almond eyes, Ellie guessed, of a Chinese Samoan. Ellie may have met her before, she couldn't be sure. There were so many of them.

As Yelena waited at the centre lane to take a right into their street, Ellie looked down Ponsonby Road towards the little patch of civility and diversity that had become home. She loved it. A couple of hundred yards in either direction would take her to brilliant Italian cuisine, or tapas, or vegan, Vietnamese, or Turkish. She could drink freshly ground espresso at half a dozen different cafes, from kosher to shabby chic, where she could sit and watch the Ponsonby Road passeggiata and the comings and goings from the brothel that looked like a modernist Salvation Army Citadel, two along from the old paint-blistered wooden steeple of the Samoan Methodists. Branko's funeral had been held at the Anglican church on the other side, All Saints. She'd got her first school holiday job behind the counter at a kebab joint nearby, and had waited tables through uni at various cafes all along the strip, most of which had lasted about eighteen months, when the first terminal tax bill arrived. You could see the constant churn of restaurants and cafes and boutiques as Darwinian, but Yelena reckoned it was more like unintended Marxism – rich men with tax problems redistributing their ill-gotten gains through their bored wives by financing them into vanity retail. At fourteen Ellie'd had her first sloppy kiss under the old Hydra sign just around the corner, before an after-ball party where she'd got so drunk she'd vomited over her date, inadvertently saving her virginity for another year. This was her town, her village, her hood, she had memories imprinted on every yard of it, yet she couldn't afford to live here any more except as her father's caregiver or as Yelena's tenant on mate's rates.

Living cheek by jowl with Yelena in her little heritage cottage just off Ponsonby Road was never going to be a long-term thing, but was for the most part, a joy. In lovemaking, as in most other things, Yelena was boisterous almost to the point of disinhibition, and it was hard to avoid hearing her dear friend ratcheting through her seduction routines in the sitting room and climaxing in the mistress bedroom across the little entrance foyer. Once home, Ellie quickly bid Yelena and Luissa goodnight and, as soon as she'd used the bathroom, was careful to fully close the bedroom door. She stripped, climbed into bed and inserted the little rubber ear-plugs, so that, with a bit of luck, she could disappear into her own fantasies rather than be an unwilling witness to Yelena acting out hers. Ellie took some deep breaths, relaxed her toes and calves and let her mind wander. Behind the number, SD 00007982, a person was appearing, still a wraith perhaps, but becoming more substantial the more she thought about him. She fell asleep wondering whether she might finally have met her match.

I'M NOT SURE what I've done. Something wrong. A new one, in uniform, blonde with scarlet lipstick and matching epaulettes, says I need better care. Somewhere else. Another room. They'll help me shift tonight. I tell her I'd rather stay here where I can still see the lights at night. She smiles her red and white smile like that striped toothpaste with the perfect name to match the teeth . . . Macleans! An American advertising construct, surely, *Ma* and *cleans*. Like Marlboro Man. Southern Man, who did that? Rocket Man. Was that really me? Is that who I am? 'Is it a dark room,' I ask her, 'this one you're shifting me to?'

'It hasn't got the views of this one, but it's still light and airy.'

She would say that. Can I believe her? What have I done? I tell her I'm sorry, I'm not sure what I've done, my memory isn't what it used to be, but I do apologise ful . . . ful . . . fully. She smiles her red and white smile and tells me not to worry. But I do. What if there are no lights in this new room? Should I go quietly into that black room? I need a plan. I had a plan. Walter was going to help me. Where's Walter? Walter had a plan. Find Walter. That's a plan. It's now or Nebuchadnezzar. It's now or . . . The Netherlands? *It's now.*

***

YOU have everything you need, Den. You do. I'm sliding through the foyer in my favourite Air Force 1s, the grey leather ones with a white swoosh, and a nicely detailed mini swoosh up by my little toe. I have my Rainbird in my curled palm, so as not to give my intentions away as I cross the crowded reception foyer to the main entrance. I'm hidden from the women behind the counter by a queue of visitors wanting directions. If I can't see them, they shouldn't be able to see me. *You'll be okay. Don't panic.*

Outside, real air embraces me. I shrug into my Rainbird. That feels better. It must be a Sunday, there are swarms of visitors coming down from the carparks, all so much younger than the elderly prisoners inside. Do I look like one of them? I expect to hear my name called. I walk as quickly as I can against the tide, up past the pharmacy and chiropodist and physio and hairdresser, on past the carpark entrances and exits, up towards the street. I've no idea where this is. It could be Timbuktu, though I've never been to Timbuktu. My father used to mention it. I see a woman coming down my side of the street from a bus stop further on. She looks a bit severe, buttoned down, permed to her roots, but she's not wearing a uniform so I take a chance. 'Excuse me, madam? Could you tell me where Auckland is?'

She looks at me a bit peculiarly through very thick glasses. 'You're in Auckland.'

I try unsuccessfully not to be surprised. 'Am I?'

'You mean the city, the CBD?'

'That's exactly what I mean, yes.'

She hesitates and I think the game is up, but she indicates where she's come from. 'That way.'

***

I'M crouching behind the bus shelter, listening for the hue and cry. I'm not sure what form that would take. Maybe sirens. Not searchlights, at least till after dark. Surely not dogs.

A blue bus pulls up. It's a darker blue, much darker than the driver's turban, which is the colour of the vine in the pseudopanax that Stan said he'd pull out. Did he do that? Where is Stan? What did I do to make him run away? I've seen countless graves of Sikhs beside the rebuilt monastery at Monte Cassino, just along from all the white crosses of my father's mates. He must be an ally. I step onto the bus and tell him I'd like to go to town, please.

'Senior citizens travel for free, sir,' he says, 'but you need a HOP card to do that.'

'If it's free, why do I need a card?'

'A very good question, sir,' he says, 'to which I have no adequate answer, except that the authorities require it.'

I tell him I used to have many cards, but now I don't.

'That is an existential question for our times, certainly,' he says, 'but it shouldn't be.'

I have no idea what that means. I look at the empty seats stretching all the way to the back of the bus. 'You could probably fit me in.'

'Why don't you take a seat just there, sir,' he says, 'where I can keep an eye out for you, and when we get back to Britomart station, you can go to the information booth and obtain the card to which you are entitled.'

'That sounds like a very good plan.' I tell him I like a good plan. I take a seat a couple of rows back from the driver, where I can see him in his little rear-vision mirror. Where he can see me.

***

WHERE is this? Hills and vales. Dales? Hills and vales and dales of houses, getting older, more trees. Where on earth *is* this? I try not to despair of arriving somewhere I know. I have to trust the driver. The Sikhs have always been allies. I clearly said I wanted to go to town and he gave no indication that he didn't know where town was. Perhaps I should have been more definitive about which town. What if the town to which this bus is going is . . . Bulls, say? I am *not* getting off in Bulls. If that's where I end up, I mustn't panic, but stay on the bus until it turns round and comes back. Where the fuck *is* Auckland?

***

PEOPLE get on. I move with them down the back of the bus. I find a seat beside the rear exit door, in case I need it. In case the cry goes up. The hue and cry. Is that correct? Isn't hue a colour? Just in front of me is a little video screen, with ads and notices. Every so often there's a view of the inside of the bus. I see a little man with white hair whose head moves when I move mine, but the opposite way. There was a word I knew for that. If I move my head to the right, the little man on screen moves his to the left. Same when I lean. It's mesmerising, waiting for the picture to come round again and reveal myself sitting on a bus, mugging for the camera. *I'm still here: there's the proof.*

***

WE'RE on a motorway to somewhere that doesn't look like Bulls. At one stage I brace against the seat in front, when it seems our bus will crash head-on into another bus coming the other way, but there is room for both. We seem to be on a separate bus-way, to one side of the motorway. That rings a bell. I think I've seen this before, not from a bus, but from a car.

***

WE start lifting towards the harbour bridge, and my battered heart jumps and thumps as I recognise it and know what I will find on the other side. The city flickers like old film through the stanchions of the bridge. The forested masts of Westhaven marina. The windowed cliffs of the city towers, reflecting the sliding sun. To my right, just as my heart hoped to find it, the string of little coves and bays with their dark green pōhutukawa fringes, running right around to the top of the harbour, where water and bush merge into the blue-green mass of the Waitākeres. I'm nearly home and know I'll never leave again.

***

MY knee is complaining – that cartilage moaning its fucking head off – as I limp around the marina boardwalk towards the harbour bridge, following the footsteps of my AF 1s, which seem to know the way better than my eyes. I must have walked here many times before because I remember the sound the halyards on the moored yachts make, a sort of tinkling noise in the wind. There's no noise today, it's all unsettlingly calm. The masts stretch away to one side, my right? Like . . . like upturned ice picks, bobbing in a turquoise cocktail. I wonder how long it's been since I had a real drink. I wonder if someone will give me a drink. I wonder what time it is. I used to have a phone that told me the time and other things. Did I lose it? I seem to remember someone at Colditz taking it away from me, telling me I didn't need that expense because I had a land-line connection to my cell. But whenever I picked up that phone, a voice asked me what I wanted to do. It so surprised me that she was always there that I couldn't answer the first few times. Then I said, finally: 'Escape.' That wasn't the right answer. I had a visit from a red and white to check that I was all right. She must have decided I was, but I'm not sure how she could know. But it was shortly after that, I think, when another red and white, or perhaps it was the same one, told me I would be shifted to another room. My father reckoned he could tell the time in the desert with his wristwatch. You point the twelve at the sun and north is halfway between the twelve and the hour hand. Which is how you find north, of course. If you had a wristwatch, you'd already know the time. Fuck, I'm a worry. *Don't panic, Den. You're doing fine. It'll be all right. Follow those shoes.*

***

THE fishermen are still here. They can't be the same ones I've seen here before, but they are, as I recall them, Asian and Pasifika mainly, trying to keep their rods and tackle and bait and catch-bins out of the way of the lycra-clad prancers and dog walkers coming down the hill. Would you call them recreational fishermen? When their families, often sitting in parked cars alongside, are hanging out for a feed? Most of the cars look like they've been round the clock more than once. I wonder what happened to my car. Had Ellie said something? Maybe she's looking after it for me. I could do with a drive. I could do with a feed. Some of the fishermen have cut lunches, but I can't take food out of their mouths.

***

I REMEMBER this long gravel drive. I know what it leads to. My AF 1s have brought me home. Except that it isn't there. There are a few blackened timbers sticking up like those masts, some broken, gaunt against the sky. The entrance to a sooty concrete cavern that used to be the double garage is fenced off with yellow tape, with signs saying *Hazard!* and *Danger!* and *No Entry.* The words are blurring as I stand there slobbering at what used to be my home. Now I remember. A terrible fire in the night. And running. And how everything seems to have accelerated from that moment. How on earth had that happened? The garden gate is still there, but I fear the worst . . .

Hallelujah! Carol's garden is as it was. The grass has been recently mown and everything looks cared for. That would be Ellie, of course, she might even have said something on one of her visits, I can't remember. Every pore in my broken old body seems to inhale, my nose and ears and eyes all breathe deeply of the plants and flowers and trees. Mostly spent, the flowers, the phlox turning yellow and the rest of them whose names I've forgotten wilting and drying, becoming wood, becoming dead. Except the roses – blessedly, there are still some roses. There's one I stop beside. I dare to hope it might be her favourite, Abraham Someone . . . not Lincoln. The little fork to the right takes me down towards the melia. I can remember that this tree is significant but I can't remember why. Can the zaps in my head be that precise? This gone, but not that. The melia is deciduous but sheds late, not leaves so much as twigs with yellowish berries, which I used to rake in late autumn at Carol's insistence. Behind the melia, the glossy pseudopanax with the blue highlights still blocks out the world and makes me safe. I'm home, I can allow myself to be tired. I take my Rainbird off and roll it up. I lie down on my back, putting the Rainbird under the nape of my neck to support my head, and stare up at the branches spreading like capillaries against the sky. And hope, as I close my eyes, that when

I open them again, this won't prove to be a dream. And that I'll still know who I am. *Your name is Den. Don't panic. You'll be okay.*

IT HAD BEEN a brilliant last day of freedom. Tomorrow she'd be back at the front line of a civil war in which every wound was an atrocity, yet barely made the headlines any more. Today she was still free, trying not to count down the hours before the first call-out, trying not to second-guess whether she was still robust enough for what she knew was coming.

Early evening found her indulging a secret vice, watching *Country Calendar*. Sooner or later, she thought, Stan and the gang from Te Kurahau were bound to feature. Knowing Stan, there'd be no notice, she'd only find out if she saw it. It was somehow comforting to know that Te Kurahau was there, and all these other hard-working people too, happy and productive, coaxing bounty from an invariably beautiful landscape where summer never ended. They weren't living in P-infested zombie towns, caught in the merciless maw of rural poverty and the Mob, or the Head Hunters or . . . She knew she was a worrywart, and one of her recurring anxieties was that she'd seen too much of the flip side of life to ever believe in goodness again. Or was that a sign of compassion fatigue, which the caring professionals spoke a lot about? The deeper, unexpressed fear was that once the well of compassion was drained it couldn't be replenished and you joined the legion of hard-hearted cynics – though, if her older brother was any indication, most of the cynics she'd met had reached that state without ever traversing altruism. They'd not spiralled down from compassion and ideals, they'd been scraping along the bottom from very early in their often privileged lives. To her, their cynicism seemed entirely unearnt. But perhaps *she* was being cynical.

After learning about harvesting seaweed, she surfed the movie channels and found an old western. She liked the horses and costumes and landscapes and wooden shopfronts with verandas, but inevitably, within a minute or two of arriving in town and dismounting at a saloon, the hero, in white hat and beige calf-skin matching shirt and chaps untouched by a speck of mud or dust, had become involved in one of those iconic, ridiculous fist-fights that go on for minutes, where the combatants take fifteen or twenty blows flush on the head only to pick themselves up with a bit of fashionable blood trickling from one side of their mouths and the odd blush of bruise that would completely disappear an hour later. She was guessing at the outcome: she couldn't watch the saloon fracas play out, felt her gorge rising even as she flicked channels, ranting at the television, calling the makers fucking cretins. Did they have any idea what one fist on bone and brain could do? *One punch?*

The anger was relatively new. She'd always been sickened by this crap, even though she realised that the reality of the action was on a par with cartoons. Was it worse than the ultra-real gore routinely on screen now? She didn't know, she couldn't watch that either. She landed on what looked like a romantic comedy. After thirty seconds she decided it was a stupidity, not a comedy, and hit the power button. She was alarmed at her outburst, the latent vitriol inside her, and glad that Yelena was out. She tried to calm herself by dredging up the remains of what had been a languid Sunday.

There'd been no Luissa this morning. Few of Yelena's friends got to stay over. When Ellie once enquired whether she had to ask them to go, or there was just an accepted protocol, Yelena had simply said, 'I like a clean start to my day.' Was Yelena brutal enough to tell her friends that, or did she couch it more diplomatically? In any case, it was a policy that worked well for Ellie: there'd been just the two of them in the cottage, no awkward breakfast scenarios or protracted farewells and false promises. And no matter how energetic the night had been, and how little sleep she might have got, Yelena was an early riser and enthusiastic day planner.

First on Yelena's programme had been an exhilarating ride along the black-sand beach at Te Henga and up into the dunes and trails behind the old homestead. The property was often used in film shoots: a lot of *Xena* and other blood-and-sand epics had been partly shot up there, and some Flame TVCs. Through those, Branko had become friendly with the owners, who had taught the girls to ride – Branko too, until he got so big no horse could carry him.

Ellie had loved the riding picnics, loved the quiet intelligence of horses, loved the way you could see their souls in their eyes. She tried to remember why she'd stopped coming. She'd been about seventeen, and had belatedly discovered boys, but it wasn't that. Carol had been diagnosed the year before, but within twelve months or so it had become pretty clear, though no one admitted it to her or Stan, that their mother was dying. Ellie had found it difficult to leave home after that. Even finding the wherewithal to go to school for her last year had been a battle. Den was hopeless, basically tried to carry on as if nothing had changed. Will was already gone and hardly ever came back, and Stan was only thirteen, a lanky, shy, awkward kid who had difficulty making friends at high school.

After Carol died, everything changed again. Instead of going away to uni at Otago with some of her mates, like Yelena, Ellie took what she told them was a gap year. A gap year with no travel, stuck in the big house with stunned-mullet Den who seemed to have no idea how much he loved or needed his wife until she wasn't there, and with Stan, who was in the fifth form and sitting important exams. One year became two, and three. Stan had more exams, then did what she had wanted to do, went to Otago. Ellie could have gone then, too, but uprooting herself to Dunedin had lost its allure: Yelena and the other girls she knew were finishing their degrees and coming back. Instead she'd enrolled in a BA at Auckland and became a student who commuted to her classes and went home. She'd gone to uni because nothing else appealed, chosen Auckland uni because nowhere else appealed, done a BA because nothing else seemed worthwhile, and maybe that was also why she'd fallen into completing a postgrad social work degree. There were slackers all round her, but it wasn't that with her. She sometimes looked back and thought her choices had all been fall-back default settings, looking for Carol's approval long after her mother was gone.

Her relationship with her mother had often been testy. Den was so much easier to read and to please. Carol was moody and demanding, applying unfair academic and behavioural standards to her daughter that, in Ellie's opinion, she didn't apply to her sons. Ellie thought, and once told Carol to her face, that this pressure on her daughter came from her own underachievement, and why hadn't she gone back to work? Carol had actually tried to slap her, but the action was so awkward and unpractised that she'd hit the point of Ellie's shoulder with the tender inside of her wrist and suffered the bruises and remorse for days afterwards. In retrospect, it hadn't been a fair criticism: since Ellie was very young Carol had filled her days with charitable work. She had raised money for

Starship Children's Hospital from the very beginning in the early nineties, and then, as the stars came out for Starship, Carol had moved on to serious fund-raising for some much less fashionable causes, like domestic violence, which was virtually ignored by both police and the judiciary back then. It was Carol who'd raised Ellie's awareness of the NGO she was about to return to work for, and it was really Carol's journalist eye that had informed Ellie's view of the world. Den had always seen the world as his oyster, a potentially exploitable commodity; it was Carol who had real curiosity about the world around her and how it actually worked, or didn't.

At Te Henga, Ellie had a regular, Brownie, an aged bay gelding who had a bad case of flatulence. On the canter, he would pop like a machine gun, which was okay as long as no one got caught behind him. Ellie had been happy following Yelena as they finished the canter along the beach and worked their way up the sandy tracks through the big dunes and scrub, heading towards Lake Wainamu. In summer, they'd drive out in dawn light, but this morning it had been still dark, and the sun had come up as they were climbing into the saddles. Ellie had been offered a new horse, a frisky black mare, light-boned and quick, but she'd seen Brownie clocking her, and his ears pricking in anticipation, and decided she couldn't be so disloyal. Up on the tracks through the dunes, it had been wonderfully quiet and calm. The big waves could sometimes sound like steam trains breaking over the rocks at the point, but today they'd been orderly and respectful as they rolled in. The horses walked into the rising sun through the broom and lupins, the summer crackle and pop of exploding seeds finished for another year. Ellie turned in the saddle as they got to the top of the ridge and looked back at the Tasman, the curving swing of ocean bathed in dark blue. By the time they got to the lake, it was reflecting the still-low sun off its surface and radiating the first shimmers of heat back at them as they came down the big dune.

She liked letting her mind flow with Brownie's gentle rhythms, allowing her thoughts to go where they might. But this morning she'd tried to wrangle them a little more, to stop projecting into tomorrow, to suppress the feeling of dread rising in the pit of her stomach. She'd consciously directed her thoughts back to SD 00007982. A picture had begun forming of the man behind the number. Though she knew the chances of it being real were infinitesimal, that she might be lost in a complete fantasy, she found it hard to dislodge.

On Friday morning, before she went out to the fertility clinic, she'd done her last delivery run for FreeLunch4Kids. For the past few months, since the house fire, when she no longer had to care for Den, she'd volunteered on Mondays, Wednesdays and Fridays to deliver lunches to children who had none. It was top-of-the-cliff intervention for needy children, more emotionally manageable than what she was used to – bottom dredging, picking up the fallen, the broken. She'd started as a sandwich maker and would regularly go down to the warehouse base at the back of K Road around 6 a.m. and spend a couple of hours making sandwiches: it was such a satisfying way to start the day. More recently, since she'd decided to go back to work and been battling every day to steel herself and to harbour her energy, she'd limited herself to delivering.

Deliveries started about nine, but on Friday she'd gone in early to see Francie, the boss, to let her know she wouldn't be available for any more runs. She'd arrived just as the sandwich makers were finishing up. And saw, as she hoped she would, Henry.

Henry ran the whole team, the core and whoever else turned

up: on Friday there'd been a group of employees from a local bank helping out as a team-building exercise. Ellie had been a little early, so she'd pitched in and helped to pack the little brown paper bags and then load them into cartons, referring to the list of schools for the day marked up on the big Perspex sheet. The mood in the kitchen and packing room was always uplifting. That might have come anyway from the feeling of doing some good in the world, but on the mornings Henry was there his presence was a big part of it too. He ran the kitchen and sandwich table with all the adrenaline and dynamics of a fitness class, played loud music and led the singalongs. He had a terrible voice but no shame, and that gave everyone confidence to let rip, even Ellie, who couldn't sing to save herself. Henry's choice of music was pretty eclectic and always upbeat, even when it was about lost love. On Friday morning, as she'd walked in past the plastic vegetable crates and cartons, George Ezra had been blaring, asking over and over again, 'What are you waiting for?'

Francie was out schmoozing suppliers, so when the packing was done and Ellie had been allocated her route and cartons, she'd sought a moment with Henry before she took off, to explain that this would be her last delivery for a while because she had to go back to work, and could he let Francie know?

'Oh no!' he'd hammed, 'not work!'

'That's exactly how I feel about it.'

'Jeez, Ellie,' he said, concerned. 'What work could that be?'

Her friendship with Henry was recent, begun since she gave up work to look after Den. It'd actually been Henry who'd suggested she get involved with the charity. He was a mate of Yelena's, an extension of the Kook A Chew crowd because he worked in the kitchen there, but he'd sometimes go out to corporate functions as

Yelena's handbag if she wanted to make a straight impression on some conservative potential client. That hadn't happened in quite a while, Ellie suspected, because Yelena was successful enough to no longer give a fuck what anyone thought of her sexuality, so Ellie had seen less of Henry, unfortunately. She liked him. He was extremely easy to look at, and his big brown eyes, it seemed to her, always carried a light for her.

It wasn't till he asked the question that she realised he'd only known her as her father's caregiver with time on her hands, not in her former guise as harried social worker. 'I work for an underfunded NGO as an advocate for victims of domestic violence,' she said, using a pat response she hadn't needed for three years. No matter how she framed it, mention of DV had always been a conversation stopper. Nothing had changed: Henry's smile faded and he seemed lost for words. She remembered what to say next to kick-start things: What do *you* do? But she already knew Henry worked as a chef in Kook A Chew till late, then three mornings a week got up early to supervise the sandwiches. So that was a no-go. As she tried to think of some other segue, she found she didn't need to say anything.

He smiled. A wide smile. He had great teeth, she thought, and eyes, and . . . stuff. Henry was by any measure a handsome man, charismatic. A strand of black hair, curly, had escaped from the red bandana he wore instead of a plastic hair-net, and fallen down across his forehead. 'What you do makes you one of the good guys, Ellie,' he said, offering a high five. 'Kia kaha.'

'Kia ora, Henry,' she said, palm on palm, a caress rather than a slap. 'E taku hoa.'

He smiled again, then looked at her, she thought – or perhaps wished – as if really seeing her for the first time. His smile faded, which was a bit disconcerting, then he said, 'Yelena told me about your dad, and you've been working here, and now I find out what your day job used to be.'

'*Is.*'

'Yeah,' he said. 'You look after people, Ellie. Hope someone's keeping an eye out for you.'

That was another conversation killer. Did she look like she needed help? What was she supposed to say? Reassure him that she wasn't Nola No-friends? She tried to turn it into a joke. 'There's always Yelena.' It sounded pathetic, even when he smiled and tried to run with it, praising Yelena.

She'd left knowing that she'd see him around another day, as part of Yelena's circle, because she'd become one of them. A pity they were all gay. With, she corrected herself, at least one exception.

Lying on the sofa in front of the dead television in the sitting room, she picked up the information sheet from the carpet beside her. SD 00007982 had become a constant companion over the last two days. As she alighted once again on the answer to the last question, the essential question, *I've been lucky. Why not share?*, she realised with a start that the voice of the ghostly Tūwharetoan had taken on a timbre and accent she recognised. As much as she chided herself about the remoteness of the possibility, another part of her kept coming back with, Why not? Henry *was* Māori, he *was* the right age, he *was* obviously a chef, and he had, as far as she could tell, a similar sense of humour to the one displayed by SD 00007982. She could hear him saying exactly those words and all the others on the sheet. Despite her admonitions to herself, she began seeing Henry's smiling face when she looked at SD 00007982, and somehow George Ezra's voice was in there too: *What are you waiting for?*

That ear-worm had accompanied her on the FreeLunch4Kids

delivery route on Friday, one she hadn't done before, through Sandringham and out over Mount Albert Road into the furthest reaches of Mount Roskill, a nest of streets she knew only too well. She'd been distracted by SD 00007982 for much of the trip, and by speculation as to whether Ezra might appeal as a name for her son. She thought it would have to go into the possibles list, though there was that American poet, Ezra Pound, who lived in Venice and was a Nazi sympathiser. Was Ezra Pound Jewish, she wondered? Surely not, if he was also a Nazi. Ezra was definitely biblical and might have been Jewish originally, but did that matter any more? Nothing was exclusively anything any more, in an ethnic sense. She'd seen Ruebens and Herschels in Herne Bay, who were, or looked like, the sons of WASPs. Who would know? So, Ezra would be a possible. Or Henry. That should be on the list too, whether or not he was . . . If he *was* SD 00007982, would he mind?

To get to the first school, a primary, she'd had to turn right into a street which she wouldn't have used if the memory had come soon enough. But she was halfway down it, where it curved slowly to the left, when she saw the house. She believed in public housing, but you could tell immediately which of the old state houses were in private hands and which were still owned by Housing New Zealand. The old staties that had gone up in the fifties in a frenzy of optimistic nation-building after the war had great bones and floors of heart timber. They could be renovated, insulated and opened up to the sun. The sections were generous, the original quarter-acres most of them, room enough for a lawn out the front, a flower garden round the fence border, a garage or carport up the side and a vegetable garden and a few fruit trees out the back. In theory, there was no reason why the Housing New Zealand tenants couldn't do the same with their land, and perhaps some of them did, but not the ones

Ellie got to visit. She couldn't bring herself to look at the house she remembered. It would be like the others, curtains always drawn, lank grass growing through an upended supermarket trolley, one corner of a grey sheet flapping on the clothesline dragging in the dirt, encrusted nappies caught by the wind in the fence, a rust-bucket parked car missing a wheel. The smell inside hit you like a slap, made your eyes water. Urine, cat and human. Old cabbage. Rotten food. Shit. Mould.

He'd stopped his fist an inch from her face. 'Is this a problem for you?' he'd asked her, then smashed it into the wall beside her head. The gib-board folded in like cardboard: her face would have been pulped. He was still smiling. 'No problem for me, eh.' She remembered the mother with the kids gathered close, all wide-eyed but clear-eyed, settled in their trauma: *This was normal.* When she'd walked out, like a zombie, she'd got in the car, driven around the corner, this corner she was driving round now, and stopped, burst like a balloon, the tears and tension flowing out of her. When she'd gathered herself, she'd rung Sergeant Tracey Costigan at the DV Unit, put the phone down and cried again. What had stayed with her was the heat of her shame as he taunted her, his smile and his smell. Rotten teeth, chemicals and beer-infused saliva, and old, stale blood. A year later he'd killed the woman. He got life, twelve years non-parole, the kids went into state care, got fostered. That six-year-old boy had little or no chance of not becoming his father. That was how it went. Circuitous. Endless. She couldn't even remember the boy's name, or his father's. But the street she remembered. This street. That house. *Move on*, she thought. *Please.*

The first school, a primary, was just two blocks away. Ellie double-parked outside the school office, took one of the smaller cartons from the boot and carried it into reception. She passed teachers on their way to class, already trailing little posses of curious kids. She put the carton on the counter. The receptionist was busy with a mother and a child who looked like a new entrant, big shy eyes, but a passing teacher, a middle-aged woman with streaks of grey, diverted from her course, thanked Ellie and went to give her the empty carton from yesterday. Ellie said she'd need to hold on to it until Monday, that she wouldn't be going back to base. 'Have to go back to work,' Ellie explained to a slightly raised eyebrow.

'Well,' said the woman to the little child. 'We'll just have to trust that another angel turns up on Monday.'

Ellie had driven across the bottom end of Mount Roskill into New Windsor and back towards the last stop, a big secondary school at the southern end of Three Kings, where she unloaded the biggest carton of little brown paper bags, the one sitting on the back seat of her car. Even the streets she hadn't been in before were familiar in a generic way. Clientsville, she'd heard some of the advocates call these patches of deprivation, the slums of Auckland, where her clients generally lived. At first glance, these weren't as bad as some slums, if you drove past and didn't stop to go inside the houses. And certainly not as bad if you just stopped at the schools. When she first began doing these deliveries, out east in Glen Innes, she thought she'd missed her vocation, that she should have become a teacher, because it was so clear to her that the schools had stepped into the community vacuums and become the neighbourhood hubs, the last state-funded agents for change and for good in this sea of market-forces wreckage. Being a teacher, saving kids, enlightening them, would beat the hell out of ferrying them and their mothers to A & E.

But the more schools she visited, the more she could see the teachers were being worn down by the extra-curricular demands, by so many small hands reaching up for salvation from material impoverishment and mental stimulation, hour after hour, day after day.

She thought about her own child or children, if she was so lucky. Was SD 00007982 the man? If he was, and it worked, what then? The percentages weren't that high. She couldn't assume her eggs would survive the thaw, and she only had eight. But *if* it did happen, what then? She'd never wanted to be a single parent; children were to have been a natural part of a loving, supportive relationship. Watching and supporting Claudia since Will left her, she'd seen first hand how consuming and draining solo motherhood could be. She knew Yelena would always be there, Claudia would do what she could, and there were other friends too. Poor Carol, she would have been a brilliant grandmother. But Ellie had always assumed there'd be a partner with a job, a salary: she never thought she'd be a beneficiary. How would she live? *Where* would she live? Carol's share of the estate would be available when the section was sold. Would that be enough for her to buy something in the part of town where she grew up? Auckland was a series of often badly connected towns and villages. Some she felt at home in, in others she felt so alien she might as well be in another country. That was the reality. She couldn't count on any help from Den, living or dead. Will might have been right about the mercenary rest-home financial template but what else could they do?

She became aware of her mobile, on silent, thrumming insistently on the coffee table. She didn't recognise the number. The voice identified itself as Meredith, the supervisor at the Sunset Road Retirement Village. She said that Ellie's father, Dennis – in case she'd forgotten the name, Ellie thought – hadn't been seen at happy hour or dinner, though that wasn't unusual of late. But after dinner they'd been alerted by the sensors in his apartment that there had been no movement inside for four hours. She was about to explain how the sensors worked, but Ellie cut her off. 'Where is he?'

'Well, he appears to have disappeared,' said Meredith.

What an odd way of putting it, thought Ellie. That someone could appear to have disappeared.

THINGS CAN DISAPPEAR in the night, while I'm sleeping. I don't know what's gone on, what's gone, until I try to use it or find it, and realise it's not there. So I always repeat my mantra before I open my eyes. 'Here lies Dennis William Sparks,' I say to myself. I know I might be taking a bit of a punt with this next bit. 'Beloved husband of Carol and father of William, Eleanor and Stanley.' Then, in case Carol is listening, I always add, 'Just testing!' But she never bites.

After I've said my prayer and know that I still know who I am, I open my eyes. It's dark. The smell of the earth I'm lying on and the ragged thrum of cicadas is comforting. I've missed both, and so many other things I can see or feel. Being cold. Trees. Branches arcing over me. The night sky beyond. Stars. I roll over on my side and find my Rainbird under my head. I sit up and shrug into it. I'm stiff and chilled. Through the vegetation I can see a weak flickering light. I push myself up using the trunk of the tree as leverage. That fucking knee never goes away. I have to lean while I catch my breath, my cheek against rough bark scored with narrow furrows. This tree, melia, I remember, for some reason. Carol and I planted it, after Will was born. This tree, still with me, trying to support me. My tears run into the rivulets of bark and down into the earth. A tree hugger, finally. I'd laughed at the very idea, long ago. What a waste. I seem to be crying a lot, and quite often can't remember why. I push off the trunk, get the knee going, begin limping back along the grass track. At the fork I turn right onto a wider track, towards the dancing light, growing stronger as I get closer. My AF 1s know the way to a couple of steps leading up to another wooden gate, where I stop, peering over at an expanse of deck, which seems both deeply familiar and strange.

The light is coming from a small blaze deep in the pizza oven, which is still there. In its low flicker of flame, I can see those gaunt blackened bones to the south of the deck where my home used to be. The kitchen area is completely razed, but the big french doors from the sitting room are still standing, in front of a cross-hatched black ruin extending back into the darkness. That edge of the deck itself has also burnt away, exposing the ash-strewn concrete foundations underneath. The rest of the deck out to the pool is still there, as far as I can see, most of the surface covered with . . . stuff. I can recognise the sun-loungers. One is made up as a bed, with a pillow and old blankets, the others arranged as chairs, but draped with vegetation of some sort. And behind the loungers is a low structure, a kind of lean-to. It has a central ridge like a tent with riders running down to the deck, burnt timber from the house, covered with see-through plastic sheets. As I watch, another flickering light comes on, one of the torches that used to surround the deck. I see a thin figure turn from the torch, carrying a red-embered stick he's using as a lighter. I step back instinctively, my knee gives way and I stagger onto the bottom step. I must have cried out: by the time I recover my balance and look up, the figure is at the gate, pointing a gun in my face. I don't recognise the face immediately, but I'd know that pistol anywhere. 'Walter!'

'Walter? Who's Walter, Mr D?'

The face is long, a boy's face, but old, too, with watery brown eyes which seem to have seen as much of the world as mine. 'I know you, I think.'

'It's Jackson, Mr D. There's no Walter here.'

'You must give me my pistol back, Jackson.'

When Jackson hands Walter to me, I must confess I cradle him to my chest like a baby.

'I didn't steal it, Mr D,' says the boy. 'You gave it to me the night of the fire when I found you on the sofa. Honest. I'se just keeping it for you.'

I'm in no position to contradict him. The boy – what did he say his name was? – opens the gate for me, and I limp up onto the deck and look around in wonder. 'My father would have known what this was.'

'What was?'

I indicate the makeshift shelter and the sun-lounger bed and chairs arranged around the table, which I hadn't noticed before because it, too, is draped in what look like corn fronds or maize. 'This is like . . . My father lived in the desert.'

'Yeah?'

'In the war.'

'My grandfather was there too.'

'Bivvy!' I'm exultant. 'That's the word! Bivouac!'

The boy is looking anxiously at Walter, who is waving around a bit. 'Does Walter have any bullets in him?'

That was something I knew, I'm sure. When the boy offers to take the pistol and put it somewhere safe, I tell him I appreciate his looking after Walter while I was gone, but I will not be separated from Walter again under any circuses. I'm deeply embarrassed because I know that's the wrong word. Circles isn't right either. The right word has gone, but not the knowledge that the word I've substituted is wrong. I must look bewildered, lost. The boy says he doesn't want to be rude, 'considering it's your house, but how come you're here? Does anyone know you're here?'

I tell him it's a long story. I've found that to be the perfect answer for questions I don't want to answer. It always stops further enquiry: no one, it seems, wants to hear long stories. But the boy is different. He's obviously waiting for me to continue. 'Enough,' I say. And that seems to be sufficient.

'You hungry, Mr D?'

'Depends. What are you cooking?'

'Warming up a can of baked beans,' he says. 'I'se gonna have it on bread. Got no butter, though.'

'Real food! Sounds wonderful.'

The boy crosses to the table, takes a small blackened pot and places it close to the fire in the pizza oven. He then clears one side of the table, pushing the dry vegetation over to the other side, and invites me to sit down on an upturned pot that had once, I think, contained a yucca near the steps to the pool. When I take my place, Jackson lays out plates and knives and forks. The pattern round the edges of the plates looks familiar to me, though much of it has been burnt off. The provenance of all the stuff Jackson has used to make himself comfortable here is obvious. Good luck to him, I think, unless the boy started the fire with this outcome in mind. No, *I* started the fire, hadn't someone suggested that? Why would I have done that?

Jackson takes a small tomahawk from beside the fire and chops some blackened timber he's stacked nearby, just a few lengths, which he feeds into the fire. He comes back to the table and cuts a loaf of white bread and lays a thick slice on each of the plates, turns the pot of beans a couple of times, sticks his finger in the top and pronounces it ready. He brings it over to the table and ladles generous portions of beans over the bread doorstops. When he's seated in front of his meal, he asks me if I'd mind if he said grace? I tell him that's fine with me, that I'm as hungry as a hunter and truly grateful for what Jackson has put in front of me and I'm happy that he thanks whoever. Jackson closes his eyes and murmurs something to himself.

'You can say it aloud if you like.'

'It's my Nana's,' he says. 'Whakapaingia ēnei kai – bless our food. Hei oranga mo ō mātou tinana – for the well-being of our body. Whāngaia ō mātou wairua – feed our spirit.'

'You don't have to translate,' I tell him. 'I'm getting the general idea.' After that, the next word I recognise is Amine.

I look at my utensils and have a bad moment with my fingers. This has happened before. I look across to the boy and mimic him, holding the bread in place with my fork in one hand and cutting with my knife in the other. I don't want him to see what I'm doing, but he does. He doesn't laugh, doesn't give any indication he's noticed, except, I can tell: he slows his movements so that it's easier for me to shadow him. Lifting the portion to his mouth with the fork. He chews, I chew. A wonderfully savoury mixture. 'Succulent indeed.'

'Is that good?'

'That is very very good,' I confirm. 'Delicious.' I watch the boy carefully for my cues and notice other things. He's looking worried. Chews twice, like clockwork, then listens, like the noise of his jaw is blocking something. His eyes are always moving around the perimeter darkness established by the weak light from the fire and the torch. Chew, chew, stop, listen. Chew, chew, swallow, stop, listen. I feel obliged to do the same. Chew twice, stop, listen carefully. 'Are you expecting someone?' I ask him.

He says no, but shortly after that, he rises from the table and stands, like a pointer dog with quarry in his nostrils. When I ask what the matter is, Jackson puts his finger to his lips. All is silent, save for the cicadas and the crackle of the fire in the oven. But Jackson can plainly hear something I can't.

'Prob'ly nothing,' whispers the boy, then seems to contradict himself almost immediately. 'Car just came up the drive.' He moves quickly from his place at the table, round towards me. 'Mind if I borrow Walter for a sec?' Before I can register the question or reply, he lifts Walter from the table and disappears through the gate into Carol's garden. I resolve to keep Walter in my pocket in future, though the boy is so obviously alarmed by what he's heard, I'm not about to deny him whatever comfort he gets from the pistol. Who knows what's out there?

JACKSON MATERIALISED FROM the darkness of the garden even as Ellie turned from the driveway into the parking bay, the swinging arc of the headlights catching him full beam.

'Mr D is here,' he said, as Ellie opened the door.

Jackson helped carry the hemp supermarket bags and blankets and pillows up through the garden to the deck, where Den was sitting quietly at the table. 'Dad. Thank God you're here.' She dropped the bags she was carrying and hugged him, then saw his plate, white bread strewn with baked beans. 'I've got some real food here,' she said. 'I'll put something together.'

'This is delicious!' he said.

'Oh,' said Ellie. 'Yes, sit, you too Jackson, finish your meal, please.'

Jackson lowered the stuff he was carrying, which Den now saw was blankets and pillows. 'Is that my bed?'

'We'll make up one of the sun-loungers,' she confirmed. 'Like Jackson's. Just for tonight.'

'Yes,' said Den. 'Just for tonight. But I'm not going back.'

'Okay, Dad.'

Den became suddenly panicked by the thought of what tomorrow might bring. 'I can't go back! Promise me!'

'Okay, Dad. Don't worry, we'll think of something.'

'I'm happy here. I'm home.'

'Yes, but . . .'

'We're sweet,' said Jackson.

Sweet? thought Ellie, trying to smile encouragingly. The section would be sold soon, and even if it wasn't, winter was coming. And . . . She was registering the changes on the deck since her last supply drop for Jackson a couple of days ago. Jackson's sun-lounger bed, not in the lean-to, out in the open, the fronds of desiccated vegetation draped over everything. What the fuck? 'Jackson, what's going on here?' She picked up a frond. It was dry and crackly. 'What is this . . . ?' Holy shit, it was marijuana. 'Where did you get this?'

'I was down picking feijoas, and I found these plants. Three of them. Just growing there, ready.'

Whenever Ellie had come to weed and water the garden, she'd

concentrated on Carol's flower beds and left the bush area and mature trees to themselves. But even so. 'How . . . ?' she began, but was cut off by Den's sudden revelation.

'Stan's birthday present!' Den said he remembered he and Stan had planted three bushes on the night of his seventieth.

'Thing is,' said Jackson, 'It'd be a shame to waste it. You can't buy this stuff, it's all synthetic shit. So I pulled it and dried it. See?'

He was indicating the lean-to. Ellie peered inside and saw marijuana hanging from the ceiling, completely obscuring the interior. When she stood up, she turned away, trying to process this latest complication, and saw the bottom of the pool, drained the night of the fire, covered in the same stuff.

'There's a shitload,' confirmed Jackson. 'Another coupla days of no rain and we'll be sweet.'

That word again, thought Ellie. This wasn't how she'd ever seen things turning out, but what the fuck could she do, apart from buy time? She'd think of something. She took the blankets and began making up one of the sun-loungers for her father's bed.

***

HALF an hour later, Ellie drove back down the driveway, clinging to the one thing that made any sense: Dad was happy. For the moment. Tomorrow, she'd think of something. Some plan for Den. Some plan for Jackson. Some plan for the fucking marijuana. How could Stan have done that? Something to say to Meredith at Sunset. That had to be a priority. When Meredith had called, she'd relayed the information the home had gathered about Den's movements, that he'd been seen up on Sunset Road mid-afternoon by the woman who was a part-timer at the pharmacy, that he'd asked her the way to town. One of the bus drivers on that route had reported to the shift supervisor picking up an elderly man who, he said, looked like Einstein's brother, in sneakers. He'd been intending to take him to the end of the line at Britomart so he could get himself a card, but the old man had exited quietly with a bunch of other passengers somewhere along the waterfront. From the moment she heard that, Ellie had known where her father was going and had managed to dissuade Meredith from involving the police or taking any further action until Ellie got back to her.

Before she drove back up the hill to Ponsonby, she rang the number Meredith had given her. Ellie was grateful to get Meredith's voice message, her shift was obviously over. Ellie confirmed, with as little detail as possible, that her father was safe and that she'd be in touch tomorrow. She'd tried to sound confident and in control, but felt neither.

This was how it had started with Jackson. Just for a day or two, she'd told herself, a sort of casual extension of her fostering arrangement, even though the department knew nothing about it. She'd got him a room in a motel she couldn't afford, just for a week, so that he could do an interview with the fire investigator sent by the insurance company. She knew she had to get him through that, or he'd be the obvious suspect. After that he'd disappeared. She'd reported that to the department, and part of her had been grateful he was gone.

She'd been watering the garden a week later, keeping her mother's flowers alive, she didn't know why, maybe mourning the house was part of it, when she'd heard a low noise from the pseudopanax at the back. A croak, like someone she knew calling her name – 'Miss Ellie'. He'd been living there like a bush rat since he left the motel, starving, his face and arms swollen from mosquito bites. Terrified his father would find him.

The fire investigator had completed his enquiry, so she'd helped set Jackson up on the deck while she found another solution. A week became a fortnight, became a month, because there *was* no solution. She'd watched with horror as Jackson Collins joined the legion of missing persons being actively sought by police. She'd pretended to share the department's concern, even wringing her hands one day over what might have become of him, though her anguish had been about her impotence, her failure to extract herself or Jackson from this procedural and environmental cul-de-sac.

As much anger as anguish if she was honest. If Jackson's father had assaulted a neighbour or a man or woman in the street as severely as he had Jackson's mother, he would have got six or seven years. But that wasn't how the Crimes Act worked. Instead he'd been given only three years, then been paroled before he'd even served out two and released to hunt his son like an animal – the boy who had been the only one brave enough to stand up in front of a judge and say, This is what my father did to my mother. The legislation, the court, the parole board, the police, couldn't keep Jackson safe, so Ellie would.

Six months later, half a bloody *year*, and there was still no obvious solution. Jackson's fear of his father was palpable, not just *with* him every moment of his day, but *in* him. She'd offered him a mobile, a little pre-pay with limited functions, but he wouldn't take it because he feared that somehow he might leave an electronic footprint his father could follow. He had no bank account, no driving licence, and lived exclusively off the food and small amounts of cash that Ellie brought him. He seemed to need so little. He rarely left the property, and then only at night, when he'd work his way through the park and along the track at the bottom of the cliff into town.

When she asked him what he did there, he said he walked up and down Queen Street 'to see some people', people he could be sure wouldn't know him. As far as Ellie could know, he saw no one, other than her. She tried to come every other day, bring him something – food, cash, a book. She'd asked him about his sister, but he told her Lila was too close to his father to risk contact. So it went on, and the longer it went on, the fewer solutions appeared. In fact, with the insurance wrangles and delays, it got easier. The heat had gone out of his case: Jackson Collins was officially gone and pretty much forgotten. But now the section was going to be put on the market, the sweet spot was souring fast.

Jackson's resurrection would be more problematic than his disappearance, and not just for him. She'd be a pariah in her profession, her career burnt – sucked in, got too close, unprofessional, allowed sentiment to cloud her professional judgement, crossed sacred professional boundaries. She was apprehensive, petrified even, but it all came down to what she'd seen, what she knew about the things she could and couldn't live with in herself. Whatever happened, whatever the consequences for her, she wouldn't help to expose this boy to the depredations of a murderous brute. Jackson had sobbed when he told Ellie that he was dead meat if his father found him. The tears, she realised, were for his father: he couldn't help himself, that's the way he was.

I'M ON A lilo in the tent at Tāhuna, my older sister Jean beside me, and Mum and Dad on creaky-springed stretchers the other side of a canvas divider. I can hear the cicadas and the sound of the waves, though they must be nearly a mile away, beyond the back-beach estuary. As I listen, the crashing of the waves on sand gets louder, then turns into Dad, roaring angrily in his sleep for some reason. I'm dreaming, because the sound wakes me and I'm on a sun-lounger on the deck underneath the stars, and the sounds aren't of anger but of torment and they're not coming from my father but from the boy sleeping nearby. I peel back the blankets, get my bare feet on the deck and try to stand, but the bloody sun-lounger's so low I have to crawl across to him. His moans have become terrified convulsions and I kneel by his side and begin talking to him, trying to calm him. 'It's all right, it's all right . . .' What was his name? I know that I know him.

My words are having no effect. The boy has writhed onto his side, turned away from me, so I put a hand on his shoulder. He reacts violently, throws his arm back at me, twisting in his bed and rising, looming over me, the tomahawk almost magically in his other hand. I have time to think that the boy must sleep with the tomahawk, before the little axe is above me, poised over my damaged head, the boy's eyes blind with terror. I scream into his face. 'It's me! It's me!'

The boy comes to himself as suddenly as he'd reacted, drops the tomahawk and helps me to my feet. 'Sorry, Mr D, sorry!'

'It's all right, it's all right, we're all right,' I repeat, as if repeating it will make it so, though I know it's too late for both of us. I know who he's seeing in his nightmare. 'Shall we have a cup of tea?'

'Nah, Mr D. Thanks, I'm okay. You okay?'

'I'm okay, you're okay,' I tell him. I think it's a joke popped up from somewhere in my lost past, but it's meaningless to the boy, so I stop agonising over its provenance. 'You'll be able to sleep?'

The boy assures me he will, and lies down again, with the tomahawk across his chest.

'Do you really need to hold on to that, d'you think?' The boy lets me take it. 'I'll put it over here by the fire.'

By the time I've placed the tomahawk by the little stack of wood beside the pizza oven and turned back, the boy is asleep. I stand there warming my bum by the last embers of the fire and look up at the stars. Stardust, we all are. Who said that? Every night we go to sleep in darkness, trusting that the world will keep turning to catch the light. My descent into the black room is arbitrary and frightening, but I have to keep faith and fight the terror that one day soon I'll stare up at these same stars and have no idea what they are. For now, they're comforting.

'Still star-gazing, Den?'

It's a voice I recognise, a voice I've been yearning for. When I turn towards it, I expect to be disappointed, but there she is, in her summer print, leaning back with her bum resting on the table, her long legs crossed at the ankle. 'You must be cold, darling,' I tell her.

'I'm never cold.'

I try to keep the tearfulness out of my voice. 'You can't imagine how pleased I am to see you.'

'Of course I can,' she says.

ELLIE CHECKED THAT the outside door was disarmed – reassuring, because it meant someone was already there – swiped her card, entered the code for the inner sanctum and stepped back into a world she thought she'd left behind.

As she entered, Rosemary stood up from her computer and hugged her, said the right things about missing her, welcomed her back, then told her they'd organised a pōwhiri for her on Friday.

'Please God, no!'

'Joking. But we will do a shared lunch.'

There were a lot of things about Rosemary that Ellie admired: she was a tall, willowy, brainy woman, early thirties now, brave and altruistic. She'd shadowed Ellie seven years ago when she was doing a thesis on domestic violence for her doctorate, then, on the strength of what she'd seen working alongside Ellie, she'd abandoned academia for front-line intervention. When Ellie left, Rosemary had taken Ellie's place as senior advocate for the adult safety team. Her academic background gave Rosemary an enviable ability to analyse and objectify, Ellie thought, and a better chance of lasting in the job. Ellie had seen the advocates come and go, flaming into anger and frustration at the daily injustices and brutality they saw, burning up with it, burning out. Ellie wished she was clearer on where *she* sat on that spectrum right now: it might give her a better steer on whether she would survive re-entry.

Rosemary had already downloaded and printed the police arrest list, with the summaries of those arrested for DV over the weekend. Sixteen today, about average from three years ago, Ellie thought, at least the number hasn't gone up. She could remember as many as two dozen. And there was one positive change – less obvious misogyny in the police summaries of the circumstances leading to the arrests. Comments like '*She got lippy so he smashed her*' were at least in quote marks now.

She and Rosemary triaged the list, eliminating the obvious no-gos, the ones who were outside the central police district covered by their agency and the assaults where a child was the victim, the preserve of the department. There was one murder, a name that Ellie vaguely recognised from the past, a serial offender. She'd seen something in the Sunday papers but had deliberately avoided it. Ellie knew she could probably conjure up a memory of the woman who was now dead, but there was no point: they had to save the living. Rosemary crossed the murderer's name off the list and they moved on.

That left eight live ones, one of them hospitalised. They did a rapid risk assessment, based on the police report, previous experience and feel. Reading between the lines of the police fact summaries, Rosemary and Ellie agreed that they could phone two and make a time to visit later. One woman they knew would be at work and would be embarrassed if they turned up there. That left five serious assaults where the offenders had been jailed and where the police had confirmed they were in the court cells and would be up in front of a judge this morning.

Ellie and Rosemary had had to assume that every one of them would plead not guilty and would be given bail, that a jaded, desensitised judge would believe that looking sufficiently stern and admonishing, and imposing strict bail conditions, would be enough to keep the victims safe. But of course the men would often go straight back to their partners and beat them again for going to the cops, even if it had been a neighbour who had made the call. Ellie and Rosemary had to get to the women first. If they were still there when the men returned, it wasn't only the victims who risked attack. To speed things up, the two women divvied up the cases on geographic lines: Rosemary would go west for three, Ellie east for the other two. She would also visit the woman in hospital on her way back into town. That was less urgent – at least for the present, that victim was safe.

Ellie left the building with a copy of the arrest list and court list, cartons of food from the donations room and some stuffed dolls and toys for the kids, whose ages she'd noted. There was a chill in the air, carried by a swell of cold air from the south. It wasn't a snow-on-the-central-plateau wind, but after a late summer of benign northerlies, it carried a bite. She thought of her father, exposed on the deck with Jackson, and her belly lurched. She should ring Meredith. She should ring Teresa at the clinic about her choice of sperm donor. One fuck-up at a time, she told herself, and imagined lifting the needle off old vinyl and moving it across the turntable to a different groove. It usually helped. She pulled out onto Great North Road and tried to remember the quickest track across town to Glen Innes.

**

SIMONE Bishop was first on Ellie's list, because her husband, Lyall, was likely to be one of the first up in front of the judge. The court list would be in alphabetical order, but it wouldn't be set down until just before the session started. The court clerk was supposed to email it through to the agency as soon as it was in place, and also keep the agency updated on progress as they worked through the list.

Ellie drove along the Kepa Road ridge, then dropped down into Glen Innes, with its established trees and gentle undulations. A town planning exercise back in the sixties, it had originally been settled with families from the Freemans Bay slums, razed in the name of urban renewal. The sections out here always surprised Ellie with their generous size, and all the little parks and linking paths must have looked great on the plans. Once the lights were taken out, though, they became dark, dangerous places too close to people's homes. Places to lurk unseen, to beat, rape and murder, then disappear. The urban renewal cycle had come full circle: those state houses on big sections were now being knocked over to make way for smaller, more plentiful units.

Old, careful habits reasserted themselves. After searching the paint-blistered wooden letterboxes for Number 66, Ellie drove further along – three houses was standard – before pulling over. Never have a strange car sitting outside the house, with a rego that could be clocked.

Before getting out of the car, Ellie went back through the summary on the police arrest sheet. Simone and Lyall Bishop had been out to a local pub on Saturday night. A neighbour, a Mrs Dempster, had babysat the three children, a five-year-old boy, a three-year-old girl, and an eight-month-old girl. An argument that started in the car, about Simone's behaviour at the pub, had continued at home after the babysitter left. It escalated to the point where Lyall struck Simone in the face, then left the house. Mrs Dempster, with what she called a bad feeling, had returned to see if Simone was okay, then woken the children and driven them all to hospital. A doctor at A & E had phoned the police, with Simone's consent. X-rays cleared Simone of a broken eye socket, and Mrs Dempster drove them home. On Sunday morning Simone reported that Lyall had been back while she was at the hospital and had kicked the door in when he discovered his wife wasn't there. He had been picked up at a friend's place early Sunday morning, charged with male assaults female and remanded in custody. There was no indication as to whether police were going to oppose bail, so Ellie had to assume they weren't.

So far, so standard. She also checked out on her phone the address for her second call-out, Alana, long-term partner of repeat offender Eric Ali Sua-Bensen. She remembered enough about him to want to be gone before he got home, so was relieved to see that Alana was only four blocks away.

The curtains at the Bishops' place were drawn as if no one was home. Inside it would be murky, probably dank. The smell always hit you first. Ellie shivered and told herself these were projections born of experience, not prejudice, but they didn't make her feel any better about herself as she opened the boot, got out a food parcel and looked for a toy or doll suitable for the three-year-old girl, Destiny, who was probably at home. She closed the boot, then opened it again and retrieved one of the agency's mobile phones. Some sixth sense about Lyall Bishop said he would be the kind of guy who might have smashed Simone's phone before he'd stormed out, to keep her isolated.

Ellie walked up the cracked concrete path, knocked on the blistered pale green door and conjured up a smile. Simone would be home, but would she be brave enough to open the door, which, on closer inspection wasn't actually closed – the latch was smashed. She called out as she knocked gently, so that Simone would know it wasn't Lyall. The door swung open with the pressure of her knock, and was caught halfway by a delicate hand.

***

THE house was immaculate: the threadbare carpet clean and unstained, the Formica benches and lino in the kitchen gleaming in the light flooding the area from the back and side windows, through which Ellie could see raised beds of vegetables: silver beet, broccoli, runner beans. There were places in the living room where the gib-board was caved in, some, Ellie suspected, covered with children's paintings, carefully framed with cardboard backing. Simone was clearly house-proud and a good mother: she'd obviously managed to get the older kids to school and kindy, and the baby was asleep in a bassinet in the corner.

When Simone answered the door, she held her hand up, strategically covering one side of her face. Ellie was careful and respectful. There was often only a narrow window to explain who you were, where you were from – crucially not from the department, who might take away her children – and that you wanted to help. The door remained open as Ellie talked, Simone's hand still up, protectively, as if to shield her from a blow. 'Is it okay if I come in?' Ellie finally felt able to ask.

In answer, Simone opened the door further, dropping her hand only when Ellie was inside and she'd quickly pushed the door behind her. 'I'm sorry,' she said in a small voice, 'I'm not at my best.'

The sight of Simone's face made Ellie wince. Her lustrous black hair was pulled tightly back into a pony-tail, so there was no hiding the black swelling closing her right eye. 'I'm really worried about you and your children,' said Ellie. 'I'm worried about your safety. Maybe the time has come when we need to look at how to get you and the kids safe?' She could see Simone slump as the tension in her ebbed. She wanted help. Ellie handed her the food parcel, then pulled the cloth doll with yellow hair from her big leather bag. 'This is for Destiny, if you think she'd like it.'

'She's at kindy,' said Simone, taking the doll. 'She'll love it. I'm trying to keep the kids to their routines, if I can.'

Simone offered Ellie a chair beside the sofa, but didn't sit herself, instead hovering anxiously over by the baby, one hand caressing the curving cane on the side of the old bassinet. She was a petite woman of about thirty, Ellie guessed, considering that she probably looked older than she was. She was somehow elegant, even in jeans, jandals and a faded cotton top.

Intuition born of experience told Ellie that this injury wasn't the first Simone had suffered, just the first she'd reported. She suggested they work through a risk assessment together, that it might be really useful in determining how dangerous Lyall was and what sort of plan they might need to keep her and the children safe. She didn't want to spook Simone by telling her that the real aim was to determine how lethal her partner was. Sometimes, just producing the checklist spooked them, and she would work through the questions from memory, but after such a long absence she couldn't trust herself to do that.

Simone didn't object when Ellie withdrew the form from her bag and they started on the questions. By the time Ellie got to the third section, how much abuse the children were witnessing, it had become clear that the police report about Saturday night had not even begun to reveal what was really going on. The blow to the eye might have been the first injury that required medical attention, but Simone revealed that Lyall had often punched her in the stomach, kicked her legs and tried to strangle her. He'd tried to isolate her from friends and family, and seldom took her out in public because of his flaring paranoia and jealousy: at the pub he'd thought she'd exchanged glances with one of his mates.

'He usually won't take me out with him, and I don't want to go, because he's accused me of that before. I don't make eye contact with anyone any more, because he might think I'm looking at them. I don't laugh at anyone's jokes, I don't talk to any of the men, only the women, and even then he's suspicious that I'm talking about him.' She looked away from Ellie, towards the sunlit window. 'What I'm doing now, with you, he'll kill me if he finds out.'

***

IT was an hour before Ellie made it back to her car. The last ten minutes of that had been on a Housing New Zealand 0800 number, on hold, before persuading someone to send out a repairman this afternoon to fix the front door. Simone had wanted to stay in the home for the children's sake. She had no family in or near Auckland, so Ellie rang the agency and tried to ascertain whether Lyall had appeared in court yet, and what his status was. Ideally, the court list would be updated by email every three-quarters of an hour, with '*Bailed*' or '*RIC*' beside their names. Remanded in custody would mean breathing space for Ellie and Simone, but Maria told her they hadn't heard yet. Ellie then phoned Zoe, a family lawyer who specialised in these cases. She was in court, but Ellie knew that if she left a message for her, Zoe would respond and do what was needed. Then Ellie arranged for new locks on the doors and windows and an alarm that went straight to the police. The trouble was, all this would take the best part of a week, a week in which Simone and the children – and the elderly Mrs Dempster – would be in danger. Ellie would have to get on to Women's Refuge and see if she could get Simone and the children there for the next few days.

She looked at her watch: 10.45. She needed to get across to Alana. First, though, she needed to know that Eric Sua-Bensen wasn't likely to be in the vicinity. She rang Maria again – still no court update. Ellie didn't have a choice: she had to take a chance that the judge sitting this morning wasn't stupid enough to believe that a patched gangsta with previous was going to abide by any bail conditions. Before she could put the mobile down after talking to Maria, it rang again. Will. Fuck.

'Had a call from Meredith at Sunset,' said Will quietly. 'She said she couldn't get hold of you, that Dad's done a runner. When were you going to tell me?'

IT'S GOOD TO feel the wind. The remains of the house give a bit of shelter from the southerly. The boy sets me up at the table with a rug over my shoulders and shows me how to strip the buds from the leaf. He seems to understand my finger problems and sits beside me, so that my actions can perfectly replicate his own. 'Here's some good buds, Mr D, you reckon?'

'Good buds.'

'See these have turned dark brown an're covered with resin, so they're ready. We strip the leaf away, careful, not touching the buds . . .'

'Right.' When I get the sticky stuff all over my hands, the boy doesn't get upset. 'We got so much it doesn't matter.'

I'd woken at first light, disoriented. Had no idea where I was at first. Stared up at the sky, then felt something hard under my pillow. Was delighted to discover Walter. Rolled out from under the blankets and rugs and fell the short drop from the sun-lounger to the wooden deck onto my complaining knees. When I hauled myself to my feet with the help of the table leg, and saw the charred skeleton of the house, I remembered where I was, and rejoiced.

The sun-lounger nearby had been empty. I remembered the boy had been sleeping there, the boy who had the nightmares. What had happened to him? Then there'd been a loud crash from within the ruins, like collapsing timber. I'd panicked and run towards the french doors, but it was only the boy, with the tomahawk, appearing from where the living room used to be, dragging a piece of blackened four by two. 'Wood for the fire, Mr D. I'll get it going.'

And he did. Then toasted some lumps of bread in the flame, and spread butter and jam over a couple for me, and brewed a pot of tea to wash it down. What a start to the day!

After breakfast, I was about to piss al fresco when he took me down through Carol's garden and into the concrete shell of the garage, to show me the track he'd cleared to the downstairs toilet, which still had water in it but wouldn't flush by itself. He showed me how to tip some water in from the plastic bucket sitting beside it. An old saying came to mind, way back from the hippy communes: 'If it's yellow, let it mellow. If it's brown, flush it down.'

The boy grinned and gave me a high five as if I'd discovered the formula for thermal, thermo whatevers.

On the way back out, we passed an old metal cabinet near the door, scorched but not burnt. One of the doors was hanging open. Inside, the shelves were crammed with pots of paint of different sizes, all used, the sides smeared with the colours of the house, with Carol's scrawl in black marker on the sides or tops: *'Undercoat, outer. Back bathroom: Wash & Wear. Upstairs walls. Top coat, tongue and groove room.'* And instructions: *'Washhouse: Okay for touch-ups but not completely the right colour!'* Carol had chosen the colours and supervised their application with the care of a Michelangelo. I had a moment of despair, a sense of waste that staggered me against the cabinet.

The boy took my arm. 'We got fresh water too.' He led me back through the gate and showed me the nozzle of the hose, followed it back to the tap, just to be sure that I remembered where it was. 'That's how Miss Ellie found me here,' he said. 'Came to water the garden. I thought she was the department.'

Back on the deck, he'd explained that we'd better clear the hut, because it might rain soon and we'd need to get the sun-loungers and the bedding back inside. He sat me at the table and brought the leaf hanging inside the bivvy, and began stripping the buds, showing me how to do it, over and over again with endless patience . . .

It comes to me as I'm sitting there beside him, whose name I can't remember, that I'm happy as I can ever remember being. I suppose, my memory being what it is, that may not be saying much. But still.

IT WAS DIFFICULT getting used to the new, straight, family-oriented Will. Ellie wasn't accustomed to factoring him into decisions about her father, or anything else of consequence, so keeping her brother informed about Den's escape had been the last thing on her mind. Even now, sharing information with him didn't come easily, not helped by his responses.

'Out in the open on the fucking deck?'

'He's got shelter. Jackson's built a little hut from bits and pieces of the house.'

'Jackson? The fucking arsonist?'

Ellie explained as patiently as she could that Will should be grateful that Jackson was there to look after Den, that it had given everyone a bit of breathing space because Den was adamant he wouldn't go back to Sunset. 'We have to think of something else.'

But Will wasn't able to move on to future options. 'Let me get this straight,' he said. 'Dad's squatting in a humpy made out of the burnt-out ruins of the house this little shit set fire to?'

Ellie took a deep breath, then thought, I don't have time for this. The alcohol and drugs might be out of his system but Will was still toxic. She hit the off button on the phone and started the car. By the time she'd completed a U-turn, so had he. Her mobile burped again. 'I was out of line, sorry,' he said.

'We'll figure it out. Tomorrow, okay?'

'What are the options we should be thinking about?'

'Will, I'm driving, I can't do this right now. We'll talk later, okay?'

AT SOME STAGE I must doze off, or somehow absent myself. When I come to, I'm still sitting at the table, as before, but the boy's looking at me strangely. *What the fuck have I done?*

'Was that your missus you were talking to?' he asks.

I'm not sure what to say. I can't remember talking to Carol just then but I know she's back. The boy isn't a doctor or a red and white, so there's no danger surely in telling the truth. 'Her name's Carol. Does it bother you?'

'Nah. She's a spirit, wairua, like my nana. I talk to my nana in my head, ask her what she thinks. What would you do, Nan?'

'Where does she live?'

'Up north, she used to. Me and Lila would go there, stay with her. You'd have liked her, Mr D.'

'I'm sure I would have.'

'She could tell stories, my nan. You ask her a question and she tells you a story. Sometimes, it was the same story, but second time around it would have a different meaning. Depended on the question.'

'It always does,' I say, unimaginably grateful for his understanding. 'You can't get the right answer unless you ask the right question.'

'That's the sorta stuff she said.'

'How long since you've seen her?'

'She passed when I was like eight, but I remember her like yesterday.'

'That's the way it is,' I say. Possibly a bit mournfully.

His long face droops. 'Jus' the way it is,' he agrees.

'I used to say something,' I tell him. What I used to do, I think, in situations like this, is tell a joke. I seemed to have one for every occasion. But they've fled. There was a saying, though. Uplifting, I think, if I can remember it. 'Life is like . . . something . . . A haircut!'

The boy is looking at me doubtfully. 'A haircut?'

'A haircut. You get it just the way you like it, but it keeps changing anyway.'

'Yo!' The boy likes that, laughs. 'My nan liked a morning tea. Got no bikkies left, so another piece of toast, cuppa tea?'

'Smoko,' I remember. 'What Branko called it. We liked to pretend we were working men.'

'Smoko,' the boy repeats. 'Do they still call it that?'

'I have no idea.'

'I never had a job,' he says. 'When I get one, I'll find out an' let you know. Why did they call it smoko?'

'Back in the day, the manual labourers all smoked. They needed their hands to work, but when they took a break they could roll a smoke.' I'm not sure how true this is, but it comes to me easily, as if it might be true.

The boy looks carefully at me, weighing something up. 'I could roll us a smoke, Mr D.'

'A smoke for smoko! We'd be duty-bound, wouldn't we? Honouring a tradition.'

'An' that,' he says.

I watch him get some papers from the bivvy, lay the papers and buds and leaf out on the table and expertly roll a fat joint. There's a definite art to it, which I'm too late to learn. The boy is such a generous companion, and what with Walter in my pocket and a joint about to be smoked, I feel for the first time that I'll no longer miss my roll-top: I have pretty much everything I need right here. The boy lights the joint, takes a deep drag, hands it to me. I hardly know him, but it's like being invited into a warm house by an old friend. I hold the smoke in and hand the joint back.

'Smoko,' he says, grinning. 'I like smoko!'

When I exhale, I see the boy through the wreathing smoke. A kindly old soul in a boy's body. In his confidence and ease around his bivvy, he reminds me of my father, though altogether gentler, nicer. He seems older and more worldly than me now. If he makes it to thirty, what a good man he'll be.

The boy hands the joint back. Oh yes, I think, dragging it deep.

He says he has a question he doesn't know the answer to. I tell him I probably won't know either, but the boy isn't discouraged. 'Is it good to keep secrets, Mr D? Or should you always tell the truth?'

'Mostly the truth, I think. If it isn't cruel.'

'I told the truth about Dad smashing Mum and they put him away.'

Oh shit. That order of secret. I need another toke, draw it in. 'What are we talking about here? There are different kinds of secrets. Some are relatively harmless.'

'This one isn't,' he says.

Through the smoke, the boy's eyes are watering. Maybe that's normal with him, I can't remember. I feel too old to bear any burdens. That time has gone. 'I don't know that I'm the best person to tell a secret . . .' I begin. I want to call the boy by his name. 'I can't remember your name.'

'Jackson, Mr D.'

'Of course, Jackson. My apologies. But therein lies the problem. I suspect this is an important secret, yes?'

'Yeah.'

'My fear is that if you tell me your secret, I may not remember that it *is* a secret and I might tell someone. More likely, though, I'll just forget whatever it was you told me, and what help is that? You wanted to share your secret and the person you trust loses it.'

'Right,' says the boy, though I'm not sure he's understood what I said. In fact I'm not sure I said what I meant to say. And can no longer remember what I did say. 'Another toke, Mr D?'

'What a good idea!' I take another deep drag. *Oh yes!*

THE SUA-BENSEN house was a world away from the Bishops'. The street was almost all private houses and Number 45 was the pick of them, a two-storey ex-statie given the full reno – double garage lock-up at the side and a big lean-to extension at the back with an ultra-modern kitchen. At least it had been when Ellie was last here.

She cruised past, parked and skimmed the police summary. It might have been a duplicate of the one she'd read four years ago, and the one before that – although the first complaint, she now recalled, had been made by Alana. A oncer. The second complaint was from the next-door neighbours – also a oncer. Within six months they'd been forced to sell up and move. This time, on Saturday night, the complaint had been made by a taxi driver who was dropping people off across the street. Alana's screams carried clearly, but his fares simply hurried inside as if they were deaf. The driver rang the cops before he took off. Alana, the report said, showed no visible injuries, refused to be examined by a doctor, but 'looked traumatised'.

At least Eric the Red, as Sua-Bensen was known, couldn't get to the taxi guy. That nickname had to be either a joke – Sua-Bensen was a big, very good-looking brown man – or a warning, to do with his gang colours or his propensity for blood. He was patched, his father had been patched, his grandfather had been patched. The proceeds of crime enabled Alana and the children to live well, but in a cage of violence.

Ellie thought about the food parcels and toys in the boot, but that wasn't what Alana and her four children were missing so Ellie left it shut and walked up the concrete path to the door. Four years ago, Alana had feared Eric, but had also been in awe of him. She hadn't believed she could ever escape him or the gang, that she had no choice but to put up with him and keep him happy. And the brutal truth was that there *was* no way out for Alana, short of Sua-Bensen disappearing off the face of the earth. They weren't married, but the violent relationship would continue until someone died. Unfortunately, it wouldn't be him.

She remembered her last Christmas drinks, three years back, with the advocates in a bar in Kingsland. After a few wines, the conversation among the women had inevitably gravitated to work maybe because it was sometimes too hard to share the daily brutality at home. The talk got funny, then it got dark.

That day, a gangsta whose partner she was helping had wished one of the advocates, Ngaire, a Merry Christmas, then told her that it only cost about five k to off someone. Make them disappear, he'd said, to clarify the threat.

'Really?' Ngaire had replied. She was close to retirement, grey-haired, with a late-middle-aged frailty about her, but she'd had the guts and presence of mind to reply that he shouldn't put ideas in her head, because if that was true there'd be a much cheaper and more efficient way for the agency to deal with intransigent offenders like him.

They'd laughed and drank to Ngaire's chutzpah, then the idea took flight, of what their world might look like if the agency started putting contracts out on the worst offenders, the recidivists, the irredeemables, the ones they knew would eventually kill.

'Just take them out,' said Ngaire gaily, sipping her rum and Coke. 'Get rid of them, wipe them off the face of the earth, and—' She'd shrugged. 'Problem solved, actually. No one will miss these bastards, no one will mourn them. Everyone associated with them will be better off. Merry Christmas!' They'd all laughed and raised their glasses again, except one of the secretaries, who'd taken the suggestion seriously. 'Wouldn't that be, like, eugenics?'

One of the other women said it wasn't about eugenics because these cretins had already procreated. It was about saving the women and children they'd already maimed.

It was Rosemary, the academic, who'd suggested it might stack up on a cost/benefit analysis: that if you could cull twenty of the worst offenders for five k each, say, that was only a hundred k per annum, an eighth of the agency's annual operating budget. 'Just imagine the effect – each year, twenty of the worst offenders are permanently removed from the agency's books, so after five years, for an outlay of half a million, you've got rid of a hundred brutal recidivists who would never offend again. You could multiply that by a factor of ten, say, in terms of the people they affected – the women, the children, their neighbours, their children's friends, the teachers, their mothers, fathers, cousins.'

'Not to mention their social workers and DV advocates,' said Ngaire. 'Multiply by twenty! Imagine the downstream savings, the millions saved on hospital and prison services, the millions more outlaid on wrap-around social services on these scum and their victims. Zip. Gone. No judge, no jury, no appeal. Brutal summary justice in the dead of night, the sort these bastards understand.'

Ellie had been right with them. Word would travel. Within that five years, she reckoned, the worst of them would be gone, and potential offenders would be warned off – there'd be a bigger bully in town. There'd be millions of dollars available for other social services, for education, health, they'd be able to mothball half the prisons.

By then the laughter had dried. It was a sober moment. That night, as the women drank in anticipation of Christmas, of being with their families while mayhem was being visited on women and children in other homes, there was a moment when they'd looked at each other in silence, both amazed and fearful at the vision they'd laid out. And how truly attractive it was.

***

WHEN the door opened, Ellie had to adjust her sightline downwards. A shy girl of about eight was partly obscured. 'Have you come to see Mummy?'

As Tanya, Ellie remembered from the arrest report, led her down the hallway, past the stairs, towards the back of the house, Ellie heard Alana calling to her daughter – 'Come and tell me who it is, darling.' But Tanya was determined to show, not tell.

'This lady was at the door,' said Tanya, as she ushered Ellie into the open-plan kitchen and dining room. Alana, now much bigger than Ellie remembered, was lying on a window seat behind the table, propped up with cushions. She had a beautiful open face, which, Ellie was disappointed to see, was registering alarm at the sight of her visitor. 'Oh shit,' she said, 'you can't be here.'

'I'm pleased you remember me, Alana,' Ellie lied.

Alana's face was unmarked, but she didn't seem to be able to get comfortable and was clearly in pain with every breath she drew. Sua-Bensen never left bruises where they were visible. Ellie was hoping that, now she was here, Alana might ask her to sit down, but her expression hadn't changed; in fact, she seemed terrified. She kept looking up, as if beseeching Ellie to do the same. Was it God she was supposed to be seeing? Then she got it: Sua-Bensen was upstairs.

Ellie had to hold her terror in, and back away slowly, as if the mad dog could actually see her, not just hear her. She raised her voice. 'Lovely to see you looking so well, Alana, but I can tell you're really busy and I've got these other people I've got to call in on.'

'Can you show the nice lady out, darling?' said Alana, the relief on her face palpable.

'But Mummy–'

'Sorry I can't stay for a cup of tea, Tanya – another time.'

The stairs were between Ellie and the front door. She had to get past them before he came down and blocked her exit. She mimicked telephoning. *Ring me.* She couldn't risk leaving her card, but Alana would know how to make contact by now, if she was able to. 'I'll call you anyway,' she whispered. 'Please pick up.'

The hallway was still empty as Ellie went past the banisters towards the front door. She daren't look up the stairs: if she did, she would break and run. At the door, she turned to the little girl. 'I'm very sorry, Tanya, that I can't stay.'

'Mummy's weeing blood.'

As Ellie walked back up the path to the street, she kept her gait as calm and regular as possible, gave no hint of the panic inside her, though she could feel his eyes on her back. She slipped gratefully into the car, but realised that, from upstairs, Sua-Bensen would have clocked her rego. Nothing she could do. *Drive. Get away.*

Back on the main street, she pulled over. She wanted to ring the district court and berate the useless clerk who'd left the hyphen out of Sua-Bensen's name so that he was called early. Instead, she tried to compose herself with one eye in the rear-vision mirror, and rang the police Family Violence Team number. You took your chances on who answered the phone, but this time she was in luck. A sergeant she'd never spoken to before answered the phone, took note of the information and told her she'd get a unit to Sua-Bensen's house as soon as one became available.

***

SHE'D had worse happen – the Sua-Bensen thing wasn't even a confrontation, really – but she'd been younger. As she drove on, she was having trouble getting her heartbeat down. Stopping her hands from shaking and sweating on the steering wheel. Keeping her eyes on the street ahead, instead of constantly checking the rear-vision mirror. If she had Sua-Bensen and his cohorts figured right, they'd be driving a late-model top-of-the-range fully tricked-out ute or SUV, or one of those American gangsta cars. But every modern car behind her, even the latest and smallest, seemed to have huge grilles, most of them blacked out. They looked like a school of sharks, with gaping toothless mouths. But she could imagine the teeth.

Once within the confines of the hospital carpark, Ellie felt safer. People everywhere, witnesses. And, if the worst came to the worst, A & E a wheelchair ride away. She usually read the police arrest report in the car, but she felt too unsettled, so she shouldered her bag and headed for the cafeteria. She decided not to risk a coffee and ordered a smoothie which, according to the menu, contained some berry with destressing properties. She was there to see Miriama Hohepa, who'd been admitted to intensive care on Saturday night with extensive injuries – fractured ribs, ruptured spleen, broken nose, eye socket and cheekbone, and concussion. 'Like a road crash', the attending officer had written. Her partner or husband was still at large. Her hands were still shaking too much to get the report out of her bag, so she decided to wing it. When she reached the thoracic surgery ward, no Miriama. The duty nurse was flummoxed for a moment: yes, she could confirm that Ms Hohepa's ruptured spleen had been removed in the early hours of Sunday morning.

Ellie was rerouted to the neurological ward. At some point the surgeons had realised that Miriama's concussion symptoms had helped to mask the fact that she'd had a stroke, most probably while she was being beaten. Ellie followed the charge sister's directions to a room at the end of a long corridor. She'd warned her that Miriama was comatose and probably unable to talk anyway, since the stroke had affected her speech and hearing. The severity and long-term effects were yet to be accurately assessed. Ellie wasn't to try to talk to her. The charge sister gave her every excuse to turn and go, but Ellie couldn't go back to the agency and tell Rosemary that.

She tiptoed into the room, as if Miriama might have magically revived, but there was no chance of that. She was a diminutive Māori woman, a couple of low bumps under the sheets, hooked up to three different tubes, one down her throat. The eye further from Ellie was covered by a bandage that extended down to the broken socket and cheekbone. It looked enormous. Miriama's other eye wasn't bandaged. The pouch beneath it was black with blood that must have drained from her broken nose.

Ellie sat there in shock. Eventually, she lifted her bag onto her knees. This evil couldn't be a one-off, surely. Even if Miriama's relationship with this monster was new, he would have committed other atrocities. She took out the arrest sheet, intending to look for previous, but didn't get past the names at the top of the preamble. The woman's partner, the offender, who had previously served three years for serious criminal assault on this same victim, was Dwayne Michael Collins. Ellie's watering eyes skated across the name, although it did ring a bell. It was the next two names that froze her: the children of this long-term abusive relationship. A daughter, Lila Hera Collins, nineteen, living at the home address out the back of New Windsor, and a son, Jackson Terei Collins, sixteen, a ward of the state, current address unknown.

Ellie bent forward and rested her head in her hands. She had to get out of here before Miriama woke up, she knew that much. Because Ellie had been unable to talk to her, any conflict of interest was still theoretical. She'd hand the file over to Rosemary as soon as she got back to the office. She stood up and started pushing the material back into her bag. She'd forgotten to turn her mobile to silent, and grabbed it quickly when it rang, missing the name on the screen.

'Ellie?' said the voice. 'It's Teresa.' Ellie knew the voice and name from somewhere but it was so out of context – *she* was so out of context . . . 'From the clinic. You were going to ring me about a donor. Is this a bad time?'

She thought of saying she'd ring back, but the day wasn't going to get any better. Sitting beside this broken woman in the neurological ward was as peaceful as it was going to get.

Ellie remembered a line at the bottom of the information sheets, the very last question, a kind of afterthought: '*Would you be willing to meet a potential recipient before she starts treatment if you were asked?*' '*I'm sweet with that,*' SD 00007982 had written. '*Up to them.*' When she asked whether it was possible to meet SD 00007982, there was a long pause before Teresa said she'd see what she could do.

Ellie thanked her and cradled the mobile in both hands as if it might be a talisman. *What are you looking for?* was the question she thought Teresa might ask. *What are you expecting to see?* Ellie was so glad Teresa had the experience and good grace not to ask, because Ellie wasn't sure of the answer. If she used this donor's sperm to impregnate her egg, there would be this inchoate soul inside her, someone new, who couldn't be known in advance. But she wanted her choice to at least be informed by elements she couldn't measure or evaluate simply by reading an information sheet. Tenderness, compassion, emotional intelligence. The child might be male. She needed to be sure that she didn't bring another beast into the world. If she was to have a son, she had to see his father, she had to ask him about his mother and his two sisters, she had to look into his eyes and see what she needed to see when he talked about the women in his life.

WILL WANTED TO fuck her then and there. He could feel his cock lifting against his jeans. Claudia had brought clean towels into the steamed-up bathroom, and when he'd hoisted pink, cherubic Archie from the water into the towel she held, his forearms had brushed against her breasts. They'd stood there up against one another, Archie swaddled between them, nestled in under the swell of her as they kissed across him. 'Stay,' she whispered. 'Stay and fuck me.'

And he would have. Yelena's mantra, one of many, would have counted for nothing. *Wait until you want it, then wait some more. Enjoy self-denial. Take the power back, the power over yourself. Saying no is powerful.* Fuck that! Two months of abstention on every level was enough: Claudia was a voluptuous fuck and he missed that. She was also so fecund she'd probably already conceived just from his hands on her tits. Luckily, the kids were better than prophylactics. He could have held off until Archie had been read his story, but then there'd be another couple of hours before Kristin was ready for bed. He could even have tried for that, but for an appointment he couldn't miss.

He climbed up to Great North, turned right and headed west, back to Grey Lynn. He remembered walking along this ridge just a couple of months ago, but it seemed as if years had slipped by. Time flies when you're high, he used to say. The converse was equally true: it sure as hell slows when you're low. And he'd had a lot of that. Learning a new business had been some help, but commercial realtors didn't work weekends, and he'd found those hardest to fill, when he wasn't with the kids.

Being in commercial property gave him a different take on the buildings he was walking past. He'd started seeing figures instead of concrete and steel: cap rates and square metre rates, and gross rent multipliers and replacement values minus allowances for depreciation. His head was now so full of this shite he felt like a fucking quantity surveyor. But Yelena had been right again. Basic needs. People needed shelter, people needed a place to sleep, a place to work. They didn't need fucking TVCs and they didn't need the crap the TVCs were trying to sell. But although Will was grateful to Yelena for the break, commercial property wasn't necessarily his gig, long term.

He'd actually enjoyed finding a lessee for the Flame building. Talking it up was easy because he knew so much about it. The hard part was cleaning the place out. Getting rid of the accumulated filmic and office bric-a-brac was like emptying your father's garage after he'd carked. Virtually every object trailed a sliver of history, and the more he threw in the skip, the angrier he got with the failure of it all, the futility, the humiliation, and the more he threw in the skip. Everything would have gone to the tip if Trish hadn't remonstrated. He'd even have ditched the Avid, which turned out to be worth fuck all anyway – there's nothing so worthless as outdated technology. Trish'd run a garage sale of the costumes and props, plastic swords and retractable knives and weaponry mainly, and kept the proceeds after slipping him a couple of hundred, and they were done. Gone, over forty years of Den and Branko's lives, and a fair chunk of his own. He was glad for the end of it. Savage, clean.

The next thing was the sale of the section. With what he knew, he could run the campaign himself, save on land agent's commission – or take it himself off the top. That'd give him some breathing space, to sort those insurance fuckers for the fire. Then . . . then he'd be able to move on. Jump. Once he found a place to land. Commercial property wasn't it. Sooner or later, he would find something else that people needed, something they would pay for. He would keep his eyes peeled for the right opportunity. And he would keep his memory keen, sharpen it like a blade on steel, for those who had fucked him over.

Looking west through the grey dusk, he saw a darker shade looming above the Waitākeres. Rain coming in. He quickened his pace. He didn't mind keeping Lila waiting, but fucked if he was going to get wet.

***

THE fish and chip shop closed the vats on Mondays, but somehow the fatty miasma lingered in the stairwell, and he was close to vomiting by the time he'd fought his way up through it to his flat. He'd scarcely recovered his breath when his mobile belched: *I'm here.* He crossed back to the door and unlatched it. She was there, in her black coat and even blacker shades. Twitchy as all fuck. But not like she was strung out on short rations waiting for the next hit, something different. Nervous. Anxious. Maybe because she didn't know why she'd been summoned. He hadn't seen her in weeks, since he told her, finally, after a few false endings, that he was finished with P, he was no longer buying. It was funny: he'd thought maybe the sex would be harder to stop than the dealing, but not fucking Lila had hardly been an issue. He'd sort of known that the fucking had always just been an adjunct of the deal. Once the ice was on ice, so was the sex.

Yelena had warned him that it wasn't so much the physical cravings that would get him, it was all the space in your head the drugs used to fill. You have to keep your brain occupied, she'd said. She was the prime example: constantly talking, doing, thinking, theorising. She was fucking exhausting to be around; no wonder she collected sponges like Ellie. Yelena had a theory about everything and most of her advice was pretty good, as long as you stayed away from geopolitical conspiracies. She'd talked about Dionysus, who she said was the Greek god of sex, drugs and rock'n'roll, whose appetite – a bit like hers, from what he could gather – was unquenchable.

There was another goddess she mentioned – he couldn't remember her name, maybe it was Eleanor – who was all sweetness and light and nurturing. Yelena said she believed in those polarities: they were presented in the gods as male and female, but she reckoned both elements were in us all. That might not be true of women like Claudia and Ellie, Will thought, but it was certainly true of Yelena. And of him. There was a part of him that still missed being out of control, the part of him freewheeling downhill with no handbrake.

Why was Lila so anxious? He doubted that she would have objected if he'd wanted to reinstate their relationship. Then she lowered her black shades and revealed an even blacker eye, the left one, completely closed. Must have been a flush right cross. Shit. 'Dad's gone loco, tried to scam the supplier,' she said. 'He's off his fucking head.'

'I'm sorry, Lila.'

'Yeah, well.' She was twitchy as, wouldn't leave the door, had her hand on the handle, like if she let it go she was lost. *Just tell me what the fuck I'm here for.*

'I know where your brother is.'

***

THE neon fish wasn't leaping tonight, so he had a clear view down to Lila, crossing the street to the crappy grey hatch and getting into the passenger side. He clocked the driver. Same guy. Her father, the white-trash whippet with a mullet. Same denim jerkin. One tattooed arm hanging out the window, with a cigarette dangling in his closed fist, swinging, impatient to be gone.

WE'RE HAVING BAKED beans on toast again for dinner, and it's as at least as good as last night, maybe due to the mahi – that's what he calls it – we've done. We've got most of the buds stripped and packed away from the weather in the back of the bivvy. There's still room for the sun-loungers in there, so we're sweet if the rain does come tonight. When I say we, it's really been the boy doing the work. I think I've been some help, but there've been a few blanks. A couple of times, I was carrying armfuls of leaf from the swimming pool up to the table, and the boy had to lead me back from the rose garden. I was deeply apologetic, but he said it was sweet – everything is with him – because I'd been talking to my missus. I can't remember doing that, but it stands to reason that Carol would like being around her roses. So he encouraged me to take some of the old leaf down to the roses after the buds were stripped, and lay it down as mulch.

I'm following his movements with the knife and fork. I think my fingers are getting better, but can that be real? The fire is keeping the shadows at bay, but the boy chews and listens, chews and listens, just like last night, as his eyes keep raking the edge of the darkness. The night definitely smells of rain, and the boy gets up to put some more wood on the fire, telling me he won't bother lighting the torches tonight because we'll probably have to take shelter in the bivvy soon. It's then, as he turns from the fire, that he sees something. It's not that he says anything, just the look on his face. I'm spooked by that, even before I twist in my chair and see the face, whitish in the dark, staring in at us from the other side of the gate.

ELLIE WAS DRIVING west along Tamaki Drive, making good time against the flow of traffic out of the CBD. She'd wanted to beat the rain. She was surprised how late it was as she left the refuge and headed back across town. The refuge, one of about ten secret addresses across the city, depended on the discretion and goodwill of neighbours who must surely have noticed the comings and goings of the ever-changing rag-tag procession of women and children.

Simone had been inventive and reassuring with her children, turning the strangeness of the house, the bunks and communal kitchen into an adventure, 'like camping'. Her lawyer had rung back and Simone's occupation and protection orders were in train. She would be able to go home on Wednesday, after the locks had been changed, all the windows secured and an alarm installed. Ellie would go with them, in case Lyall was there and the orders needed to be immediately activated.

She was bone-tired but floating. She'd done a great job of remembering all the shit about the job, but had forgotten this part, the sheer exultation when she managed to put together a safety plan that had started to work, and a woman and her children had successfully taken the first huge step to safety.

At the end of Quay Street, Ellie dived out of the thickening traffic, turned under the overpass and threaded through the streets behind the Viaduct Basin to the chandlers and kayak and paddleboard shops at Sailors Corner, then on to Westhaven Drive, which took her around to the base of the harbour bridge, now lit up and looking even more like a giant coathanger.

She couldn't imagine any other work that could possibly give her this degree of stress or the same suffusing high of satisfaction. And Teresa had called back. Tomorrow after work she'd go to the clinic and meet SD 00007982. That he was willing to meet her was in itself a good sign. Maybe he'd be the one. Maybe she could love her life again.

The rain seemed to be holding off. She'd get to Den and Jackson before it arrived, make sure Den stayed warm and dry overnight. Then what? She didn't know. Pity there wasn't a refuge for the old and bewildered that didn't cost and arm and a leg. Or maybe there was: if she couldn't find it, who could? She had to think about the best way of telling Jackson about his mother. She'd rung the hospital late afternoon and there was no change in Miriama's condition. Serious but stable. She'd spare Jackson the details.

She pulled into the driveway and edged up the dark bush-lined tunnel to the parking bay, swung right and was alarmed to see a grey hatchback already parked. It wasn't a car she recognised. When she passed the passenger window, she saw the red ember of a cigarette flare. It was Lila, sitting smoking quietly in the car. In dark glasses. She blew smoke out the window as Ellie leant in. 'You're better not to go up there,' said Lila. 'Sorry.'

**

ELLIE began running up through the dark garden, then slowed, fearful of what she might see, willing herself to take the next step. Steps. Then she heard Jackson's voice, plaintive, followed by a terrified scream, cut off, then silence, which she was drawn into, as fast as she could go, through the garden gate and up to the deck, where she could see a figure framed in the fire from the oven, lifting the tomahawk, about to bring it down on someone or something lying in shadow. She screamed. The figure, a man in a denim jerkin, whipcord thin and quick, turned towards her. The slumped form on the ground must be Jackson, she thought, because her father was walking into the firelight now, drawing a pistol from his pocket, for God's sake. A pistol from props, some kind of souvenir from Flame. Maybe Will gave it to him after the clearout. He pointed it at what must be Dwayne Collins, Jackson's father. Den was screaming 'Enough! Enough!' in a strangled voice, close to tears. He didn't sound like her father. His voice was so frightened and querulous it sounded like a falsetto. 'Leave the boy!' The man smashed down on Den's arm and the pistol arced across the deck and clattered towards Ellie's feet. Den was yowling in pain, Jackson whimpering from the shadow.

The man raised the tomahawk again. It was so clear what was about to happen. He would cleave Jackson's skull like a gourd. She picked up the pistol and ran at him, yelling. He suddenly pivoted from Jackson to her and raised the tomahawk a couple of feet to the right of her left eye. The man was calling her a cunt as if he knew her. 'Do-gooder cunt.' She remembered a line from some western: 'Never bring a knife to a gunfight.' Instead she'd brought a play pistol from props. His mouth was open in front of her, exuding the same stench as the man in Mount Roskill who punched the wall beside her head. Something chemical. Something rotten. The teeth, those that weren't missing, were brown or black – she couldn't tell in that light. The rancid mouth was spitting at her. She closed her own mouth as his hoick hit her pressed lips and rolled down her chin. 'Useless do-gooder cunt.' He had a thin, reedy voice to match the sneer on his white, unshaven face. He didn't give a fuck about the pistol, must have realised it was a fake. His left hand went for her neck, maybe to hold her head in place for the tomahawk. She cursed her useless fucking father and his useless make-believe world and wished the gun was real and jabbed the barrel at Dwayne Collins' eyes because that's all she could do before the tomahawk smashed her. The gun seemed to come alive, jolted in her hand. She was looking with surprise at the pistol, hardly noticed him falling away, sideways, twisting with the force of the bullet, then head first to the deck.

Her father was there beside her, dancing, exultant, holding up his arms like a victorious boxer. 'Walter, you little bottler!'

She looked at him. 'Walter?'

'Walter worked!' he crowed, 'after all these years!' Then, as if by way of explanation of the obvious, he indicated the pistol, now hot in her hand. 'I was keeping him for something. I had a plan, I knew I had a plan, I'd just forgotten what it was.'

There was someone at the gate, opening it, coming in. Lila approached her father tentatively, as if expecting him to rise up in a rage. He was face down, thin and flat against the decking, the filthy mullet piled up on the back of his head, one side of the bloody bone-splintered exit wound. He looked like a dead possum. Road kill.

Lila bent over him, as if to take his pulse or see if there was anything she could do. But it wasn't a heartbeat she was looking for inside the greasy denim jerkin. She withdrew a wallet, then ferreted in the pocket of his jeans. She stood up with a bunch of keys, pocketing the wallet inside her black coat. 'I'll get rid of the car for you.'

Jackson was stirring, trying to get up. Lila looked across at her brother. 'He's had worse,' she said, then walked across to the gate and disappeared into the darkness of the garden.

What the fuck happens now? Ellie looked at Jackson, trying to get to his feet. She should help him. She should. She couldn't move.

Den did it. He seemed enlivened. Maybe he was concussed or maybe the blow he took had shaken up a connection and some synapses were back in play. Jackson was getting his bearings as Den helped him to his feet, staring at his father. 'Is he dead?'

Ellie just nodded. She didn't really know but it seemed pretty clear. Should she tell Jackson she was sorry? She wasn't. She was still hyper, the adrenaline had nowhere to go and her whole body was starting to shake.

Jackson limped across to the corpse. He was bleeding from a wound in his head, the blood running down into his mouth. He sucked some in and spat it down on his father. Then he turned to

Ellie and Den, his face shining with blood in the light from the fire. 'Should we bury him, you reckon?'

'Good idea!' said Den. 'The roses!'

Ellie looked at her father, his wild hair dancing in the light, as alive as she'd seen him since the night of the fire, but obviously losing it. 'Roses?'

'Blood and bone. Carol says the roses like a good feed.'

winter

THE NEWS, NOT entirely unexpected, but a shock anyway, had come late Friday afternoon. Stan was sitting at the big outdoor table – a slab of macrocarpa, religiously oiled with linseed over the years but now massively ravined by sun and rain – with Lester, who had rested his crutches on the back of his chair and stretched out his left leg so the scar could catch the winter sun. The knee looked red and fierce, Lester's old skin pulled tight across the wound by stitches and staples barely containing the swelling underneath. Lester resented the artificial knee: it was a sign of weakness, that the unremitting toil of living sustainably off-grid had worn him out and forced him to seek help from a medical system he'd shunned. He'd had no choice: there'd been so many things he could no longer do.

The main winter power source, a little hydro unit that sat in the watercourse on the other side of the house, relied on an intake further up in the bush. This kept clogging up, and during his first winter here, after the Wwoofers had flown like godwits back to the northern hemisphere, Stan had been the one who'd clambered up the rocky gorge to clear bracken and dead foliage from the grate so the water could flow and keep the little turbine whirring. Even back then, seven years ago, neither Lester nor Penny could get up there. Now there were others who could do that for them, the twins, or even nine-year-old Nathaniel, agile as a possum. But Lester would at least be able to clean the big solar panels, shifted, for accessibility, from the roof to a patch of north-facing slope nearby.

There were things Stan needed to say to Lester, and now was the perfect time, here in the last rays of the short winter day, looking out at Lester's beloved Kahurangis. It was Lester who had articulated the vision that had originally drawn Stan to Te Kurahau: 'We're building an alternative to the violent and acquisitive society around us.' That had seemed so simple, so self-evident when Stan was twenty-five, but now, at thirty-two . . . He owed Lester a decent discussion, an expression of his doubts, even if the older man ended up hurt and, possibly, angry. But Lester wasn't just worn out physically, he was pretty much talked out these days, so the longer they sat there with the sun falling at their backs and lighting up the snow-capped peaks in front of them, the more difficult it became. Stan had left it too long. Where would he start? With a half-truth? Was a lie better than an omission?

When he finally mustered some resolve to begin the conversation and looked across, Lester's eyes were closed. Stan marvelled again at the strength of those old bones, bullet bald pate melding to high forehead, falling to the granite lines of nose and cheekbones, the lower face framed by a white beard that hugged his jaw and climbed up to his temples. He looked like an Amish elder. In the seven years Stan had been here, Lester had become closer to him than his own father. He was thinking exactly that when Jackson came up the track through the gardens.

Lester didn't approve of cell phones, the power they demanded from the storage batteries, but Jackson had been able to keep the mobile Ellie had given him powered up by the battery of the old house-truck where the Wwoofers lived in summer. Pretty much every other day Jackson would trek down to the little hill of pines where he could get patchy reception. He would keep in touch with his sister, he said, but mostly he called Ellie, his 'guarding angel', and as a result, Stan was better informed about his family than he'd been since he first left home at seventeen.

Through Jackson, Stan knew that his father had suffered a blitz of those unseen strokes and had been left so debilitated he was now living in a secure dementia facility in Herne Bay. Yesterday, when Jackson had called, Ellie had been visiting 'Mr D'. She had warned Jackson that Den was down to two words, 'Excellent!' and 'Enough!', which began and ended the conversation, with nothing in between. But when she'd put Jackson on, Den had recognised his voice and said other things.

'What things?' Stan had asked.

Jackson had been reluctant to say, so Stan speculated that his father had been rude.

'He was never,' said Jackson.

Turned out that Den had spoken a kind of code. 'Down tools,' he'd said. 'Lights out. Smoko!'

Jackson said it was kind of an in-joke, but seemed troubled by Den's words, and had gone down to the pines today to make a follow-up call. Stan was about to call out, 'What news from the front?' but something in Jackson's gait, perhaps the urgency, stopped him. Jackson was silhouetted by the lowering sun, straggly hair flaming red. When the sun dropped behind the mountains across the valley at their back, the last range before the wild west coast, it instantly took both light and heat, and Stan could see the details of Jackson's thin face, tight and tense. Chill rose up from the ground, hit the bare skin of Stan's face like a slap. He shivered and knew.

***

NEXT morning, Stan wanted to get started before anyone was up and about, so he wouldn't have to replay the goodbyes of last night. All those 'See you soons', hugs and kisses, even from the men. Stan was convinced that men like Aaron and his older brother Will – perhaps even Lester at times – saw something weak and wounded in him, so when it came to man-hugs and handshakes, Stan braced himself and tried to get a decent purchase, make a strong grip. He felt like a fraud, particularly with the kids, his home schoolers. The adults, other than Aaron, might find it easier to understand once they knew, but in the meantime he had to go. He couldn't stay here with his secrets.

He'd woken at 5.30, dressed in the same outfit he'd worn to his father's seventieth, when Will said he looked as if he'd just stepped off an R. M. Williams clothes-horse. Fuck Will, they were Rodd & Gunn, a label he'd never heard of before he saw their window display and walked in. He put some old undies and socks in his day-pack, a toothbrush, a razor, then stood at the centre of the yurt for a moment or two, and looked around for something else to pack. After seven years here, there was nothing else to take away, except the books he'd packed into a small carton last night. They were the ones Rachel had given him and which he felt he should return. After they'd confided their dysfunctional families to each other, she'd quoted Tolstoy – 'All happy families are alike; each unhappy family is unhappy in its own way' – but told him not to bother reading the old Russian because unhappy families had given rise to some wonderful modern literature, real and funny and dark and strangely uplifting. So he'd read the novels she'd given him: Anne Enright's *The Green Road*, A. M. Homes' *May We Be Forgiven*, Jonathan

Franzen's *The Corrections* and Maggie O'Farrell's *This Must Be The Place*, and now he couldn't leave without them, though the Franzen was touch and go – so many pages of unnecessary detail, so many trees that could have been left uncut. When he looked about, there really wasn't a lot he would miss. The yurt had been a good shelter, not much more. It had a small wood burner, which struggled against the lack of insulation from the plastic windows.

He closed the door behind him and moved out into the cold darkness, past the outdoor kitchen with a gas grill that died when the wind turned to the east, and pissed in the grass beside the composting toilet. He wouldn't miss that kitchen, or the dunny you had to be so careful only to shit in. The Toyota Estima was parked next to the house-truck. He'd been intending to load the books in the back, then wake Jackson, but he should have known better: the kid was there, ready to go, as he'd been every morning since he'd first arrived.

'Yo, Stan.'

'You ever sleep?'

'Like a baby down here. Give you a hand? You got a suitcase?'

Stan told him this was it, and asked if there was anything else Jackson wanted to bring.

'Got everything I came with.'

That was true. The same clothes he was wearing when he got off the plane, and the flax kete he'd been carrying, which looked as empty now as it had been then. Ellie hadn't been specific, just that Jackson needed a break from Auckland. 'Who wouldn't,' Stan told her.

Stan shrugged off his day-pack, laid it beside the carton of books and lowered the back door. When he turned back, Jackson was looking out towards the north-east. He pointed at a cluster of stars low in the sky. 'Matariki,' he said, 'Happy New Year, bro!'

Stan recognised them as the Pleiades cluster, Tien Mun, heaven's gate, in China, not that he'd been able to see the night sky in Shenzhen.

'My nan told me the big star would be her, and the six little ones would be the eyes of her tamariki, my mum and her sisters and brothers, and her mokopuna, me and Lila, all of us always watching out for each other.'

'Cool,' Stan said. What he really wanted to say was: Where the fuck *are* they?

'She said we should all get together this time of the year, to look back on what's happened and make a plan.'

'A plan?'

'Y'know, what to do next.'

Jackson didn't strike Stan as disingenuous. Maybe it was just his way of asking what the future might hold for him. But Stan had no idea: after he'd delivered Jackson back to Auckland, that'd be over to Ellie.

'Nan said she made that up,' Jackson continued, maybe to let Stan off the hook. 'The bit about her tamariki and me and Lila. Nan said some people thought the ariki part stood for chief. Like, for you, it might stand for your dad, his eyes looking down at us.'

Stan looked up at the cluster and realised that he hadn't once thought of his father since hearing that he was comatose after suffering a massive stroke. Maybe that was the point Jackson was making. 'Let's go,' he said.

***

AS they traversed the gravel track down through the paddocks to the ruined bridge and forded the river, Stan tried not to think about whether he would ever see the farm again. They turned at the T where the farm entrance met the shingle road down the valley to the sleeping town, then joined the two-lane blacktop leading east out of Collingwood.

He'd driven this road so often. The pictures in his head were of mountain ranges on his right and the curving bay on his left, as he followed the tunnel forged by his headlights through the darkness. Jackson made no further attempt at conversation. Stan was grateful for the silence, and for winter. This road in summer was full of tourists, many in vans just like his, rent-a-dent crapola, big enough to sleep in, store some food and a gas cooker, but no room for a dunny – the signature vehicles for the notorious freedom campers who shat their way across the country. In turn, vans like Stan's got shat on by the locals, dirty looks, blasting horns, cut off by big utes charging past, pointed questions as soon as it parked. It would be sort of okay as soon as his accent declared him a local, but sometimes even that didn't help. Stan felt like saying, Hey, I shit in a compostable toilet at home. What do you do?

Tourism was the lifeblood of the district, and many of the locals now relied on clipping the tourist ticket in one way or another, but the co-dependency had become increasingly fraught. Stan couldn't be sure that the divisions and tensions weren't here before he came, but they hadn't been as patent. They passed an idyllic spot beside the Tākaka River, bulldozed and landscaped so vans like Stan's couldn't hide.

The tensions weren't all imported. Further back, they'd passed a side road leading off to the Te Waikoropupū Springs. Stan wondered whether a sign he'd seen last summer was still there, placed prominently in a paddock just before you turned onto the little road that led down to what was reputed to be the purest water in the world, sacred to local iwi. The last thing the tourists saw before they entered the reserve was a sign put where it couldn't be missed: '*Wanted: Person or Business To Market Spring Water.*' For Lester that sign summed up the obscenity of commerce, its encroachment on the valley. And, with that at least, Stan could not disagree.

As they crossed the bridge before Upper Tākaka, Stan looked for and saw in the grey mist of dawn, the huge herd of dairy cows down beside the river. Sure, the farmer had fenced off the water, but there was no way that number of animals could graze on porous alluvial soils without leaching nitrate, piss and shit into the river and aquifers.

Light was filling the sky as the old Toyota began struggling up the big hill. The road had been washed out in several places by Hurricane Gita, and most of the repairs had been completed before the latest weather bomb wrecked it again. They'd had to reinstall traffic lights to control the remaining one-lane track across the precipice of slips above and below the road. Stan marvelled that the road was open at all. When he'd seen the huge clay gullies which had opened up and taken whole hillsides down into the ravines, he'd despaired that the road could ever be safely reinstated. For people like Lester, the isolation caused by the torrents of rain and mud and debris wasn't a bad thing, and he rejoiced that the area might once again be dependent on coastal shipping for supplies in and out, because that would at least kill industrial dairying. But for Stan it was a warning that the vain little constructs of man, like roads across wild terrain, would fall victim to the new climatic normal. Just one harbinger of many that urged him to get back over the hill while he still could.

***

GITA and that weather bomb had also been a disaster for Te Kurahau. Lester liked to say the Kahurangi National Park was their backyard, but that wasn't strictly true. There was a slice of much darker green on the last small hill at the bottom of Te Kurahau land, rising beyond the organic gardens and pasture, which had been planted in pines by the previous owner. That had been part of a much larger belt of pine plantation between the end of the farm and the beginning of the bush that ran up to the snowline. Lester had always preferred not to see it: he hated pine forests, partly because they smothered any native diversity, but mostly because they were commercial. But that belt beyond the farm was gone, clear-felled by a forestry company two months ago, the dark green now mottled grey scored with huge yellow slips. The foresters had gone by the time the bomb hit, but they'd left live fuses: huge piles of slash and off-cuts that had been swept downstream and had wiped out the old one-way wooden bridge, the only vehicle access to the farm. The bridge was still down, but so was the river, and their vehicles could get through the ford as long as it wasn't raining in the mountains.

The real damage was to the river, their beautiful river with its gravel bed, where they would have summer picnics and parties with the Wwoofers on the bank by the swimming hole. Now it was a silty mess from clay sediment and slash and sludge. It had become clear that if Te Kurahau and everyone further downstream, wanted compensation from the forestry company they could, in the words of the yellow-helmeted bastard who appeared to be one of the owners, 'whistle for it'. Using the reviled court system to sue for compensation for their bridge would be, in Lester's opinion, almost as bad as having to rely on the medical system for a knee that worked. Stan doubted it would happen.

In the meantime, they needed to rebuild the bridge and work out how to pay for it, and that's what they'd talked about last night in Lester and Penny's house. Stan and Jackson had joined Aaron and Malcolm and Isabel around the big table made out of two doors lashed together and overlaid with marine ply, while Penny oversaw the huge cast-iron woodburner oven and water heater. It looked like a giant Aga, but was in fact designed locally and made by some guy in Motueka, freighted over the big hill in pieces. The open-plan kitchen/dining/living room was still warm from the bare concrete floor: there were no rugs, no carpets, to inhibit its heat-retaining and releasing properties. Lester and Penny had angled the eaves of the house to give shelter from the sun in summer and let it fall on the concrete pad in winter; between the woodburner and the floor, the house was never cold.

The kids, Nathaniel and the twins, Jasper and Sarah, came and went at Penny's direction, Nat and Sarah bringing wood, Jasper at the basin washing and chopping the pumpkins, kūmara and Brussels sprouts Stan and Jackson had lifted from the garden that morning, along with the leeks already in the pie. Penny, in her mid-seventies like her husband, face weathered nut-brown, framed by white hair urchin-cut, long, scrawny limbs anchored by a bit of belly these days, looked as if she'd go on a lot longer than Lester, but even she had slowed considerably in the years Stan had been here. Lester stayed in his armchair, with his leg raised, close enough to contribute his bob's worth if he felt moved to do so.

Malcolm, as usual, had led the discussion. Listening to his discourses about pine forests or any aspect of organic farming, you'd never know that he'd turned his back on a career in corporate

PR. And yet you could see the vestiges of that former career in the way he smoothed the edges when personalities clashed, the way he mediated and found a way ahead that everyone could buy into. His wife Isabel matched Malcolm so perfectly in build and colouring – both were small, wiry and sort of prematurely wizened – that you might think there was a bit of narcissism going on, if you didn't know them. Twelve-year-old Jasper and Sarah already looked like their parents' miniature doppelgängers.

Isabel was more introverted than Malcolm, less voluble, but equally kind and generous. She'd been in IT and had built the Te Kurahau website, which made it easier to contact any Wwoofers who were interested in coming this far out of the way. Te Kurahau had no wifi, but Isabel could feed the website every couple of days via the free wifi at the Golden Bay Cafe in Collingwood. Stan usually found an excuse to go with her, just for a change of scenery. Which was telling, now he thought about it.

As well as the twins, Malcom and Isabel had an older daughter, Maddy, fourteen, boarding at high school in Nelson. She'd been home-schooled from the age of seven by Stan, and he sometimes wondered if his teaching had been partly responsible for Maddy wanting to go to a real school over the hill. Maybe that was just the way it went: none of Lester and Penny's five adult children had chosen to come back to Te Kurahau. It was a matter of private sorrow to them both, though they lived in hope that one of them might decide to return sooner or later, with their grandchildren in tow.

Clear-felling their own pines on the little hill at the bottom of the farm would give them more than enough cash, said Malcom, but they'd have to live with the risk of erosion until the new natives developed decent root systems, a four- to five-year window in which the soil was increasingly vulnerable, due to the frequency of bad weather. Stan listened as Malcolm talked about an alternative concept: continuous harvesting, where batches of mature trees could be felled every year and replanted in mānuka. The batches they felled would have to be big enough to allow sun and light into the fledgling mānuka, but not so great that the root system holding the surrounding land together would be made unstable. Malcolm reckoned that over, say fifteen years, if they were careful, they could replace that pine forest with mānuka, which would give them as much high-grade honey as they could eat.

As well as financing the bridge rebuild, Te Kurahau needed a modicum of actual money for petrol and parts and regos for the vehicles, rates and so on. Some of that they got locally by bartering their produce, and they could always sell at the Nelson farmers' market, or offer lessons in organic farming, and Isabel and Malcolm would run open days for $25 a head if they were really desperate.

Te Kurahau also had a capital fund, a trust fund created by Lester and Penny, since augmented by the proceeds of Malcolm and Isabel's family home in Lower Hutt and by an apartment that Aaron and Rachel had sold back in Tel Aviv. They couldn't risk spending any of the capital, but the interest from the fund was never enough, particularly since the rate had dropped post GFC. Finding enough cash to survive was a constant struggle, even with the unpaid labour of the Wwoofers. The pine forest was a unique opportunity. But Malcolm's concept wouldn't give them the big immediate cash injection they'd get from clear-felling – enough to rebuild the bridge and cover everything else for a year or two.

Aaron, an ex-Israeli Army engineer, was the beekeeper, wielded the chainsaw on the old logs for the winter fuel, kept the tractor and implements going, could fix anything, from the hydro to the house-truck, hunted wild goats and had become the co-operative butcher, assisting the local man, Selby, who killed and butchered whatever beast would provide their meat for the following twelve months. And every year Aaron would say the same thing, as he wielded the knife: this cow or calf or pig has had a wonderful life, but for this one *very* bad day. Selby had a sign back up the valley that probably freaked some of the passing tourists – '*Home Kill Professional*', with a number to call. Aaron was a tall, dark, spare man of few words and bleak moods, which Stan found intimidating, and even more so since his wife Rachel had gone back over the hill. You didn't waste small talk on Aaron, you didn't just pass the time of day. Whatever you said to him would be gravely considered, as if it might be a rebuttal of the theory of relativity. Inevitably disappointed, Aaron would regard you with what looked like mild contempt, through grey eyes which must have seen life and death up close. He was in favour of clear-felling, of taking the cash and the environmental risk, until Lester weighed in from his armchair. 'We do what is right, not what is lucrative.' And that was that, debate over, even for Aaron.

But not in Stan's head. His eyes had drifted up to an A3 sheet plastered against the macrocarpa cladding at the end of the table. Lester had told him it was Te Kurahau's founding document, and that what had been crossed out was as important as what was written. The sheet was actually a blow-up of the Riverside community's statement of intent, created back in 1990 when that community was still Christian Pacifist. Lester and Penny had been members until 1998, nearly ten years after the statement had been written, when they'd left the community at Lower Moutere and come over the big hill to found Te Kurahau. The first word crossed out was therefore '*Riverside*', which had been replaced by '*Te Kurahau – The School of Vital Essence*'.

Jackson had had a problem with that translation when he first saw it some weeks ago, whispering carefully to Stan. 'Vital essence? What's that?'

Stan said he understood it was a translation of the 'hau' part of Te Kurahau.

'Nah,' said Jackson. 'Hau is, like, soul.'

Stan said he liked the sound of that, but they'd better keep it to themselves. He was humouring Jackson, because so many of the words on that A3 still spoke to Stan's vital essence. Or soul, for that matter. And Lester's abrupt closing of any debate over their pine plantation had once again contradicted one of the tenets up on the wall: '*We choose to share responsibility in policy making, discussion and planning . . .*' Was that reason enough for leaving Te Kurahau in its time of most need? Or an excuse to justify his own selfish ambitions?

The tensions and divisions within the larger community had all come, according to Lester, on the back of commerce, driven by the almighty dollar. He could paint a clear national link between commerce and agricultural opportunism – land use that veered violently between whatever commercial fad held sway at the time: sheep, pinus radiata, dairying. Stan had never made it to Europe, but some of the Wwoofers had eventually given voice to their dismay about what they'd found here in what they thought would be nirvana. They said that much of Germany and France were still rural and had preserved a mix of forests and meadows for centuries. They'd shown him photos from home of rural beauty that made much of the countryside here look like the victim of short-term rapacity. And that was before news came from over the hill that all the blackcurrant bushes were being torn out because the Malaysian company they were supplying had reneged on contracts after finding cheaper suppliers in South America or India or wherever. So the hops that had been ripped out in the eighties were being replanted on the back of a boom in craft beers.

Lester, thought Stan, was like an old fire-and-brimstone preacher from a western. Self-sustainability was his mantra and he railed against the evils of commerce, which was reducing the globe to a polluted hell. That was what had driven him and Penny from Riverside community, as both words and cross-outs further down the A3 sheet showed:

> *We reject private ownership and private profit.*
> *We choose limitation and equality of personal income.*
> *We aim to be self-supporting and to produce goods of*
> *the best quality at a fair price.*
> *We do not want to escape from the world, but to*
> *use our pooled resources to help it through service to*
> *others and practical involvement in social, peace and*
> *environmental movements.*

But what had happened to their river proved, Stan thought but lacked the guts to articulate, that the world could no longer be kept at a distance. Even here in the furthest reaches of Golden Bay. So here they were, in dire need of cash. And there was salvation, Stan knew, sitting at this very table. But salvation had kept its mouth shut.

Te Kurahau had been the perfect sanctuary for his troubled twenties, a place for him to take refuge and recharge and think about what he wanted. He'd arrived with a bunch of young Germans, medical students, with whom he'd camped overnight at

Torrent Bay on the Abel Tasman track. He'd heard a joke, that if you fell on that track and broke an ankle, not to panic, there'd be a German doctor along within ten minutes. Stan reckoned you'd be unlucky these days to have to wait that long. He'd followed the Germans here, and when they left, he'd stayed.

He was proud of his contribution to Te Kurahau, and profoundly grateful to it for rescuing a confused young man with the oppressive humidity and humanity of Shenzhen inside his head. He'd come home at the end of 2010 after two years teaching English as a second language. The Foxconn scandal had just broken, but even before the suicides of those young workers, Stan had picked up from his ESL students that they were mice on the wheel. He'd come home with a sense of hopelessness, that the human race was doomed. Te Kurahau had given him a stable base, rescued him from depression, changed him from being a boy who didn't know what he wanted to do to a man who did . . . He'd thought. Now that man was having his doubts. Te Kurahau was a knot he didn't know quite how to start untying: if he pulled on the wrong strand, he might entangle himself further.

Stan still believed what Te Kurahau had taught him, that there was a kind of personal salvation in planting the soil and growing things. His experiences in the Shenzhen concrete ants' nest might have precipitated that, but he'd probably also inherited something from his mother. His strongest memory of her was being in the garden, Carol in big-brimmed sunhat and gloves and loose cotton chinos, waving her trowel as she explained what she was doing. He'd found that Carol was also a weird connection to Te Kurahau, since so many of the back-to-nature people he met had lost their mothers to cancer – Lester, Isabel, Aaron and Rachel, when she was here.

And parts of that A3 still spoke to his soul:

*We accept all human beings as our brothers and our
sisters and choose to behave towards them with love
and not violence.*
*We strive to develop a fruitful, beautiful countryside
and to make our living in ways that do not harm
the planet: and to study and put into practice safe
horticulture, farming and living.*

But now there was this itch that he'd tried to ignore but couldn't.
He now knew he *could* live sustainably, he could feed and clothe
himself and his family, if he had one, for as long as he lived, and
probably live longer doing it that way. But was that it? For the rest of
his life, until he was old and worn out like Lester? Was *this* it? He'd
felt that question inside him for perhaps the last year, without real
resolution. Until two weeks ago: it was weird how circumstances
conspired to test vulnerabilities.

Stan had never had to pool his assets into the capital fund,
because he'd had none. He'd given himself and his labour
wholeheartedly and it had never been a problem: you gave what
you had. The doctrine of no private ownership had been easy
enough to accept when he had owned nothing. But a fortnight ago,
$500,000 had been credited to an Auckland account he'd thought
was moribund. He'd tried hard to believe in Lester's dictum that
money and commerce were false gods, until that moment. He'd no
idea that money could be an instrument of truth.

It wasn't just the money. There was something else he couldn't
allow himself to even think about last night in front of Aaron, with
those grey eyes boring into him. Stan feared that if the thought
was out there, floating in the ether, Aaron might pick up on it
telepathically. He'd felt an incipient erection in his jeans and was

glad of the big table shielding his lap as he desperately tried to keep thoughts of Rachel at bay.

***

THEY climbed the last of the switchbacks before the road wandered across the flat summit, where dwellings could be seen among the gorse and scrub and mānuka. What did they do up here in the clouds, these people, Stan wondered? Surely no one could endure a daily commute down to Tākaka or Nelson from here?

He pulled the van over to a shingle picnic area gouged out of the side of the hill. He and Jackson got out and looked back towards Golden Bay, unfurling itself in the rising sun, snow-white then green melding into blue as the land fell from the Kahurangis to the sea, then curved round to the mists of Farewell Spit.

Stan became aware that Jackson wasn't looking at the view, he was looking at Stan. 'You're not coming back, eh.'

Stan couldn't trust himself to say anything, or look away from the view.

***

GOING down the other side, tiptoeing through the endless switchbacks, listening to the van's suspension stretching and compressing, down to the red light where the one-lane tarmac ahead looked like a high-wire strung across precipitous clay gouges above and below, Stan had time to look out at another spectacular view, the coastline arcing eastward towards Nelson.

He was unsure why he'd chosen Nelson to come back to, in what turned out to be a long, hot, glorious summer as 2010 morphed into

2011. Maybe because it was pretty much unknown, and he could look at it with alien eyes, like the backpackers and Wwoofers he'd hooked up with, working for their keep round the district, picking, sorting and packing fruit.

He'd only ever been to Nelson once before, as a fourteen-year-old. It was shortly after his mother died, and someone – it must have been his father – had thought it a good idea to get him out of his home environment and send him down for a holiday with his paternal grandparents, Lance and Dorothy. They'd picked him up at the airport and taken him to a caravan in Tāhuna Motor Camp, a site they returned to year after year. The caravan's wheels had been removed and it sat on old railway sleepers. He'd slept on a stretcher under the awning. Until that point, Stan had seen very little of them, probably because, as Lance made clear at every opportunity, Auckland was an abomination on the face of New Zealand and he wouldn't be seen within coo-ee of 'that shit-hole'.

Lance, it turned out, was a tyrant, even asleep, when his buzz-saw snore rocked the caravan. No wonder Dot's eyes looked so unpresent most of the time. Neither of them once mentioned his mother. Maybe they had always disapproved of Carol, Auckland born and bred (of parents who also both died young), or maybe they thought the best way to deal with grief was to pretend it didn't exist.

Stan remembered very little about those two weeks, except one day when he'd been swimming in the gentle waves of Tāhuna Beach. He'd swum beyond the tiny breakers and kept going until he was far enough out to see the whole arc of the beach and the Richmond Range rising up behind. He'd turned away from all that, and floated on his back looking up at the sky and then out to where the sky met the horizon. The thought had come to him that he could just float away, towards that horizon, that that was the best thing that could happen. He floated out there for at least an hour. It was such a benign beach there were no lifeguards, and Lance would be snoring under the umbrella as Dot tried to lose herself in a 400-page romance. As time passed, the idea settled calmly on him, that he would simply drift away. Another boy at Springs, a year older than Stan and also known as a 'social retard', had topped himself by jumping off an overbridge on the north-western highway. Drifting off to the horizon seemed an eminently better way of doing it. And maybe it would have happened, if the tide hadn't turned and brought him back to shore. His eyes were closed to protect him from the salt, but he heard children's voices and splashing, and when he turned over in surprise, his feet touched the sand.

Now he could connect the dots and understand why his father had been so emotionally inept when Carol died, given his parents, but back when a grief-stricken teenage boy needed his father to come closer, Den had been lost in his own grief, and lost to Stan. He'd been *so* lucky to have had an older sister. He was sure of one thing from that time: Ellie had saved him.

'Bro,' said Jackson gently. 'The light's green.'

***

LESS than an hour later, they had crossed the Riwaka plain and the Motueka River Valley, and parked at the Riverside Cafe, the old converted homestead beside the road at Lower Moutere, where Rachel served them breakfast. She was waitressing for friends who had the lease from the community, and was staying in the Riverside Sojourn, a board and batten not far from the cafe, the beginning of the community's houses, which circled up the hill around a central park. When they'd come in, she'd been warm and welcoming but all business, getting them settled at a table and coffees under way. When she came back with the flat whites – Jackson still couldn't order one without a chuckle – she said she'd booked them on a late-morning flight to Auckland.

'Can I show you something?' she said to Stan. He rose and followed her around the corner to an alcove that led to the loos. She stood in front of him, blocking the entrance, took his hand and placed it on her breast above her heart. 'Just me,' she said, then kissed him, pressing herself up against him. 'That's all,' she said, 'I've got work to do.' She walked past him, back towards the tables, then turned and smiled at the rod in his moleskins. 'You might need a moment to compose yourself.'

Back at the table, Stan watched Rachel move about the big room, engaging, graceful. She was in jeans and brocade blouse but he knew that underneath she'd be wearing a plain black leotard, which he'd been hoping for an opportunity to peel off her later, but the timing of the flight would stymie that. She was an Israeli, born of parents who'd shifted to Tel Aviv from the US when she was three. She could remember nothing of Ohio – unsurprisingly, she said, after having gone back there for a look – but still had, to Stan's eyes and ears, something of an American sensibility and accent, a languid ease of speech and movement.

Stan found her surprising, in a good way. She peered myopically at the world through rimless glasses framed by long hair that fell from a central part, sort of John Lennon, circa *Imagine*. The glasses appeared to be too heavy for her nose and needed to be nudged back in place, always by her slender middle finger, never the index, with her ring finger and chunky opal prominent, and her pinky held out as if she was politely taking tea at Buckingham Palace. Maybe it was just a nervous habit now, like a tic, but the glasses and falling hair gave her a bookish air that was thoroughly justified. She'd majored in English literature and then become an editorial assistant at an international publishing house. Rachel seemed extraordinarily well read – she'd read all the classics and many authors Stan had never heard of, mainly Americans, mainly women. She still had an editor's eye and strong opinions, named names, mostly American, mostly male, authors, she said, of bloated egotistical tomes, often late in their careers when – and this, Stan thought, might be the nub of her objection – they could probably bully their editors. Stan didn't feel qualified to argue, but felt perhaps Rachel needed to write to quell her inner critic. One day, maybe he could give her the time to do that.

There was another side to Rachel, a side that sat peculiarly with her bookishness, a driven energy also at odds with her appearance and with the way she moved and spoke. Maybe it came from the kibbutz where she'd volunteered as a teenager, where she'd met Aaron, and which he'd pulled them out of when some of its elements became privatised. She was a worker, who got things done efficiently and without fluster, whether labouring in the gardens, or home-schooling the kids at Te Kurahau, which is where she and Stan had made a real connection. Stan flushed at the memory, and tried not to devour her with his eyes, as she effortlessly covered the tables in front of him. She also had a kind of certainty and decisiveness about her which Stan found very attractive and a bit intimidating. He possessed so little himself, he found it hard to trust in others.

She was certain, for instance, that medicinal cannabis was the wonder drug of the future, and had contacts with the green fairies around the province who would try and supply those in desperate straits. Some of them had been prosecuted, but Rachel had a powerful belief and had been the advocate for the trial plot at Te Kurahau, overcoming even Lester's objections. The plot had failed, not through any genetic problem with the plants, as Jackson had made clear with his stories of success in Auckland, but because they'd been paranoid about it being seen and had planted it in a clearing in the pine plantation that hadn't got enough sun or rain.

When he and Rachel had begun whispering about leaving Te Kurahau, they'd planned to take advantage of public and private opportunities within Nelson to teach English. There were ESL pods for foreign students within some of the established high schools and privately funded intensive courses for adults who wanted to combine tourism with study. But that was before Stan's manna fell from the sky. When Stan confided his windfall to Rachel she'd come up with another altogether more ambitious scheme for how they might make their way out here in the world.

The idea had arisen when she'd learnt that the supplier of fresh lettuces to the cafe, Ron Halston, wanted to sell his hydroponics operation and retire. The lettuces were, apparently, a viable business in their own right, but Rachel could see huge potential in a different crop. She was convinced that legalising the supply of medicinal cannabis would be the first step towards decriminalising recreational use. She'd followed developments in states like Colorado, where growing and selling the plant was huge business, not just for smoking, but in creams and oils and the hemp itself. Big Pharma and Big Business was already gearing up for it here in anticipation, but experience in the States proved, she reckoned, that boutique suppliers of quality product would also have a future, like the makers of artisan craft beers. The success of craft beer was all around them in the Motueka Valley, with thousands of hectares being converted to hops, the tall poles marching across the valley like vineyards for giants. The set-up costs were rumoured to be so great that most of the owners needed foreign investors to help them cover the development, not to mention the harvesting and drying infrastructure. Whereas Ron's lettuces, she said, were easily managed, already paying their way and they could transition into cannabis gradually, as the law and the market changed. To Stan it all made tremendous sense in theory: it might be a way of turning his windfall into a productive, even lucrative, way of life.

Five hundred thousand dollars had seemed an impossible amount of money for a man who had no credit card, no mobile phone and who'd thought he had no bank account until all that money landed in it, courtesy of Will selling the section and releasing his mother's share of the estate. What did you do with such a vast sum of money? What could you possibly spend it on? The lettuces would be a springboard into the world of commerce, a head-first dive into the deep end in fact, but driven by the thing he most loved doing: growing plants.

Rachel had had a preliminary meeting with Ron and Wendy Halston at the cafe, in which, as agreed, she'd deliberately not mentioned cannabis, and had arranged for them to go and view the operation this morning. They'd have time to do that and get to the airport. That was Rachel. The only item she'd left off the agenda was the leotard peel, but that might have been difficult anyway with Jackson riding shotgun.

After breakfast, there'd been time for an update on Nathaniel, and another quick teenage pash in the alcove leading to the loos, before Rachel finished her shift and joined Stan and Jackson in the Toyota. They drove further into the gentle hills of Moutere, up on to the Old Coach Road that ran north–south along a ridge between

Upper Moutere and the coastal highway. There were views west to the big hill and the Kahurangis beyond, and east to the coast and city. They were looking on the eastern side for a letterbox with a number, but needn't have bothered: the glasshouses were visible through established trees in a dale scalloped into the side of the hill.

***

RON Halston was a ball of energy and enthusiasm, a bit dusty round the edges, but otherwise not a man for whom retirement seemed imminent. He'd got out of dairy farming in Southland fifteen years before, he told them, and that had proved to be the right move at the right time. Now he wanted to sell his lettuce business. Stan was too polite to ask why this timing seemed so right.

When Stan told Ron and Wendy, who seemed like the anchor around which Ron swung, about the late-morning flight he and Jackson had to catch, Wendy said she'd get a cuppa ready, and disappeared back inside the brick-and-tile bungalow, as Ron led Stan, Rachel and Jackson back down the shingle driveway, bordered by bare-branched silver birches and liquidambars, to the central glasshouse. Ron told them it had been moved here from the Grove Street area in central Nelson, known as 'little Italy', where one of the Italian families who'd settled in Nelson had built it to grow tomatoes.

Inside, there was a field of green lettuces extending from where they were standing at the western end, for about seventy-five metres to the far end, all at waist height, growing in what looked like lengths of spouting, which Ron called gullies. These sat across rails, and as the lettuces matured, they were gradually moved down the shed, from seedlings at the far end, to mature plants ready for picking, the ones right in front of them. When Jackson exclaimed that was a shitload of lettuces, Ron smiled and gave them the figures – twelve to fifteen thousand in this one shed, which, with the other sheds, produced six thousand lettuces for sale every week.

'Would the wholesale price the cafe pays be about the norm?' asked Rachel.

Ron confirmed that the outlets he supplied around the area, mainly cafes and restaurants, but including one of the supermarket chains, paid about the same, with seasonal variations, and he also grew and supplied fresh herbs, coriander, basil and parsley. He picked a lettuce out of the gully right in front of them, showed them the lovely white roots – brown, he said, meant trouble – then popped it back into its hole. He showed them the electric pump in the corner which pumped water up into the overheard pipes running the length of the shed, and then down into the two hundred and fifty gullies, a litre of water a minute down each one.

'Five hundred litres a minute,' said Jackson.

'A shitload of water,' confirmed Ron with another smile. He showed them how the water dropped down from the gullies after passing through the roots of the lettuces and returned to the pump. 'Each time the water passes through the tank, nutrients are fed in automatically, with sampling machines that measure conductivity and the pH levels. It's all controlled electronically, but it has to be constantly monitored by the human eye, because if it goes wrong, you'll get a shitload of damage real quick.'

Jackson chuckled, but Stan was feeling a bit dismayed, seriously out of his depth, even before Ron started talking about acid burn and tip burn and the need for the big fans in the ceiling to keep the lettuces transpiring.

Ron walked them through the other three sheds, the ones he'd built himself. The two big ones were single-skinned plastic, not glass. 'Things grow better under glass,' said Ron 'but it's harder to clean and when the panes break they're a bastard to access and replace.'

Stan, seriously awed by the hinged roofs and automatic venting systems, asked roughly how much it had cost Ron for each of these sheds.

'Best part of a hundred thousand for each of the big ones,' said Ron, 'and only slightly less for the smaller propagating shed because it's double-skinned for extra warmth.'

Stan could feel his huge wad of money diminishing with each informational sally. He'd arrived here with a fortune, and now it didn't look like enough for a deposit.

By the time they left the sheds, he was overwhelmed by the cost and complexity of the operation. He tried to catch Rachel's eye, to telegraph his anxiety or just to get a steer on how she was responding, but she had eyes and ears only for Ron. Jackson, oblivious to their plans, was also rapt. His stream of questions and comments indicated a more than nodding acquaintance with hydroponics.

Ron was no fool, and as they started walking back up the drive to the house, he asked Jackson where he'd acquired so much of his 'good oil'. Jackson kept his head down and muttered something about a 'cuzzy up north with a garage'. Ron just laughed, said he hadn't come down in the last shower, so Stan, emboldened by the cat being more or less out of the bag, and despondent about their chances of acquiring an operation of this size anyway, asked how easily the operation would transpose to growing cannabis.

'The devil's lettuce? Not something I know much about, son.'

This time, Rachel's eyes found Stan's. She dipped her head and pushed her glasses up her nose: this wasn't the plan, he was going off piste. Oh well, thought Stan, we're stuffed anyway. But Ron surprised him.

'I'm too old a dog to learn new tricks,' he said, 'and I'm from a pretty conservative background, so I don't want to touch the stuff. But marijuana, from what little I know, would be a helluva lot easier to grow than lettuces, and a lot more lucrative, I imagine.'

'Really?' said Stan, the black cloud lifting. Rachel's head had lifted too, and she was smiling.

'Only thing is, you'd have to factor in one big cost that we don't have with lettuces: twenty-four/seven security. We've already had one of those big fans nicked by some local pot-heads. If you grew commercial quantities of marijuana here, it'd be like the opium growers in Tasmania: you'd need armed guards shoulder to shoulder the last two weeks as the crop ripened.'

***

UP at the house, over cups of tea and freshly baked cheese scones, Wendy talked about their former lives, dairying in Southland. The bitterly cold, dark mornings, crunching through the frost, the doors always open, mud being traipsed through the house. Her words resonated with Stan. Farming at Te Kurahau might have been as far removed from industrial dairying as it was possible to get, but cold and mud were agricultural constants, it seemed.

'When we sold and went to see the bank manager,' said Ron, 'he was stunned that we weren't tapping him up for a bigger farm, more cows.'

'Coming here was the best thing we ever did.'

'Down there we had no contact with the people who consumed

what we produced. Here, we deliver fresh lettuces and herbs most days – as you know, Rachel – and get instant feedback.'

'Brickbats and bouquets,' said Wendy. 'But mostly bouquets. Ron loves those relationships with customers.'

'You'd be good at that, Rachel.'

By God, thought Stan, there's a twinkle in the old guy's eye. Possibly picked up by Wendy too. 'Are you married?' she asked.

'Yes,' said Rachel.

'No,' said Stan.

Wendy chuckled. 'Clearly not to each other then.'

'None of our business, of course,' said Ron. 'But you do need to be a good team, and from what I've seen, you've got the makings, with your right-hand man here.'

Meaning Jackson, who had said very little, apart from 'Nice scones', to Wendy. 'My nan used to make ones like this.'

Stan had a moment of euphoria when he realised he might just about be able to buy the business, after Ron told them his accountant had valued it at 'just under a mil', on a gross turnover of four hundred thousand a year. Stan knew bugger all about borrowing, but with a fifty per cent deposit and four hundred k coming in annually to pay any interest, surely the figures would work. Meaning they could live in this house with brick walls and insulation sitting at the top of the rise where it caught the sun, and if there was no sun you could throw a switch and central heating would keep it warm as toast. With an indoor kitchen with a gas hob that didn't blow out in an easterly. With rooms you could walk into and out of, with doors you could close. A room for Nathaniel and one for Jackson, if he stayed. An indoor toilet you could piss and shit in at the same time. And land of your own, three hectares of land! A green sward above the sheds, rising to a knoll with a paved area and bench where you could sit and contemplate the coast rolling around to the lights of the city at night. An orchard you walked through to get there, with established trees, plums and pears and apples, and raised planters behind the house where Wendy grew her vegetables, and flower beds. Enough grassland for sheep you mightn't own and wouldn't kill, just sell grazing rights to a neighbouring farmer. Maybe they could have a milking cow, maybe they could be self-sustaining here, with a cash-flow they'd never had at Te Kurahau. And there was a prize-winning winery just up the road where they had summer concerts, and easy access to the city and the Saturday market. An income. Money. Responsibility yes, but autonomy. Not having to run every thought past the co-operative. If he wanted to grow cannabis commercially, he could.

Stan wrenched his concentration back to Ron. He handled the weekends, he was saying, but on a weekday there were two full-timers, one in the propagating shed and one overseeing the big sheds, then part-time pickers and packers and deliveries, and there was always ongoing maintenance 'that you can't do yourself'. It gradually dawned on Stan what 'gross turnover' actually meant: all these costs would have to be paid out of that, before any interest, and before any money actually landed in their hands. After tax.

Then Ron said the obvious, which made Stan feel like such a fool: that the business was distinct from the land and buildings, separately valued, which would also have to be bought.

'RV one point five,' said Ron.

Stan didn't know what RV meant, but it didn't really matter. The overall price was two and a half million, not 'just under a mil'. He was wasting his energy on an impossible dream. 'I'm sorry,' he said, 'I don't think we can do it.'

'Fair enough, son,' said Ron. 'Only you can know that.'

'What he means,' said Rachel, pushing her glasses up on her nose, perhaps to hide the flare of dismay in her eyes, 'is we'll have to work through the figures.'

'Sure,' said Ron. 'Your accountant and lawyer will have a lot of questions.'

'Right,' said Stan. He had neither accountant nor lawyer and no more questions.

'If you give me your email, I'll send everything through.'

Stan didn't have an email distinct from the Te Kurahau website, and he didn't want anything going there. But what was the point sending anything through anyway? Before he could say so, Rachel gave her email address, care of the cafe, as their 'point of contact'.

Whoa! thought Stan, and rose abruptly to his feet.

'Of course,' said Wendy. 'You've got a plane to catch.'

Ron walked them to the car. Stan pulled open the door, which creaked with rust. Does this look like someone with two and a half million? he thought. But Ron seemed unperturbed. Said it was a big decision, and he was happy to give them a couple of weeks' grace before he put the broker on the job. He'd prefer not to have to pay a broker's fee.

Stan drove back down the driveway to the glasshouses, then up to the road, his face tight with humiliation, not daring to look at Rachel or say a word.

***

THE silence lasted all the way along the Old Coach Road ridge to the highway, then right around the coast until they were on the straight into Richmond. Stan was accustomed to Jackson saying very little, but when Stan caught a glimpse of the boy in the rear-vision mirror, he was clearly feeling the tension. Rachel had been studiously following the scenery, face turned away.

Lester was right. Commerce had inserted its ugly maw into their relationship and Stan, instead of being full of love, was full of doubt. He should never have confided his windfall to Rachel. Had that influenced her departure from Te Kurahau? No, he had to remind himself, her departure – their affair – had pre-dated that money landing in his account. But that was what money did: made you suspicious of other people's motives. And yet Rachel had said she knew what she wanted, and it was him. Stan wasn't so sure that she should be so certain. After Aaron's tyranny of mood, he probably appealed as a salve. Stan suspected that the same weak and wounded quality in him that alienated the likes of Aaron and Will perhaps appealed to women like Rachel, who might need some respite from domineering masculinity. Who knew? He didn't any more.

Maybe the stakes were too high for them, even without the lettuces. Rachel had walked away from Te Kurahau, left her husband and her son. Stan wouldn't have dared ask her to do such a thing, but she had. How long, though, before she began comparing him with Aaron's sheer competence on every front? How long before she began resenting him for the separation from her son? And for losing everything she owned to Te Kurahau? Maybe their relationship had already run its course, a means to an end, a springboard to jump them out of Te Kurahau, for her to get out of her unhappy marriage? Might their closeness and empathy be a by-product of sharing their poor-me stories, where they could cling together in victimhood and a desire to escape?

On the Richmond straight, she finally turned towards him, pushed up her glasses. He glanced across, found her eyes. She'd been crying. 'I'm sorry if I was out of line back there.'

'Two and a half million? We're dreaming. We shouldn't have left them hanging.'

'It's worth their wait,' she said. 'You know what the broker's commission would be if they sold on the open market?'

'No idea.'

'Me neither. A lot, though. Hundred grand, maybe?'

'But it's fraudulent to let them believe we have any hope of raising that kind of money, isn't it? Can you see us walking into a bank? Explaining to the manager where we've been for the last ten years? Why we're going to be a great risk borrowing two mil to run a business when we know nothing about payrolls, GST . . . Fuck, we don't even know what we don't know!'

Rachel stared out the window again, though it was flat and featureless now as the hedge-rowed paddocks dwindled and transitioned from rural to suburban. 'We can learn. Ron will help set us up. We can pay someone to do what we can't.' She turned back towards him. 'I can see us there, can't you?'

Stan shook his head, not in denial but in hopelessness. He *had* seen himself there. And he'd seen Rachel there with him. 'Yes,' he said. 'That's the trouble.'

'I didn't want to close off the possibility before we'd explored it properly. We don't have to walk into a bank. There are investors around, the guys stumping up for the hops conversions. An American's behind the big conversion down the road from the cafe. Maybe he'd be interested in a quicker return than he'd get waiting for the hops to mature.'

'So we wouldn't be our own bosses?'

'Is anybody? Were we really our own bosses at Te Kurahau or just victims of group-think? I'm certainly not my own boss when

I'm waitressing. Who'll be the boss when we're teaching? It's more important that we're doing something we value, and that we have a financial interest in its success. I love the thought of the lettuces, even if the cannabis never happens. Delivering our fresh produce around the area, connecting with people, being part of a wider community.'

Stan made a left turn onto the Richmond by-pass, an ugly semi-industrial assault on their senses. Stan felt lost. Rachel's hand reached out and covered his on the steering wheel. 'It's true that your money changes everything. It gives us a chance. I wish I had something to contribute. I wish I hadn't put my share of the Tel Aviv apartment into Te Kurahau. I wish. I wish. But it's your call, I accept that.'

Stan didn't reply, but his thoughts kept coming back to the opportunity for a new life. It was the right business. Ron had nurtured his outlets. He wasn't dependent on one customer. He had a great operation, doing something that would give Stan and Rachel maximum satisfaction, whether it was conventional lettuces they grew or the devil's. He needed to talk to someone who wasn't Rachel.

At the airport, he parked in the kiss-and-drop zone and grabbed his day-pack from the back, as Rachel moved across into the driver's seat. Jackson was already out, waiting patiently with his kete. What the fuck would he be making of all of this? 'Your books are in the back, Rach.'

She adjusted her glasses. 'That sounds ominous.'

'Nah,' he said, leaning in to kiss her.

'We never got to do that.' She smiled.

'What?'

'*That.*'

'Too busy agonising about money.'

'We won't make that mistake again,' she said, her open palm caressing his cheek. 'Love to your dad and the family I've never met.'

***

INSIDE the terminal, they sat in plastic chairs and watched the departures board tick over. Stan tried to convince himself he could find satisfaction in teaching, that if he taught as he preferred to, responding to the pupils, not being too directive, it could be a lot like growing a plant. He grimaced, hearing Rachel telling him the simile sucked. His mind drifted back to money. He asked Jackson what sort of return the marijuana in Auckland had brought in. 'I'm not interested in where the money went,' Stan clarified, 'just how much it got on the open market.'

'Dunno,' said Jackson. 'My sis got rid of it. Ellie said Lila could keep what she made and use it to build wheelchair access for Mum.'

It was the first time Jackson had mentioned his mother. It was always Lila. Stan wanted to ask what had happened. Presumably the wheelchair was a recent development? There were questions there to be asked, but Jackson's mobile buzzed. He instinctively stood, to help reception, and pressed the phone to his ear. After no more than a few seconds, the kete dropped from his other hand onto the polished lino. Stan picked it up. It was empty, apart from a desiccated flower of some kind. Maybe a rose, thought Stan, judging from the thorny stem.

Jackson looked stricken as he gave the mobile to Stan. 'It's Ellie.'

***

ENGAGING with the outside world was one thing. Auckland was another. The isthmus looked like it was nesting in an oil slick, both harbours gun-metal grey with an oleaginous patina where shafts of sunlight penetrated the low cloud and struck the water. Stan looked down and felt sick. Auckland was, as always, something he had to wade through. Somehow, he had to get to the other side, the flight out.

The arrivals entrance broke in front of him, swinging back like drafting doors in a sheepyard. He looked up and there was Ellie, standing beside a row of men in grey suits holding signs. She turned, saw them, ran across. Stan had time to think that she looked different, longer hair, taller – though that couldn't be. She was beaming, that was the word. She looked as if she'd lost weight, a psychological shedding as much as a physical one, as if she'd broken out of a carapace. When she hugged him, she smelt like citrus, she smelt like the best part of coming home. When she pushed him back to arms' length to look at him, she saw his tears and assumed they were for their father. Her eyes filled then. Den had been in a coma for the last twenty-four hours of his life. 'The doctor said he might still be able to hear, so I told him we loved him. I told him you were coming.'

Stan pulled her close again, not wanting to say anything to betray himself, or let her see something in his eyes that might have told her his tears were for her, and for his mother. Still.

Ellie turned to Jackson with outstretched arms. He seemed to stand passively in her embrace, holding his kete, and Stan was worried that Ellie was embarrassing the boy, until he saw Jackson's face over her shoulder, an enormous smile, his eyes half closed in rapture.

***

'I'M parked over there.' She pointed to the far side of the drop-off area, which she was scanning. 'But Lila said she'd be here.'

Jackson nudged her arm and directed her towards the far end of the drop-off zone, where two figures were locked in verbal conflict on the footpath beside a silver Prius. Stan could hear the raised voices, particularly that of a young woman, yelling in the face of a traffic warden. 'Oh shit,' muttered Jackson and hurried towards her. 'Hey sis!'

Lila immediately abandoned the warden to run towards them on dangerous-looking high heels. She looked a helluva lot more upmarket than when Stan had last seen her, a twitchy twig with a shaven head doing her hip-hop schtick at his father's birthday. She was wearing a sheepskin coat with a big wool collar over some sort of mini-skirt. The thought came to him: that's where the marijuana money went. That's okay, he told himself, it wasn't mine. When she reached Jackson, Lila launched herself at him and they twirled as she kissed him. The warden, still watching, thought this a pantomime of major proportions. 'Nice try!' he yelled.

Lila gave him the fingers. This was obviously Jackson's first view of his sister's transformation. He was shaking his head in wonder. 'Jeez, sis, you're looking–'

'Just Karen fucking Walker!' said Lila, doing another twirl, holding out her coat so Jackson could see her shimmering skirt and top.

'Uber aren't permitted to pick up passengers here,' said the warden. 'You can drop off, but not–'

'Tell this arsehole,' said Lila to Jackson, 'that you're my brother and I'm taking you home for nothing, for love.'

'She's my sis,' began Jackson, dutifully.

'They're brother and sister,' said Ellie. 'I can vouch for them.'

'And I suppose you're related too,' said the warden.

Stan half expected Ellie to have a go at the man – the old Ellie would have – but this new, less combative version just smiled politely. 'I'm parked over there,' she said, indicating the squat concrete building at the other side of the crossing. 'So why don't you do your job and move on.'

The warden, a middle-aged man who had probably seen better jobs, couldn't resist a last rejoinder before taking Ellie's advice. 'Why don't you all just get in your cars and fuck off.'

Lila just grinned, then gave Ellie a big hug. 'Sorry about your dad. That's how it's s'posed to be.' Stan didn't get it, but Jackson and Ellie seemed to understand.

The obvious warmth between Ellie and Lila was a surprise. When Stan first heard Jackson describe Ellie as his 'guarding angel' he thought it an endearing malapropism, but it had grown on him as an accurate description of his own bond with Ellie, made strong by so many shared hurts, especially Carol's death. That was what ultimately defined their relationship, changed it from just sister and brother, to what? 'Guarding angel' covered it. There was something similar between Ellie and Lila, a crisis shared, or a disaster survived, an intrepid journey completed: a bonding, a binding. Stan felt a pang of jealousy, which he quickly suppressed. Jackson and Lila had nothing, while he had always sipped from a silver spoon.

Lila was opening the passenger door to the Prius. 'Hop in, bro.'

Jackson hesitated a moment, then solemnly shook Stan's hand. 'Thanks,' he said. 'Hope you get the lettuces.'

He eased himself into the passenger seat while Lila smiled back at Ellie across the car roof. 'See you at the funeral.'

So there was to be a funeral of some kind. Den had been agnostic, as far as he knew, and Stan couldn't imagine what form such an event would take. An extended commercial for himself probably, with music over.

***

IT had only been nine months or so since he was last here, yet there seemed to be massive changes to the industrial estate surrounding the airport. More roadworks, roundabouts, traffic lights, under-passes, overpasses, more enormous sheds with ostentatious branding for freight couriers, hotels, motels, God knows what. Monuments to the world of commerce, a world which he seemed hell-bent on joining. Ellie negotiated the first roundabout and had time for a sidelong glance. 'You're looking good, Stanley. Got your good threads out of the closet, I see.'

Stan nodded.

'And Jackson looked great. How was he down there?'

'Good,' said Stan. 'Easy company, fits in with whatever's going, works bloody hard.'

'Thank you for taking him. He needed a break from Auckland. His mum had a stroke, after she was beaten up by his father, who seems to have disappeared. With a bit of luck he'll never come back.'

'Right,' said Stan. 'Jackson didn't really say anything, and I didn't think I could ask.'

'And the lettuces?'

Ah, so she'd picked up on that. He was going to tell her anyway. There was something about being in Auckland that made the plan, played back for Ellie, seem less preposterous. Maybe it was being around so much commerce, so much endeavour, so much wealth. Even the new motorway tunnel, which projected them out onto the old north-western like a cork out of a bottle, made the impossible seem less so. And yet, the story had no happy ending that he could see. Other than possible employment for Jackson, if it had gone ahead: he would have been the ideal manager of the two big sheds.

Ellie would like that bit.

And she did, he could tell, even though she listened to it all in silence. Then, after another little spell, she said, 'You couldn't have known this when you were talking to Ron Halston, of course, but you must realise your deposit is now a million, not half a million?'

'Sorry?'

'Your share of Dad's estate.'

Holy fuck, he thought, looking out at the looming Sky Tower. This is what Auckland does. Kills you but gives you money.

Ellie was taking the Western Springs exit. When they stopped at the lights, she asked him to drive. She was blind with tears.

***

STAN drove them up the Bullock Track and through West Lynn on Richmond Road, as Ellie wiped her eyes and admitted she'd taken the wrong exit. Stan didn't mind: these were the tracks of his mid-teens at Springs. Yes, there were new cycle lanes and definitely more traffic, but the map in his head still worked. Ellie gave him the rough itinerary of the next few days. They were meeting this evening at a bar in K Road, tomorrow, Sunday, was free, and their father's memorial service was eleven o'clock on Monday morning, at All Saints, where Branko's had been.

'Did Dad find God then?'

'Good God, no!' she laughed.

When Stan wondered aloud whether the Anglicans were okay with hosting services for non-believers, Ellie said churches had to adapt to a more secular world.

'Couldn't think of anyone more secular than Dad.'

'He had a spiritual dimension too.'

266

'Did he?' Stan didn't mean to be challenging, but couldn't help it. She'd always defended him. 'Does a belief in the power of advertising count?'

Ellie ignored that, told him he'd be staying with Will and Claudia as there was no room at Yelena's little cottage. Stan had just assumed that Ellie would have a place for him, as she always did. Jesus, home and hearth with Will. Could he make it through two nights with his older brother? He'd have to book a flight out on Monday afternoon, flee as soon as the service was over.

Ellie directed him left onto Ponsonby Road, down a block or two, then suggested he find a park. 'Will wants to meet you here.'

'Where?' They were just past SPQR, surrounded by Tex-Mex places, bistros, Thai. It was too late for lunch, surely.

'Over there.' Ellie was pointing across the street to what looked like a menswear outfit in a shopfront squeezed between a women's fashion boutique and a poke bar, a typical stretch of Ponsonby Road's two-storey mix of masonry and weatherboard: unevenly shabby but inexorably becoming chic. She grabbed his hand. 'Give Will a chance,' she implored him. 'He's been great, getting the section sold. And this last little bit with Dad hasn't been easy.'

**

AND she was right. Stan found Will at a small table in the central well of what seemed at first glance a menswear boutique, but was also a cafe and barbershop. Will was communing with his laptop, but quickly rose when he spotted his brother. Stan wasn't sure what to expect: a handshake, a man-hug or a punch on the arm. Turned out to be a man hug of epic proportions. Will, shorter but more powerful, gathered him into a fragrant embrace – was Old Spice still a thing? – and murmured 'Bro, sad times, but good to see you,' with what appeared to be sincerity.

When Stan said he was sorry he hadn't made it earlier, Will quickly absolved him. 'Better you didn't see him,' he said. 'He wouldn't have known it was you. Last time I saw him he looked at me as if he was the same old Den, then said, "I should know you. I think I've seen you before."'

'Jesus.'

'Poor old bastard was terrified most of the time. Didn't know who he was, where he was. Kept trying to do a runner. He was locked in, didn't know why. We should be glad for him that it's over.'

'End of an era,' said Stan, not knowing what else to say.

'That's why they're eras,' said Will, not unkindly. 'They have a beginning and an end.'

His designer stubble was gone and the hint of belly in the slim-fit white cotton shirt that hugged his torso seemed to signal a softer Will. Instead of the usual barrage of sarky observations and put-downs, Will actually asked him questions, once he'd got Stan settled with a cup of coffee. He was happy to tell Will about the lettuces – the devil's ones too – because Will was exactly the sort of cynical capitalist who would shoot Stan's plans out of the sky, so he wouldn't have to torture himself for one more second with the possibility of the lettuces being a viable business. He could dismiss the whole idea and move on. After Stan, prompted very gently by occasional questions, had laid out everything Ron Halston had told him, Will confirmed that though another half-million would be landing in Stan's account within six weeks, courtesy of Den's estate, Stan's figures still wouldn't work – one and a half million was too much to borrow.

So that was that. A pity, really, that the conversation was at an end, because Stan had found it a profound relief to be finally talking to his older brother about something they could connect on. He loved Will's certainty, the way he talked about millions of dollars as if they were crumbs on the floor that could be gathered up or swept away. Even the brutality with which Will was burning up his dream appealed: the lettuces needed to be put out of their misery.

Except that wasn't where Will was going. Stan couldn't borrow a million and a half. What he needed was a partner, a silent partner who would put up another million, and then the partnership could borrow the further half-million. 'Now *that* would make the figures work,' said Will.

'Would it?'

'Absolutely.'

'So all I need,' said Stan with a laugh, 'is a silent partner who would put up a million dollars. How would I find someone like that?'

'You're looking at him,' said Will.

'Fuck,' said Stan.

'Does that mean you're pleased?'

'I'm, I mean–'

'Why not. I trust you, I think it's a viable enterprise and, like you, I've got a million looking for a home.' Will handed Stan a card. 'Get your man to email the guff through. We'll get my lawyer and accountant to look at the figures and we'll talk to the money. I'm serious,' he said, as if there was any doubt.

Stan, in shock, took the card and inspected it. White, black lettering, '*William Sparks*' on one side, a mobile number and email address on the other. That was it, no description of his business.

When Stan looked up, a lanky, very thin man in a suit and no tie had sidled up to Will. 'Nick Preston,' said Will, 'my brother Stan. Nick's a creative for a major.'

Stan glimpsed red, rheumy eyes behind designer glasses and a nervous tongue wanting to talk. Before he could, Will pushed Stan towards the barber shop, speaking over his shoulder to the thin man. 'Grab a seat, Nick, short black for me, be with you in a sec.' Will was ruffling Stan's hair. 'What *is* that look? New Romantic meets hippy?'

'More like don't-care meets who-gives-a-fuck.'

'I get it. Style by omission, style by neglect. But we can't ask for serious money looking like that.'

Stan let himself be ushered into the barber's, wondering if this was what happened when your parents were dead. Older brother goes all paternal and the children are forced to be nicer to each other because now there's no one left to blame, no one to adjudicate, take sides, pull warring siblings apart. Maybe Will was making a pitch to be head of the family. Nature abhors a vacuum and so does power: the king is dead, long live the king! Whatever, this new Will seemed an improvement on the old.

A young Asian man in a black apron asked him to take a seat in one of three big steel-framed chairs, as Will gave instructions. 'Sharpen this kid up, Patrick. Give his head some edges, f'chrisssakes.' As Stan sank into the chair, Will got up close to his ear and pointed to the big mirror along the wall in front of them. It reflected the lanky man, making his way back from the counter to a table. 'See that cunt? Every dollar he owns or can borrow or steal will be mine.'

This sudden flash of what seemed like genuine hatred, and the old Will, was unnerving, but Stan tried to stay calm as Patrick asked if it was okay to start with the hand-piece before he went to the scissors. 'Sure,' said Stan. Anything about to happen in Auckland was out of his control; he might as well relax and try to enjoy the ride. And he did, as Patrick mowed his locks to a controllable length, then went to work with the scissors. Stan's dismay at the amount of hair falling to the floor was mollified by the rhythm of Patrick's hands on his head, the way he scooped a fillet of hair in two fingers, tapped the scissors gently on his skull as if to anchor them, then cut. Scoop, hold, tap, snip. Stan gave his worries away and watched Will and the other guy in the big wall mirror.

Preston was sitting at the small table with his knees together, elbows on the table to stabilise himself, bony hands clasped together. He looked like a praying mantis, but Will was clearly the predator, one hand dancing up and down on a plastic-backed file, face down on the table between them. When Preston reached for the file, Will flattened his hand on it. Baulked, Preston's hand went to the inner breast pocket of his suit. He extracted a white envelope and slid it across to Will. It was unsealed. As Will took a quick peek at its contents, Preston fumbled the file, which dropped to the floor. The contents must have spilled, because Preston retrieved only an A4 sheet of what looked like stippled foil. Stan could see that Will was pissed off as he rapidly reconstituted the file, before handing it back to Preston. Preston quickly stood up and left.

When Stan's focus returned to his own image, he saw the soft hair that had framed his face was gone. His head looked suddenly bony and square. Would Rachel recognise him? That life down there was already starting to recede, Auckland seeping into him like the tide reclaiming mangroves.

'At least your head's got some corners now,' said Will when Stan was released back to the cafe, 'but those clothes are thirty going on pensioner.' Will must have given the nod to the young woman hovering by the nearest clothes rack: she arrived on cue. 'Can we find something a bit less Grey Power AGM-ish?' he asked her.

'Sure,' she said. 'Shirt?'

'And jacket and shoes,' confirmed Will, steering Stan towards a changing cubicle, then hanging on the curtain as Stan started unbuttoning his shirt.

'Look,' Stan began, 'I can get by with what I've got, I don't want to spend–'

'Those pants look a bit billowy too,' said Will, closing the curtain.

Everything the young woman, Emily, handed through the curtains was chosen by Will and everything was colour co-ordinated and sharp – even the snouts of the blue-black leather lace-up boots with exposed stitching. 'Just stick it all on, and give us a gander,' said Will.

Stan did as instructed, as items came through the curtain: stretch cotton chinos in what Emily said was 'sand'; slim-fit dark blue stretch cotton shirt; the boots; a Donegal weave wool jacket in 'rust'. Stan looked at himself in the full-length mirror and hardly recognised the urban hipster staring back. When he stepped out of the cubicle, Will and Emily made approving noises.

'Doesn't it all look a bit tight?' said Stan, lifting the jacket so they could see the shirt and trousers.

'Fitting,' said Emily. 'Like, way to go if you've got a bod.'

'Dunno about the shoes,' said Stan, 'but maybe I'll take the jacket.'

'We'll take the lot,' said Will, drawing a bundle of purple notes from the white envelope. 'My shout. Ems, can you stick his old gear in a bag? He can wear it when he gets back to the farm.'

'I'm not going back to the farm,' said Stan.

'Exactly.'

When Emily disappeared into the cubicle with an extravagant paper bag, Stan tried to get in front of Will, put his hands up in front of his face. 'You can't do this, Will.'

'Why not?'

'It's too much! It's not me!'

Will put the notes and the envelope on the glass counter and grabbed Stan's hands in both of his. 'Bro. Give it a chance. See if you relax into them. If you don't, you've still got your old gear sitting there waiting for you. Okay?'

Stan was unused to this quality of attention from Will. While it came with implicit criticism of his previous style, or lack of it, it seemed born of kindness and concern. Surely it would be churlish to object to such a change in attitude after all these years. And it *was* seductive. But . . .

When they walked outside, Stan, carrying the bag with the remnants of his old shell, was hit by the chilled breeze welling from the south. His ears and the back of his neck felt suddenly cold without the protective hair. There was something else. All those fifties in that white envelope, which Will flicked onto the glass counter like a croupier paying out a lucky call. Stan didn't know quite how to put it. 'Ellie said you were working for Yelena.'

'Yesterday's paper,' said Will. 'Yelena was great but I prefer being the owner driver.'

'Of what?'

'Fuck, where did I park it?' Will looked up and down, the low sun yellowing the eastern side of the street, traffic crawling through the after-school jam. A private-school bus pulled out of the stream long enough to disgorge some uniformed young toffs, its arse still poking into the traffic and drawing ire from the fog-horns of the

SUVs backed up behind. Stan watched the bus edge back into the stream, its place immediately taken by a black Porsche driven by a blonde. Into this hopped one of the young uniforms from the bus. Stan hoped home was more than two blocks away, but doubted it.

Will seemed to remember where he'd parked his car and pointed across the street to a graceful-looking SUV, power curves sculpted to a blunt end. When Will strode out to the middle of the road as if he owned the place, Stan felt obliged to follow. Will nodded to the traffic coming the other way and walked on. As Stan scurried with him, one of the cars braked hard and gave them the horn. Will flipped the bird, and Stan felt a perverse reassurance that Will 2.0 hadn't completely reformatted the original version. When they got to Will's car, the badge on the back confirmed it was a Tesla X. 'Stand back,' said Will, as Stan reached for the door handle, and the whole door rose like a wing to admit him. 'Fuck,' said Stan.

'I've gone green,' said Will. 'Within reason. Where it's fun. This fucker can smoke a Porsche off the lights.'

Stan thought Will had forgotten his question about work, or decided to ignore it, but then he pointed back across the street. 'Not just a coffee shop, not just a barbershop, not just a menswear retailer. You go in there and you're captured by all three. That's the future – diversity.'

'Like,' asked Stan, 'fingers in a lot of pies?'

'Some middle-man stuff, clipping the ticket as the money runs past,' said Will. 'Some commercial property, using what I picked up from Yelena, but also other things, diverse services, products. You see Lila at the airport? I'm a silent partner in her Uber. Working with people I like, people I trust. You know what Den and Branko and the hippies called money?'

'Bread?'

'Yeah. And there was another one: lettuce. Let's you and me make a ton of lettuce.'

***

LATER, walking from Will's place up onto Great North, heading along to Kook A Chew to meet Ellie, Stan's overriding impression of Auckland was of happiness. Ellie seemed happier than he'd ever seen her, and Lila at the airport, and even Will, confirmed when they'd arrived at the Ariki Street villa, with Claudia patting Will's nascent little pot belly fondly as if it was a flower she'd nurtured. And everything that followed: a contented Will with Kristin sitting on his knee telling him about her day, Archie demonstrating to Stan how his yellow plastic digger could pick up blocks and drop them. Stan marvelled at the change in dispositions since he'd last been here. Had someone slipped some ecstasy into the city's water supply? The only potentially discordant note came when Will told him the undertaker had couriered over a USB stick she'd found in Den's Rainbird jacket, his favourite, the one they were dressing him in, in case the family wanted to see him.

'I don't,' said Stan. Someone – it must have been Den – had thought he should view Carol. She was cold as marble, unrecognisable, with the ghost of a smile that looked like a grimace of pain the undertaker had tried to airbrush.

'Nor me,' said Will, 'and Ellie's already said her goodbyes.'

'He's not going to have an open coffin at the funeral, is he?' asked Stan.

'His will said specifically that he didn't want that.'

Bully for him, thought Stan, pity about Mum. 'So what's the point of dressing him up?'

'I think,' said Will, 'that's just what they do. Dressing for dinner even if you're eating alone. Old school.'

Stan picked up the USB sitting on top of an opened yellow and red courier envelope on the coffee table. 'What's on it?'

'No idea. Probably nothing, we'll open it later, if we can.'

As he worked his way east on Karangahape Road, past rebuilt Victorian shopfronts and apartment conversions that used to be office blocks, Stan realised that not all Aucklanders were drinking from the same happy tap. Quite a few of the newly renovated shopfront entrances contained misshapen, often faceless bundles of clothes, sometimes with a hopeful tin out front for coins, sometimes supported by a plaintive handwritten cardboard sign. He couldn't remember there being so many homeless. On the other hand, the woman working the corner of K Road and Hereford opposite Joy Bong had been plying her trade there when he was still at school, in what looked like the same ski jacket and short woollen skirt. Stan's new outfit and shiny shoes increased the guilt. By the time he reached the new Tesla showroom – Will wouldn't have had to come far for his new car – Stan had cleared his pockets of change.

He crossed the overbridge and looked across the road to the lights of Kook A Chew. It was early evening, but the Saturday-night party had already started out on the footpath, the stand-up tables lost within circles of happy drinkers. Stan contemplated the evening ahead with a mixture of trepidation and resolve. It had already been a long day with more new people in it than four months of winter at Te Kurahau would bring. He was accustomed to big holes of solitude, patched by contact with the few and familiar. He felt emotionally exhausted, but that was outweighed by the prospect of being with his guarding angel.

He didn't see Ellie until he was among the throng. She was at a leaner with a couple of others. He recognised Yelena, but not the dark beauty she was with, and not the guy in what looked like black overalls with his back to Stan, and his arm around Ellie's waist. Yelena saw him first, and did an exaggerated double take, calling 'Stanley, is that really you!' as she slid off her stool and came over to take his hand.

'Will got me a makeover.'

'Did he ever!' Yelena grabbed his hands and smooched him on the mouth. 'Fuck all that French air-kissy stuff.' She held him away, to appraise him. 'You used to be soft and rounded, now you're all edge.'

'Will wanted sharp.'

'Now why would he want that? You're not letting him in on the lettuces, are you?'

Fuck, thought Stan, Ellie's told her. It'll be all over Auckland soon: Stan and the Lettuces, like a children's book. Before he could answer, Ellie was there, taking one hand away from Yelena, reading him. 'It wasn't a secret, was it?'

'Nah,' said Stan. But enough about the fucking lettuces.

Ellie kissed him and she and Yelena led him back to the leaner. Yelena's friend was closest: she introduced the exotic-looking Asian as Lavinia. Stan shook her hand politely, thinking maybe part Filipina, maybe Malay, as Ellie turned him towards the smiling man in black. 'My friend Henry.'

Henry's handshake was firm and friendly: Stan didn't feel the need to macho it up, a good sign. Stan was also relieved to see that Henry's black look was entirely professional: a double-breasted chef's tunic, with matching trou and black Crocs. Crocs? Henry saw him looking, laughed. 'Don't tell Nike and adidas,' he said, 'but if you need to be on your feet for six hours, these are the go.'

Stan liked that, but was still thinking of a rejoinder when Henry turned back to Ellie. 'Speaking of which, I better get back to my hot stove.' He kissed Ellie. 'See you later.' Turned back to Stan. 'My condolences about your dad. I'm glad you're here – Ellie's been pretty cut up.'

Stan was watching Ellie watch Henry go, weaving through the tables, a word for everyone he passed, until he disappeared inside the restaurant proper. Ellie was still watching the air he'd displaced.

'Will sends his apologies,' he said. Ellie wrenched her eyes back to him, but took a moment to focus. 'Said he was still on the wagon, didn't want to risk it.'

'Good on him,' said Yelena.

'It's kinda weird round there – happy families. He's a changed man.'

'Yes and no,' said Yelena.

Yelena's comment seemed to galvanise Ellie. 'He's been fantastic around the whole Dad thing,' she said.

Stan wanted to follow up the intriguing ambivalence of Yelena's comment, but she slid off her stool and took Lavinia's hand. 'We're going to mix and mingle. You guys have a lot to catch up on.'

'She's great,' said Stan.

'She's my best friend in all the world,' said Ellie.

'So,' he said, 'nice man.'

Ellie was hopeless at hiding her feelings. Her eyes spilled love. 'He's the one,' she said. 'Sounds so simple, seems so easy. He's just a lovely man.' As she described Henry, a separated father of one, with a five-year-old, Frieda, just started school, and their plans to open a deli cafe on Te Atatu Peninsula where Henry lived, a western branch of Kook A Chew resourced by Kath and the team, Stan felt something he'd never encountered before with this shining-eyed sister, a small envy, that he'd belatedly been supplanted in his sister's affections. This made Henry real, in a way no previous boyfriend had been. Stan kissed her and raised his glass, another thing he'd never really done before with any degree of sincerity. 'To you and Henry, sis. How wonderful.'

***

STAN hardly ever drank alcohol. There was none at Te Kurahau, not because of any edict, it had simply become irrelevant to their lives. One summer Malcolm had developed an enthusiasm for making mead from a big honey harvest, but it had been undrinkable. He'd talked about making cider, but when he researched it, their orchard had the wrong variety of apples. So by the time he'd drained his second tall G & T, Stan was already feeling pissed and told Ellie he'd better not have a third. The tables were heaving, Yelena and Lavinia had disappeared, and there were no stools left for them anyway. Stan was feeling animated, less self-conscious, more connected to everyone around him, part of this noisy, friendly little nexus of humanity. Ellie was encouraging him to have another G & T. 'What the hell,' she said. 'How often does this happen?'

Them being at a bar together? Their father's demise? Ellie had drunk more than him, yet didn't seem unduly affected. 'You're used to it,' he said.

In reply, she slid her tall glass across to him to try. Bitters and lemon. 'You've gone the Yelena way?' he asked her. 'Hopefully not for the same reasons.'

She smiled at him and said, 'Cone of silence?'

The words instantly conjured up the closeness of their childhood and teens. Inspired by watching reruns of *Get Smart*, Maxwell and 99, wonderfully naive stupidity which they'd both loved, they'd created an equally silly but protective protocol. They would lean forward until their foreheads touched, so neither could see the other one's eyes or facial reactions, and any words they whispered to each other were more like transference of thoughts, which evaporated harmlessly into the air and were lost, but still known. He and Ellie could say anything under the cone of silence.

'Really?'

'Really.'

Stan turned and swayed forward. His forehead touched hers. And yes, it was a silly thing to do at their age, particularly in a crowded bar, and he was more than a bit pissed, but he closed his eyes and breathed Ellie in and the magic seemed to work: the background noise faded and he inhaled her whisper as much as heard it. 'I've missed my period. For the first time in my life, I've missed my period. You're the only one who knows.'

Stan sat back, smiling. A couple of years ago, Ellie had told him about the frozen eggs. It was such a big moment. He knew he wasn't supposed to respond – that was the deal – but he was allowed to grin.

'It's been the most awful couple of months of my life,' she said, trying to smile. Now the words tumbled from her, out into the noise around them. 'Before the coma, Dad had just enough brain left to know that he ought to be making connections with what you were saying, but for the life of him he couldn't make any. So he was in agonies the whole time, hearing this stuff sliding past him that he knew had some meaning, but just wouldn't stick. Knowing that he was under lock and key, but not knowing why. Knowing that something dreadful was happening to him, but not knowing what. It would have been better if his brain had been obliterated in one fell swoop, than the bit-by-bit dismantling of everything that made him who he was.' Ellie seemed determined not to cry, which made it worse for Stan. 'That's what happened in the end, of course. One huge stroke . . . I wish it had happened sooner.'

Stan took her hand in his. He'd been protected from all of this, down there at the school of vital essence.

'And I couldn't cut it at the agency any more. Couldn't. Had to resign.'

'I didn't know that,' said Stan. 'What happened? I guess Dad's situation . . .' He felt sorry for his sister. Will wouldn't have been a lot of help, though clearly he had been some. Ellie losing her job. His father losing *his* vital essence. He should have been here, helping his beloved sister bear the load.

'Not because of Dad.' Ellie looked at him for a couple of beats and Stan thought she was about to call on the cone of silence again. Instead, she just shrugged, then continued. 'I'd decided to use a sperm donor,' she said. Stan felt he might be missing connections because he was pissed. 'But when I met him—' She began shaking her head. 'He wasn't a bad man, but he wasn't the right man. He wasn't *my* man. And in the middle of all this darkness and despair, Henry. And maybe, a baby.' She was crying now, but smiling. 'I can't believe my luck.'

***

BY the time Ellie dropped him back at Will's, Stan had had another G & T and was feeling no pain – or anything much at all. When he waved Ellie goodbye, climbed the front steps and stood on the wooden veranda, he couldn't remember the combination for the door lock. It was a typical villa, big bay-windowed bedrooms either side of the front entrance, so he was trying not to make a noise, unsure what time anyone went to bed in the city. Judging by the heaving bars along K Road, never. But he didn't want to wake the kids. He was still standing there, trying to remember the number Will had told him: it was a year, 19 something. He was thinking that maybe it was the year Will was born – what year was that? – when his brother opened the door.

The happiness drug had worn off. Will was edgy and brusque, as he asked Stan to follow him down the hallway to the big open-plan area at the other end. He was barefoot, in T-shirt and shorts. There was something terribly wrong, Stan thought, in dressing for summer in the middle of winter. His yurt had been cosy enough with the log burner going, but he still had to wear some serious fucking clothes!

'You need to see this,' Will said. He was indicating his laptop, open on the kitchen table.

'What is it?'

'A suicide note.'

'A what? Whose?'

'Your father's.'

My father? thought Stan. That was a worry. Will seldom referred to *his* father as anything other than Den. The way Will said it made it sound as if whatever *their* father had done was going to be dropped at Stan's feet. But, a *suicide* note? Ellie had been very clear: his father had died naturally, in a coma as a result of a massive stroke. What the fuck was Will talking about?

Will had pulled out a chair for Stan, so that he could sit in front of the screen. All he could see was a big red arrow. 'Ready?'

Stan was still struggling up to speed. 'Dad left a suicide note on your computer?'

'On the USB the courier delivered,' said Will. He pressed

the arrow on the screen and the pixels quickly crystallised into a beautiful view of the harbour. Stan pointed to the screen in recognition. 'Yes,' said Will testily, 'it's from Den's loft. Just watch and listen.'

'It's the magic hour,' said Den's voice, over the rich imagery, the sun so low that the water was a purple river. 'My last.'

Stan looked across at Will, unsure whether he was up for this. Will had flopped into one of the huge overstuffed armchairs and was staring resolutely out the window to the water feature at the edge of the deck, lit blue-green like a waterfall in a grotto.

When Stan's eyes returned to the screen, Den was speaking straight to the camera, looking younger and healthier than Stan remembered him, standing four-square in that way of his, in front of the balcony from which he'd shot the previous sequence. 'I don't wish to be melodramatic,' he said, 'but by the time you see this, I'll be gone.'

Stan suppressed the urge to giggle. *I don't wish to be melodramatic, but . . .* A quick glance at Will confirmed that he should take Den's words seriously. What could he have possibly said to have so upset Mr Light and Sweetness?

'None of us know how we're going to finish,' Den continued. 'How it's going to end, though end it will – as they say, there's a tragedy in wait for each of us, sooner or later.'

That did the job. Any urge to laugh drained out of Stan, as Den proceeded, quite formally, with a speech he'd clearly put some time into preparing.

'My time has come, sooner than I would have wished, but I suppose that's a common complaint. In so far as I thought about it at all, I wanted my demise to be peaceful and dignified, replete with all the things I needed to say to you, my nearest and dearest.

But if Dr Jeetan is right, that probably won't be the case, and by the time I get to my natural end, I may not even understand what's happening or who I am, or, dear children, who you are. What a bugger that would be, eh, to follow my story for seventy years and not know the ending!'

Den's attempt to chuckle at his little joke became a catch in his throat and the screen went to black for a moment. When his face came back, he was composed once again, though in a different part of his loft, now sitting in his big chair beside the bed. 'I don't want that. I don't want to die in ignorance and terror. Selfish and controlling to the end, I know. I'm sorry if it's a shock when you find me, and I'm sorry for any distress my taking matters into my own hands, as it were, might cause you. But believe me, the lingering alternative would be so much worse, for you and for me.'

There was another cut, and Stan had time to think about what Will and Ellie had told him about the final days, which Den had prefigured exactly. Christ, if he'd known what was about to happen, why didn't he go through with whatever he was planning? Had he panicked, lost his nerve?

When Den's face reappeared on screen, it was jerky. Den was holding his mobile, still in selfie mode, and moving, walking back and forth across the loft, the picture careening in and out of focus, and the words that tumbled out of him seemed more like an impromptu postscript to what he'd planned to say.

'I got so many things wrong, and my worst sins were visited upon my children. I don't know why I couldn't see that when I needed to, but, unfortunately for you, I was an egotistical idiot long before I became a father, and had trouble changing. Then there was Carol, darling Carol, whose death was the single worst thing that has ever happened to me. In my grief, I became lost in my own selfish little hell and was incapable of being the surviving parent and adult that you needed me to be. For that, I am so sorry. It may be a complete waste of time to say that at this late juncture, far too late, but I want you to know that I know what I was.'

Stan was both moved and angry. Where had *this* man, this father, been?

'Part of my decision, of course, is pure vanity. I want to be remembered as I am, not as what I would have become. But much more than that, I don't want to die in terror, understanding nothing of what's happening, not even understanding my own demise. Does that make me a coward? I can't answer that. None of us can, until we're in the same position. I hope that time never comes for any of you, but it's certainly come for me. I can only hope you remember me fondly. As foolish, yes, but fond.'

Den's face faded, replaced by the view of the harbour from his balcony. The deep purple of the harbour had become a dark maroon. 'The magic hour,' said Den's voice, over a slow fade, 'the world bathed in the softest light, achingly beautiful because it signals imminent darkness.' On cue, the screen went to black, as what sounded like raucous elephants revealed themselves to be bellowing guitars, out of which a voice, not Den's, insinuated itself. *Into the distance, a ribbon of black . . .*

It wasn't a song Stan recognised, but Will did. 'Pink fucking Floyd! Would you fucking believe it?' Stan wanted to laugh – it was so Den – but couldn't in the face of Will's incandescent anger. The old Will, back in all his fiery darkness. 'The old cunt,' he said, waving at the laptop as Pink Floyd blasted on. 'Couldn't help himself, even at the end. Mawkish sentiment and bloated ego.'

Stan's head was still whirling. 'So, he'd intended to–'

'Top himself, yes. He had a pistol.'

'When was this?'

'Look at the date on the file. He recorded that on the day of his seventieth, just before the party.'

'So,' said Stan, still struggling, wishing he hadn't had so much to drink, or that Will had left this until morning. 'After the party, he was going to–'

Will was still pacing, talking as much to himself as Stan. 'We didn't need the fire. Fuck, if I'd known he had a plan, we'd have the best part of another mil from the insurance payout for the house.'

Stan couldn't look at Will, stared at the black screen with the music still blaring out. When Will said he needed to take a piss, and disappeared down the hallway into the bathroom, Stan stood, shaky. There was nowhere to go. He wandered down the hallway, questions forming, as Pink Floyd followed him. He eased the front door open and shut it carefully behind him, as the bull elephants launched into a final reprise.

***

THERE were new laneways running parallel to Ponsonby Road, which Stan staggered into, seeking to avoid the garish light of the street itself, but they turned out to be extensions of clubs and restaurants, back terraces of vodka and whisky rooms, refuges for furtive smokers, not thoroughfares. Full of big people, young people, his age but from another planet, many of them huge, women busting out of too tight, too skimpy, too short, in groups taking selfies, singing songs to the camera, al fresco karaoke, big men in black, dressed like the bouncers they maybe all were. Despairing of pushing his way through, Stan went back around onto the street. The fat of the land had always been the townies' description of rural life, but everyone he knew at Te Kurahau was as scrawny as him. In his new gear and blistering shoes, he might look like he belonged, but he felt like an alien. Where do all these people come from? Who are they? What do they do? All these people, young like him, pissing their lives away. He could talk. He was pissed too. Pissed, distressed. Everyone was in the same boat, pissing up to relieve the despair. How did you catch hold of your rushing life and make it meaningful? Over the background noise of shouting and singing and arguing and laughing voices, the music of live bands was leaking out from the small venues he passed, the drums sited up against the street end so they didn't overwhelm the space, the tinny whack of snare drums signalling another bar, another band, long before you got anywhere near them, and long after you'd passed, these cracks puncturing the air like pistol shots. This was how it had been when his mother died. The numbness. Nothing had changed. The years between were meaningless: he'd done nothing, changed nothing. He was fourteen years old. The rest of his life, Rachel, the lettuces . . . What was he thinking? It was all bullshit. Will was selling meth – that page of foil that had fallen to the floor, full of tabs. That's what Yelena had been trying to tell him at Kook A Chew. Of course Will wanted to invest in legit businesses, he needed to wash his dirty money. Lila's Uber, probably a great front for delivering meth. Clean and green? What a fucking nerve! Money wasn't just money, Lester said, money was what you did to get it. The lettuces were fucked, he was fucked, Will was evil. *We didn't need the fire.*

IT WAS TOO early for Henry. He wouldn't have finished work and it wasn't his polite knock, but a despairing hammering. When she opened the door to a barefoot brother carrying a sock-stuffed shiny new shoe in either hand, his first words were: 'The fire. It was Will. He admitted it!'

The change in Stan since she'd dropped him off was stark – his new clothes already baggy on him, his short hair sticking out in clumps as the gel disintegrated, his eyes wild. Ellie didn't know quite what to say, so she hugged him close, like a baby, trying to pacify him. He pushed her off. 'Didn't you hear what I just said? He admitted it!'

'I heard,' she said, and tried to conjure up as much shock as she could. 'That's awful.'

That might have worked with most people, but not with Stan, even drunk. He gawked at her, open-mouthed. She'd seen that incredulous look before, in her clients, when what was about to befall them and their children at the hands of their partners or the judges or the department was revealed. 'This isn't news to you, is it,' he said. It wasn't a question. 'You knew!'

'I didn't *know*.' She needed to deflect him, buy some time. 'Will never said anything to me. But I sort of realised it only made sense if it was him. If Dad was no longer living in the house, Mum's half-share would be released. It was about the money.'

'You should see the video,' he cried. 'Dad was terrified about what was about to happen to him. He knew exactly what was waiting for him, and he wanted to die with dignity.'

'I know he had a plan.'

'You knew he was going to top himself?'

'Not at the time, no. Much later, when it was too late.' Ellie wanted desperately to stop the questioning, cauterise the revelations until she'd had time to consider how much Stan should be told. She asserted her older sister status, told him Yelena was in bed, he needed to have a shower and get some sleep, she'd make him up a bed on the sofa, they'd talk in the morning. While he was in the shower, she put sheets and a duvet on the big sofa. When he emerged, it was clear his new clothes hadn't stretched to his undies – they were supermarket specials with white strips of elastic showing where the cheap material had disintegrated. He looked so thin and exhausted and vulnerable that she had to stop herself from weeping as she pulled the duvet over his bony chest. To her relief, his eyes closed as soon as his head hit the pillow. His last words were almost a sigh. 'Tomorrow, we've got to call the fire investigator, maybe the cops, okay?'

'Okay. We'll talk about it tomorrow and decide. Let's sleep on it.'

***

BUT sleep didn't come easily. She rang Henry to warn him Stan had overindulged and was on the sofa. Henry got there before she had to ask, told her to take care of her little bro and he'd see her tomorrow. She hadn't told Henry she'd missed her period; she'd wait until she was sure. That was okay, she told herself, she was simply being sensible, controlling the release of information, not harbouring a secret. She'd once thought, when she had no secrets, that they'd be corrosive, undermining. But secrets, she'd learnt, could be a binding agent for those who owned them. Serious secrets. Like arson and murder.

She'd expected everything to change, but not for the better. She'd done something unimaginable, notionally evil, and by her laws of simple morality, a good person who does bad suffers for it. Her world *ought* to have changed. Yet nothing much did initially, as she waited for a storm of remorse to break over her.

The low point arrived the day after they buried Dwayne Collins in the rose bed. The rain had come. She'd pulled a sickie and driven through the downpour to Te Henga, jumped on Brownie and gone to the lake. God knows what Vicky, the owner, had thought was going on with her – unrequited love maybe: maybe townies appeared quite often on dreary days to ride their sorrows away. She'd ridden Brownie into the water up to his withers. She was soaked anyway, the saddle and blanket were sodden. She took the pistol from her parka and threw it as far as she could. Just before it hit the surface, she half expected an arm to rise from the water and catch it, like Excalibur, except that the sleeve would be dark blue with police insignia on the shoulder. But it splashed and sank. She'd taken off her parka and driven back to town with the heater on full blast, shivering so hard she had to hang on to the wheel for dear life.

She never went back to the agency. After another duvet day, she'd phoned in her resignation. She ought never to have returned in the first place. Her failure was in not recognising that her work there was done, or, more accurately, that work was done with her. That had been clear even before she'd taken another person's life.

She'd gone back to volunteering for FreeLunch4Kids, shortly before it was revealed to be owned by a supermarket chain. The shock of finding that you'd been volunteering not for a charity but to serve the ends of a commercial entity that had found a lucrative way to jettison its surplus was mitigated only by the turmoil that followed among the volunteers. There'd been meetings and coffees, lots of excuses to be in the same space as Henry and talk about things that mattered. At an angry meeting between the volunteers and the representatives of the supermarket and the 'charity', Henry had stood up in the middle of the venom and said the most important thing he needed to know was whether the kids were still going to get their lunches. She loved him right then. Afterwards he accepted her offer of a drink. They'd gone to a little tapas bar where he wasn't known, and she'd basically thrown herself at him. Luckily, he was coming just as hard the other way.

All that time she'd been waiting for the guilt to engulf her, waiting for overwhelming remorse to paralyse her, for the turpitude of what she'd done to wring her out and leave her hanging, morally bereft . . . But nothing came. She couldn't summon up any kind of feeling about the demise of Dwayne Collins, apart from revulsion at the memory of his bloodstained mullet.

It helped that no one else gave him a second thought either. Those darkly hilarious pre-Christmas speculations in that Kingsland bar were truer than those women could ever have hoped: *no one* missed Dwayne Collins. In fact for those who knew him, the world was a much better place. Ellie might have expected exactly that for Jackson, Lila and Miriama, of course, but it went much wider than that, as those women in the bar had speculated. The agency didn't have to try to execute a safety plan for Miriama when she was invalided home, the state didn't have to pay Collins the dole, or fund his trial, or his imprisonment, or any futile attempts at counselling and rehabilitation. He became a zero on the state and agency spreadsheets.

And it quickly became clear the police also didn't give a toss. Lila, who was living with Miriama, told Ellie the police wanted to interview her mother about the assault. For reasons Lila didn't need to explain, she was uncomfortable being around cops. Jackson by then was with Stan in Golden Bay. Ellie was reluctant, but what could she say?

Detective Sergeant Tracey Costigan had turned up, acted like Ellie was her best mate and lamented her resignation from the agency. Miriama was in a wheelchair and struggling to talk, so it was a one-sided conversation, blessedly short. Afterwards, Ellie walked Tracey to her mufti car, and without asking a single question got the unofficial police narrative: Collins was an incorrigible recidivist on the run with serious criminal charges hanging over him, who must have used his criminal contacts to get out of the country. He might surface in Oz when he'd inevitably commit another crime and be deported, or he might come back to try it on again with Miriama. They'd deal with that then, but in the meantime they'd live in hope that the nasty little shit would cross serious crims in Oz who would put a bullet through his head and save everyone some grief. As Tracey wished for that bullet in Collins' head, Ellie tried to turn her wince at the memory of him lying face down on the deck into into a wry smile. 'Sadistic piece of shit,' said Tracey, as she reached her car. 'The world is so much better for his absence.'

That was the moment, when DS Costigan drove off without a backward glance, that Ellie's world finally tipped on its axis. She was swaying on the footpath and had to prop herself up with one hand on the door of her car to keep from falling. It had been gradually becoming apparent, but that was the moment it really hit her: that of her many and various good works, of all her acts of kindness and compassion, the very best thing she'd ever done was shoot a man in the head.

Perhaps, with a good lawyer and a sympathetic jury, what she'd done wouldn't be murder, but it *was* homicide. She had taken another human being's life. She had killed. She had clung to the car door until the horizon settled, then gradually let go and realised she could still keep her feet. She could walk. She could step forward into this new world, with its very different moral parameters.

When she'd told Stan she didn't know that Will set fire to the house, it was sort of true – in the sense that Will had admitted anything to her. But somewhere in her marrow she'd understood that Will and Lila had provided each other with alibis that night. And just as they'd never discussed the fire, she and Will had never discussed Collins' death. They didn't have to. Lila knew everything, so Will knew everything: they were, she and Will and Lila and Jackson, inextricably bound together, a disparate little family with a black hole of secrets at their centre, a centripetal forcefield pulling them powerfully into the same orbit. And Stan had to be drawn in there too, somehow.

Freeing Lila and Jackson from their father's brutal oppression was a gift beyond anything they could have expected, but Ellie didn't want their gratitude tested by police interrogation. She knew her action had begat other, unintended consequences. She'd tried not to think about Will and Lila, but she'd seen the instant lift in both their fortunes that could only have come from exploiting the vacuum left by Dwayne. She'd found that she preferred her brother being a dealer than a user. It was that pragmatic, that selfish.

Things were about to change for her little brother, and nothing she said or did could jeopardise his bright new future. Or her own. She was thirty-eight and, she hoped, pregnant. It wasn't at all the sort of world she'd worked for, or thought she'd be bringing a child into. And yet. That world, its essential nature, was something she couldn't control, though not long ago she'd been naive enough to think she could. She imagined squeezing Henry's hand, and feeling the answering pressure. It was enough. She slept.

***

WHEN she awoke, it was just before seven. There'd be a couple of places already open up on the strip, even on a Sunday. She'd grab her skinny little brother and get some folded eggs and bacon and mushrooms and spinach into him, or a three-egg Benedict on big hash browns, washed down with espresso, and see if she could keep his mouth full long enough to talk some sense into him. When she dressed and tiptoed through to the sitting room to wake him, the sofa was empty. His new shoes and socks were on the floor where he'd left them, but Stan and his clothes were gone.

STAN WAS STANDING on what was left of the deck in front of the levelled site when he heard her car coming up the drive. He'd never seen the blackened ruin. He'd fled back to Te Kurahau from the motel up the road the morning after the fire. The absence of the house was shocking, what used to be there now an expanse of bulldozed earth with surveyor's pegs marking out the dimensions of the footings for a new home. The only remnant of the old house was a square concrete-lined crater where the garage had been. He remembered they had all run down the stairs into that garage and then out onto the parking bay, where they'd counted heads, as the house began shooting flames behind them. Will and Lila were missing, of course.

He was trying to sort that chaos. It didn't help that last night's poison had swollen his brain, pushing it against his skull so hard it felt bruised. The first voice he'd heard that night, rousing him from sleep, had been Jackson's, he was sure – even though he hadn't come into Stan's room. Had he heard his voice before the panicked beeping of the smoke alarms? He couldn't say. Had Jackson been given a heads-up by Lila? At Will's request? Even Will wouldn't want their deaths on his conscience, surely.

He turned away as he heard Ellie calling his name, and padded in his bare feet down the steps, through the gate and onto the cold wet of the grass path. He could see her coming towards him, at the far side of the rose garden, now a patch of thorny sticks apart from a couple of Cecile Brunners, still showing a tiny pink flower. He saw Ellie stop suddenly, frozen to the spot. She wasn't looking at him, but at something right in front of her. Her face flushed, then crumpled with relief when she spotted him. He didn't want her to be relieved. 'I can understand now why the insurance company wouldn't pay out,' he said.

She answered warily, slowly, as if bone tired by the whole subject. 'Does it really matter? Most of the value was in the land.'

'It doesn't matter that he burnt our house down?'

'I'm not saying it doesn't matter,' said Ellie, then began talking as if by rote about the good things Will had done, how he had sold the land to Georgie, who, it turned out, was as interested in what she called a 'clean canvas' as she had been in the original home. More importantly, Ellie said, Will had found a buyer who wanted their mother's garden preserved, and that was the main thing.

Stan was incredulous. 'Burning the house down is okay because he got someone to preserve Mum's garden?'

'You don't understand,' she said.

He admitted that he didn't understand, and even though she was becoming distressed, he determined to harden his heart and not crack. 'Then there's Dad,' he said. 'His last agonies.'

'You really want to talk about that? I was there with him through the worst of his terror. Where were you?'

'*He* could have avoided it all! He wanted to. He had a plan, which Will took away from him.'

Ellie shook her head, hopelessly, and the tears spilled as she did so, as if a glass inside her had been tipped. 'He's gone. Let him go.'

But he couldn't let Will go. 'And he's selling meth.'

'I think so,' she sniffled.

'I can't take his money.'

'Yelena thinks you won't have to.'

Stan felt as if he was being stonewalled by the person who had always spoken truth to him. There was something he wasn't getting, some subterranean change he couldn't read. Ellie had done a moral somersault, from being Will's accusing conscience to his apologist. What had happened to her? He hardly needed to ask. 'He's got something on you,' he said.

She didn't bother to deny it. 'You don't need to know.'

'But it's something.'

'In the end, he's my brother, like you.'

'I didn't burn my family home down to rort Mum's will, I didn't condemn my father to die in agony, I don't make a living out of selling amphetamine to addicts!'

She looked away, to the rose garden, those little buttonhole roses, the only flowers in the middle of winter. When she looked back at him, her face had gone limp, as if she'd given up fighting something inside. 'Cone of silence?' It was a plea, more than a question.

Stan looked up at the bare branches of the melia, its bones outstretched in silent supplication to the grey sky. 'No,' he said. 'I don't want to know.'

He didn't look at Ellie, and it took a while for her to speak, and when she did, she sounded beaten. 'Most friends have a shelf life, Stan. Lovers don't always last, social circles change, governments get voted out, empires rise and fall. But families are forever, good or bad.'

'Sounds like a mafia manifesto,' he said.

'Was that a joke?' she asked. 'Look at me!'

When he did, he was already sorry for his flippancy. She looked wild-eyed and lost.

'There are truths and lies we have to live with,' she said. 'And necessary secrets.'

He thought of his own recent experience at Te Kurahau, *his* secrets, kept from those who had sustained him for most of his adult life.

'Don't cast us adrift, Stan,' she implored him. 'Don't cast me adrift. I may have made a terrible mistake, but don't forsake me. Please.'

He felt his heart turning. Her distress rocked him. What right did he have to sit in judgement on the sister who had saved him? He was in the act of breaking a marriage, of separating a nine- year-old boy from his mother. How could he of all people be party to that? Then there was his dishonourable exit from Te Kurahau, turning his back on his second family as soon as he scored some serious money. Doing a runner with the dough. Glasshouses weren't just for lettuces.

He remembered the central tenet on the A3 pinned to the wall above Lester and Penny's dining table: *We accept all human beings as our brothers and our sisters and choose to behave towards them with love* . . . He'd always considered the profound beauty of that aspiration to be its inclusiveness: *everyone* was your brother, *everyone* was your sister. And yet how could you aspire to love humanity but not your own kith and kin? His blood brother might be a step too far, but he was freezing out his sister by birth, his sister by life, his sister who had saved him.

There was a new world coming, and his day in Auckland had given him some indication of the challenges it would bring. Could he embrace the new and still hold on to the best of the old? He didn't know. What he did know was his love for his sister. He stooped and held Ellie in his arms. 'Sorry, sis,' he said. 'Sorry.'

When he held her away to see if she'd stopped crying, she was wiping away tears. 'It's all good,' she said, trying to smile. 'It's all good.'

ACKNOWLEDGMENTS

My gratitude to Suzy Butler, John Daniell, Dr Jeffrey Fetherston, Fertility Associates, Timothy Giles, Chris Hampson, Sir Bob Harvey, Dennis Hitchcock, Irma Jager, Dr Darryn Joseph, Linda McDougall, Michael and Caroline McGee, Patricia McGee, Mary McGee and Creative NZ.

And, as ever and in particular, I'm indebted to the upstanding, dedicated little team at Upstart Press, Kevin Chapman and Warren Adler, and to my editor, Anna Rogers.

- The quote on page 16 is from Helen Garner's essay 'White Paint & Calico', collected in *Everywhere I Look,* published by Text Publishing – thank you Helen and Text.
- On page 19, 'They fuck you up, your mum and dad' is from Philip Larkin's 'This Be The Verse'.
- On page 54, 'May God bless and keep you always, May your wishes all come true' is from Bob Dylan's 'Forever Young'.
- On page 106, 'Rage, rage against the dying of the magic hour boss' is based on the line from Dylan Thomas' 'Do Not Go Gentle into That Good Night'.
- On page 143, the verse is from John Keats' ode 'To Autumn'.
- On page 285, the line *Into the distance, a ribbon of black . . .* is from Pink Floyd's 'Learning to Fly'.